A SHADOW

WALKING

Can love and integrity survive austerity?

To Louise, with love + best wishes,

Anne xx

ANNE TODD

ISBN 978-1-913036-16-4

I AM SELF-
PUBLISHING

🐦 @iamselfpub
www.iamselfpublishing.com

For MPJ
28.05.53- 28.12.16
With love

And for Hartley Coleridge
November 2008-September 2019

Fear no more the heat of the sun…

Prologue

Life's but a walking shadow…

Death changes everything, and we're all touched by it at some point in our lives – like food and friendship and sex. We all have our worlds altered for ever when someone close to us dies. Death can change the way we feel about other living people, or ourselves, as we realise that we won't walk this earth for ever.

But there is another mysterious force which also changes everything. I have never, ever believed in love at first sight, and I still don't – it's a myth perpetrated by the purveyors of simplistic romances. For me, it took two weeks. Then I was held in its grip until it was torn from me, leaving me falling into blackness, utterly abandoned, like a shadow walking aimlessly through pointless days. Eventually, losing love taught me something about myself – that I am the type of woman who can function without the support of a partner. I have done so, and will continue to do so, if I have to, for the rest of my life.

Part One
A Poor Player

Chapter One
Autumn Term, 2016

"Are you with us, Miss Weston?" (He never called me Alison.)

"Depends where we are, Mr Barker."

Replies like that never went down well, especially on the first day of term, although others around me would snigger quietly to themselves. Putting a cheeky head above the parapet could bring down disproportionate and counter-productive opprobrium, but I have to say that never bothered me. Quite the reverse. That might explain why I was a lowly jobbing English teacher rather than a manager at thirty-eight.

My boss, the delightful Mr Barker, head of the English department at Hebble High School, probably saw me as an immature, outspoken and thoroughly irritating iconoclast. I certainly hoped he did, at least – I worked hard at that, but only to wind him up. In fact I did care, passionately, about my pupils, their opportunities and the way I could help them all achieve their full potential. I also cared very much about Hebble High, an institution in which I'd worked for fifteen years. Out of school, I lived alone. After a couple of devastating experiences, I preferred my own company.

I didn't have many close friends at all, and no-one at work, although I got along pretty well with most of my colleagues superficially. They were pleasant enough, but their concerns outside school simply weren't mine. They probably thought I was aloof and arrogant, but there was a limit to the amount of time I was prepared to waste discussing their sick babies or errant partners.

In fact, I preferred the company of many of my pupils. They were a noisy, irreverent bunch, a few of them brighter than I would ever be.

("Miss, what exactly *is* the difference between a myth and a fable?" Try explaining that spontaneously in front of thirty grinning fifteen year-olds!)

I'd certainly had some difficult moments in the classroom – name me a teacher who hasn't – like the time I blacked a pupil's eye. It had been an accident; I'd been standing at the side of the class, between desks, when I made a flamboyant gesture while reading a poem, exactly at the moment a rather ebullient boy turned his head towards me. My knuckle connected unexpectedly with his eye. The next day he came in sporting a splendid blue and purple bruise around a swollen eyelid. The rest of the class wasted no time telling me I was "gonna get done for assault", but then someone said to the boy, "What did yer mam say when yer got 'ome?"

The boy looked sheepish.

"She said, if I didn't stop messing about in lessons she'd black the other one an' all!"

I think I liked most of the parents almost as much as their kids.

But on the first day of every autumn term I suspect I felt exactly like their offspring, anxious and apprehensive about what was to come for the next seven weeks – some dreary days, impossible workloads always unfinished, time crawling, the bullying, the fear of inadvertently doing the wrong thing, the scorn. Sometimes I wondered, during the inevitably sleepless night before, whether I'd even make it through the school gates, or instead slink off, silently screaming, in the opposite direction. Education was such an important element of my life, but the beginning of September, I reflected, as I turned my little car right off the main road and up the hill next to the school, had always been depressing.

Hebble High was invisible from the main road that ran through the valley on its way into Lancashire. The building, which squatted half-way up a steep hill behind a group of semi-detached houses next to the road, was originally erected before the Second World War, but was mothballed until 1950. It was built to accommodate far fewer pupils, so, with its increasing popularity, the central part had been obliged to expand with a series of ad hoc extensions – it had the air of a large ship surrounded by random flotsam. Inside, the steepness of the site meant a preponderance of staircases and some interesting children-jams at the change of lessons.

Entering by one of the doors that opened from the front drive, noticing the usual September smells of polish and newness, greeting everyone I hadn't seen for six weeks, laughing about the summer, I forgot the anxiety for a while. That normally lasted until my first encounter with the Dreaded Barry.

At first, that year, the beginning of the autumn term had been no exception. There was the usual dreary Departmental meeting in an almost-empty classroom (the pupils didn't arrive until the following day), gazing out over the front field, an area of grass in front of the school, and away to the lowering rock edge beyond, looming over us on the other side of the valley.

But on *that* first day, a day I won't ever forget, the preliminaries to the opening of the school year had been rather different. Normally we convened to gloomy news about GCSE and A-Level results being poorer than average, senior staff being concerned about our performance, radical changes being threatened, blah blah blah. But for once, we'd hit the jackpot. Our examination results had been outstanding, for once. So the customary bollocking couldn't happen, which left the curmudgeonly Barry Barker and his equally obnoxious sidekick and Second in Department, Simon Benn, rather short of dire warnings. The best they could manage was that we'd better keep this standard up, or Questions Would Be Asked next year.

"Of course, it just demonstrates that the Government *has* got it right. More examinations, tougher standards and rigorous discipline are clearly bearing fruit. Long may it last."

This was Benn – consistently political, authoritarian, officious. And, because he took himself so seriously, always hilarious.

I stifled the desire to point out the inconvenient truth – our school was about as far to the left of official policies as it was possible to be; we catered well for all ability levels, we didn't stream in English and the school had a superb reputation for dynamic and popular extra-curricular activities. No, this meeting was almost over, I needed caffeine and we had twenty minutes before the full staff meeting. Unpalatable facts would have to wait, with the promise of them providing useful ammunition at a later date.

A particular strength of Hebble High School was the value its Head placed on all its staff. One of his most welcome initiatives had been the creation of a post for a member of the kitchen staff who, thirty minutes before every morning break, cranked up the large coffee machine in the staff room and put out a supply of new-made biscuits. The first day back was no exception, and I could smell the ground beans as soon as I walked in.

"You did admirably well in there – I could see your jaw twitching when Old Bonkers kicked off."

Rosemary was one of my fellow sufferers in the Department, one who wasn't averse to delivering a rapid kick to the shin under the table if things started hotting up. Like me, she valued her coffee.

"Yeah, well, it's not that I'm desperate for caffeine or anything like that. I'm keen to get into the Theatre, *obviously* – I didn't want us to miss being introduced to all the new faces and to hear dear old Brian telling us how well we've done."

"Liar! The only thing that vaguely interests me is this new deputy they've appointed. I hope it's a woman who'll value what we do and not some ambitious career type who'll persuade Brian to toe the Party line about academic rigour and ditch the innovative stuff."

"God – I never thought about that! What if they make me abandon—"

"They surely couldn't – there'd be outrage from everyone."

Was she right? Did I really have the support of my colleagues on a project I'd promoted the previous term? I was about to find out.

Ten minutes later we trooped down to the Theatre. It was a great venue for drama, music, public speaking – far more than a space with a stage, which is all many other schools have. We were incredibly lucky – it had been transformed and kitted out by the millionaire father of one of our brightest pupils, who had done spectacularly well in performing arts. It boasted a professional-standard lighting and sound system, all controlled from a proper computerised switchboard in its own elevated room behind the tiered seating, as well as wall-mounted cameras to film productions and project special effects onto the stage. The school hired it out regularly to local groups (a useful source of funds) as well as putting on vast amounts of dance, music and drama. But on the first day of term the tiered seating could easily accommodate all employees for the opening staff meeting. Brian Welch, our much-respected Head, felt we were all part of the same team, so everyone – teachers, classroom assistants, cleaners, office-staff and caretakers – all met together.

The seats filled up rapidly and the space buzzed with shiny, apparently energised people itching to get going – once they'd seen who'd joined us for the new school year. But at first we looked down onto a cluster of empty seats arranged in a semi-circle on the low platform in front of the stage, as we waited to welcome Brian and his entourage. Then the door to the foyer opened, and in they came – the Head, his senior staff team and the two Deputies, Carol Carter and the new... man. Bearded, quite casually-dressed, smiling but perhaps slightly embarrassed – and unexpectedly familiar.

Brian stood up.

"Good morning everyone, and welcome back. I hope you've all enjoyed your summer, and are looking forward as much as I am to another stimulating and productive year. I'll say more about our tremendous exam results in a moment, but first I'd like to introduce your new colleagues, beginning with the man on my right, Martin Prescott Smith..."

I realised sickeningly that my past and the present were about to become uncomfortably tangled, and I didn't like it at all. Not one little bit.

How in the name of all that's sacred am I going to deal with this?

Chapter Two

1998

There was absolutely no doubt that Cath had chosen the right cottage, as far away from home as we could possibly be. We'd toiled away in a stuffy factory all summer to save enough money to afford it; we were nineteen and just finding our independent feet. The cottage was in Mawgan Porth, nestled at the foot of a steep hill, a comfortable stroll away from the Cornish breakers, so that we could hear the surf from the front bedrooms, or watch the rugged grass and the sea birds from the room at the back. But we weren't there for the views.

I'd first met Cath when I was eleven and she'd joined my school in Halifax. We'd hit it off from Day One and been inseparable for the next seven years. Unable to bear the idea of losing touch at the end of grammar school, we'd engineered places more or less together in Manchester, where she was reading botany at the University. By 1998, I was at the end of my second year of an English and Social History degree at Manchester Metropolitan.

Cath was a pretty, soft-faced young student with waist-length hair and dancing eyes, whilst I was of similar height, blue-eyed, long-haired but at least two sizes bigger. Cath wore the clothes I could never fit into, with an innate sense of style. What's more, she was confident and outspoken, never afraid to give her opinion, but fair-minded and loyal. She also had young parents – her mum was only twenty years older than us, and far more trusting and easy-going than mine.

My mother disapproved – she thought I was easily-led and she'd said, when we were fifteen, "Catherine is a bad influence. You're not to see her anymore!" Of course I'd completely ignored that. Bless her, if only she'd known the half of it – we'd enjoyed the freedom of our first year away from home with a wildness entirely typical of two grammar school girls.

Needless to say, it had been Cath who had first plunged into the pleasures of a serious relationship, although it wasn't with someone she'd met in Manchester. Pete had initially been no more than a casual friend, a funny, irreverent Army corporal, a school-mate of a nice bunch of blokes we'd met at a club when we were seventeen. He was tall and easy-going, with a lazy smile and a wicked sense of humour – I could see why Cath had finally fallen for him (along with the fact that he couldn't keep his hands off her, which must have been nice, I used to think wistfully). Pete treated me with brotherly care, always on the lookout for someone suitable for me.

None of his mates had shown the slightest romantic interest, and I was hopeless at flirting with strangers – growing up as an only child and going to an all-girls' grammar school had left me clueless and self-conscious. But I was quick-witted and good at banter, always ready with a foil for outrageous comments, and I generally felt comfortable with our new male friends, which was a start.

When Cath realised that Pete was to be a serious and probably permanent presence in her life, she was keen to have some time with him away from the watchful eyes of her parents. She was still based at home in the holidays, and although they'd accepted Pete, there was no question of bed-hopping when he stayed the night. And as Cath once remarked, fumbling around in the car had been exciting at first, but extended skin to skin action was pretty awkward. Plus, she wanted to wake up next to him. So the idea of a holiday in Cornwall in a hired cottage looked like the way forward – but only if she made it respectable by taking me along and lying a bit.

That didn't sound like much fun to me until she assured me that Pete had roped in the services of his room-mate, a lance-corporal, to make up a foursome.

"You'll get on really well," he'd said on his previous leave, "he's got a great sense of humour and he's a bit of a rebel, like you. Trust me."

What choice did I have?

***

The fortnight didn't start well. By eleven pm on the first Saturday there was no sign of them, and no phone call – which wasn't surprising, since they were driving from Suffolk (where they were stationed, repairing helicopters). I was sleepy from the sea air and a long shared drive in Cath's mother's car, generously lent to us for our holiday. Cath said she'd wait up for them, but at one in the morning she too had given up. I had sloped off to bed much earlier.

The next morning, hearing male voices from the kitchen, I tottered carefully down the rickety stairs, opened the latched door and emerged into the sunlight. Through the door into the front room I could see a couple of quilts and some pillows on the floor – they must have crashed out downstairs when they finally arrived, to avoid disturbing us too much. Their kitbags were lying on the carpet with washbags and combat jackets strewn around, and a couple of cases, one of which had an enormous white and red Snoopy painted on it, with the words 'Chirk Bank or Bust' written underneath in large bubble letters. I had no idea what that meant.

Pete was sitting at the table with Cath on his knee; opposite him was a grinning, fresh-faced young man of around twenty with smiley eyes – far from the fat spotty little oik I'd been dreading.

"Hiya, Allie," he said, "I'm Martin."

Chapter Three
2016

I don't think I've ever been prone to melodrama – I can keep pretty calm in most situations, take a deep breath and do what needs doing. But sitting in the theatre, staring at a man who'd been everything to me eighteen years ago, and who'd caused me such pain for so long, rendered me suddenly unable to breathe, or stop shaking.

I considered walking out, then rapidly rejected it – the last thing I wanted to do was draw his attention towards me. I looked down – I wasn't going to meet his eyes – and numbly heard what he was saying, totally unable to listen. Then I heard him mention the Integrated Curriculum, and in spite of myself, I started to pay attention – and to notice anxious glances from my colleagues. This was *my* baby.

It was an initiative I'd raised last term with Brian, something in which I passionately believed. Put simply, it involved a co-ordinated approach to subjects, initially in the first two years of secondary school. I'd pitched it to our Governors alongside Brian, an enthusiastic and supportive Head, and after forty minutes of listening and intense questioning, and a frank exchange of views when I'd left the meeting, they were convinced.

They wanted to trial this new way of teaching in the second half of the autumn term, provided the rest of the teaching staff agreed, and they wanted me to take the initiative in organising the preliminary cross-curricular planning. A promotion to a new post of Key Stage Three coordinator was on the cards, Brian told me later, if it went down well. All I had to do next was to sell it to my teaching colleagues. After some initial doubts, and a lot of faculty discussions, we'd resolved, almost unanimously, to give it a go, as the Governors had hoped we would.

Martin Prescott Smith was still speaking. I drifted back to attention.

"You're probably wondering why this over-promoted drama teacher is banging on about something you'd already decided to introduce—"

"I didn't decide," muttered Barker behind me. Predictably he'd been hostile to the whole idea, egged on by his sidekick. I noticed neither of them said anything out loud, though.

"—and I'm certainly not here to take charge of the project or undermine the good start you've already made. It's just that we rolled out something similar a couple of years ago at my previous school and it was a huge success. I want to support you all and maybe help you avoid a few of the pitfalls we identified."

I felt a collective relaxing of shoulders and sighs of relief, which I would have shared had it been anyone other than Martin Prescott Smith. He was presenting himself as a really decent addition to the staff and the IC team. Huh. But he was also a Deputy Head, so technically one of my bosses. Was I now either out of the project leadership, or would I be expected to work alongside him? Which would be worse?

As we shuffled down the Theatre stairs, heading for another interminable Departmental meeting to collect our timetables and teaching groups, the Head hurried towards me.

"Can I borrow Allie for ten minutes, Mr Barker? We need a quick chat."

"Not happy, Brian – we've got a lot to get through, but if you must…"

Brian scooped me up with his arm behind me and ushered me out of the opposite door, through the foyer and towards his office.

"I'm really sorry you hadn't had prior warning about that – it must have sounded like a real kick in the teeth. I was going to tell you about it first thing, but I was delayed. Come and be introduced properly…"

The trouble with Brian was that he was just so *nice*. Avuncular, positive, supportive and so, so enthusiastic – but with a steely determination to give everyone at Hebble High a memorable, valuable experience. The staff both respected him and enjoyed his company, and so did the kids. I was convinced that they saw him as another dad, albeit a slightly more authoritarian one – and perhaps we did, too. But not a dad I wanted to confide in, at least not at that moment.

Martin was already in his office, with his back to the door, busying himself with a small coffee machine.

"Martin, let me introduce you to Alison Weston, the driving force behind our budding integrated curriculum."

He turned and looked directly at me for the first time in fifteen years. His face had aged, of course, but the perceptive eyes and the calm expression were the same as ever. And was that a slight twinkle I detected? The heartless, smug, sanctimonious *bastard*.

Right. Let's see who's really an actor.

I held out my hand.

"Pleased to meet you – and I'm sure I've seen you before somewhere, your face is slightly familiar, but I can't quite place it. Have you ever worked round here before? In the theatre somewhere, maybe?"

To give him his due, his expression hardly changed, although his eyes hardened slightly, as if he was remembering. He was good – very good.

"Um… yeah, I was in Mother Goose at Bolton Octagon, but it was years ago and I'm sure you wouldn't've…"

"That's it! I took some kids on a Christmas trip from my last school. It was very funny."

It was actually dire, and the last time I'd set eyes on him; Cath and Pete, along with our friend Alec, had left him a thoroughly caustic note after the show, and I'd walked away telling myself it was finally over – closure.

"I can sense you're going to get along really well!"

Brian was virtually rubbing his hands together with glee.

"Oh, and there are a couple of other things – when you see your timetable, Allie, you'll notice you have an extra free lesson last thing on Wednesday; Martin will also be free then, so you can use it as planning time together before you hold cross-faculty meetings on Wednesdays after school. And I've given you a shared Year Seven class so you can have some hands-on with the delivery of the IC after half-term." He turned to leave.

Oh God – just when I thought it couldn't get any worse.

"That's really great – thanks, Brian. I'd better get back or I'll be in trouble. So I'll be seeing you tomorrow afternoon, then, Mr Prescott Smith? In your office?"

"Excellent, excellent – I'll leave you to it!" With that, dear old Brian swept out.

Martin looked a touch discomforted, but far from mortified, much to my disgust.

"Allie, I'm sorry. I hope this isn't going to be too awkward for you. When I took the job I had a feeling you worked here, but I'd no idea you were in charge of the Integrated Curriculum project…"

Liar, liar, liar.

All the staff details were on the school's web pages, so he must have known perfectly well that I taught here before he applied. Why had he done it? And now I had to work with him. I needed to think, and I certainly didn't want a Deep and Meaningful Conversation now – or ever, probably. He had hurt me too much, and it had taken me years to recover. On top of that, Mr Barker was waiting for me.

"Sorry, got to go."

Chapter Four
1998

"Hi!" We were smiling politely at each other, not sure what to say next.

"How was the journey? What time did you finally get here?"

Martin glanced at Pete, who was wrapped around Cath, in no position to speak and still clearly involved in the long hello. Finally, he surfaced and muttered something about being pretty knackered and needing to get his head down for a bit (a grinning statement loaded with as much innuendo as he could muster), and he headed for the stairs with Cath in tow.

Awkward. Or at least it could have been, except that Martin's shoulders were shaking with silent laughter; I was nearly choking too, in an effort not to pass some inappropriate comment. Then we distinctly heard a regular squeaking of ancient bedsprings and the kitchen's central light fitting, directly under the main bedroom, began to shake ever so slightly. I gestured towards the door, Martin nodded and we stepped out into the bright sunlight of a Mawgan Porth August morning.

A rocky track from the cottage went steeply downhill to a sandy, half-moon beach with cliffs on each side that rose precipitously from the spiky sea grass and dry sand at their feet. It was about eleven, and the high sun made the water sparkle and dance. We walked towards the sea for a couple of minutes, then stopped simultaneously to breathe in the view and the warm salty air.

"Blimey!" was all Martin said.

"Yeah – Cath chose this place well, didn't she?"

"She certainly did… How long have you two known each other?"

"Since we were eleven, at school. She started half a term after everyone else and I was told to show her round. We just clicked – we seem to think in the same way about most things – we've even been known to go shopping separately and come back with the same stuff."

"Yeah – it's the same with Pete and me most of the time... but I may be a bit more... well, for example, we watched Zulu last year – totally unacceptable portrayal of a brutal war, I know, but... what a film! That bit when they sing 'Men of Harlech'! I used to watch it with my dad, it's one of his all-time best favourites. Anyhow, I tried, but I couldn't persuade Pete to go down the NAAFI in war paint."

"Did *you*?"

"Of course."

I had a brief and somewhat alarming vision of a squaddy arriving in the canteen with coloured stripes on his face – what a clown. Like me.

"I once rode a horse up the front drive of our school disguised as Cousin It from *The Adams Family*!"

"Wow – how come?"

"It was an end-of-term hockey match, Year Thirteen against the staff. We decided we'd do it in fancy dress with a horror-film theme and I loathed hockey, so it was a good way of having a laugh and getting out of playing. You should have seen the faces of the silly old teachers when I went past!"

Martin grinned at me and nodded.

"Impressive! Pete told me we'd get on because we were both bolshy sods with the same sense of humour."

"Did he now?"

***

We'd reached the shore. I was itching to get my toes into the water, but Martin, like Pete, had travelled in his combat kit – they weren't really supposed to, he said, but they'd risked it to save time at the end of their shift in the workshop. They'd had their stuff packed and ready the night before they were due to leave, and stashed in Pete's car (his beloved Audi, bought with a huge Forces discount) for a quick getaway; they'd been given permission to start their leave as soon as their shift ended.

Martin had left his jacket in the cottage, but those boots looked like they'd take some shifting. Paddling would have to wait. So we headed for the rocks instead, and settled on a shady bit of sand, facing away from each other, our backs comfortably sharing a boulder. The sea shushed and whispered away down the beach, and a couple of gulls wheeled silently overhead. I closed my eyes. The sun gradually bathed us in light as it moved across the sky, and we sat in contemplative silence for a while. I felt surprisingly relaxed, although after a while it was just too hot, but probably a bit too soon to go back – months had passed since Pete and Cath had been together.

"You asked about the journey?"

"Did I? Oh yeah. All right then, how was it?"

"Well… it was a slow start because we had to finish some work that needed doing before the beginning of next week. We didn't leave till nearly seven, and we hadn't realised what a long drive it is from Ipswich to Cornwall – the best part of three hundred and fifty flamin' miles! We had to stop to eat, then there were traffic jams on the M25. It was maybe two am by the time we got to the right area. Then, of course, we couldn't find the bloody cottage. When we did, we thought we'd cracked it because the door was unlocked, but we didn't realise we'd only be in half of it, and the old dear who owns it lives next door."

"Oh no! You didn't go into the wrong bit…?"

"We certainly did. Pete had this stupid idea that Cath would be impressed if she woke up to him kissing her."

How typical was that? The great sloppy sod!

"Oh God, he didn't…?"

"No! The old girl put the light on and started screaming before he got anywhere near, but it must have been one hell of a shock – two hulking great uniformed squaddies standing at the foot of her bed."

He looked at me and we both grinned.

"And?"

"Well, when she'd calmed down a bit, she admitted it was an easy mistake to make in the pitch dark, and since we were clearly serving our country, she'd overlook it and allow us to stay."

"I should flippin' well hope so – we had to pay in advance!"

"Pete went out for flowers at first light, and he's been round to apologise again – turns out her late husband was some Army big cheese, and he's only been dead six months…"

"Oops!"

We sat on in companionable silence. We must have dozed, but I had no sunscreen or sunhat and no idea how strong the August sun could be at midday. When I woke up it was blazing directly onto my face; I have dry, sensitive skin and it must have looked scorched. I felt awful, suddenly - my face was burning and I had a banging headache.

I groaned and Martin opened his eyes and half turned towards me.

"Are you ok?"

"Not sure – think I might have been out in the sun too long – should have put a hat on. Think I'd better get back." I scrambled to my feet, thirsty and a bit dizzy. It suddenly looked like a long hike back to the cottage. Martin rose easily, springing up in one move.

"Come on, soldier, quick march!"

"Piss off!"

"I could put you on a charge for that."

"I'd like to see you try!"

But he grabbed my hand and unceremoniously hauled me up the beach. It wasn't quite the sort of first contact I'd wanted.

Chapter Five
2016

"Oh, here she is… been hobnobbing with a new Riley, have we?"

Predictably, Barker and Benn referred thus to all members of the Expressive Arts faculty, since they were convinced their more talented colleagues lived The Life Of… I made no response. Benn looked grim.

"Well, since you've finally joined us, here's your timetable, but there's a mistake on it – you seem to have gained an extra free."

"Ah yes – sorry, it's no mistake. Brian's just explained that it's so that I can plan the integrated curriculum with Mr Prescott Smith before each Wednesday after-school meeting of the IC Committee."

"What? *Really?* I'm not having that. And you've got one Year Seven class for only two periods? This is *outrageous.*"

"Well actually, I'm sharing that class with Mr PS so that we can deliver some of the new IC and monitor how it goes. So he's going to be teaching a proper subject, instead of, as you'd put it, poncing around in the Theatre. Think of it as gaining an extra teacher."

"Huh, Mr *PS*, is it? A typical afterthought, obviously."

Shit, I'd slipped up there. Martin had always signed his letters MPS, even in the days when he was just plain old Martin Smith, middle name Prescott. But of course I couldn't possibly know that, could I?

Mr Barker looked grim, but we moved on to our various GCSE teaching groups and A Level groups, and the rest of the meeting passed without incident.

There were six full-time English specialists in the faculty: Rosemary Robinson, Paul Waters (a young and ambitious postgrad with an MA and a ticket to an Academy pending), and Muriel Lord.

She was a one-off, fortunately. Although inexplicably she hated Benn and Barker with a passion, and made her feelings known at every opportunity; she seemed to hate everyone else as well, including the kids, and herself, probably. She had a habit of sitting with headphones on during our meetings – I couldn't help but admire her. Then there was me, Benn and Barker. To make up the timetable we drew on the services of several enthusiastic members of other faculties, and on the whole we'd been pleasantly surprised by their different perspectives and approaches. I make no apologies for admitting that they'd helped me greatly in constructing the outline of the Integrated Curriculum.

"I suppose you want to say a few words about this *ridiculous* scheme you've lumbered us all with?" There were five minutes left before the end of morning school, we were hungry and itching to sample the free lunch provided on all training days, and then begin the final preparations for tomorrow's onslaught of excited pupils.

Great timing, great intro – cheers, Barry.

"Oh yes, thanks Barry. Don't worry, there's not much to say – just that the first meeting of the Steering Committee will go ahead in the LRC tomorrow after school, as planned last term. Faculties have selected their reps, and it looks as though I'm remaining in joint charge, so there could be a space for another English rep if anyone'd like to volunteer? No pressure, just an opportunity…"

I saw Paul Waters look up, but before he could say anything, Benn kicked in with, "I think I'll go for this." There was a quick exchange of glances with Barker, and a slight smirk.

"Excellent, Mr Benn – I'm sure you'll bring your wealth of *experience* to bear, and bring this… *project* back to reality."

Pompous twat. The perfect end to a perfect morning.

Chapter Six
1998

What was wrong with me? I'd only known this bloke five minutes, and already I was obsessed. Granted, I was nineteen and no doubt at the mercy of raging hormones, but I'd been conditioned by my mother's archaic moral values into being nervous around men and wary of anyone who seemed to be interested in me – in my earlier teens, my self-esteem had been so low I thought that if they showed the slightest hint of fancying me, they automatically must be a bit weird and pervy. If I'd had a brother, like Cath, or been to a mixed school, I perhaps wouldn't have seen blokes as a threatening sub-species, or compensated for that by being super sharp and sometimes cutting around them. Pete and his mates were different though – relaxed, funny and more than capable of dealing with my defensive nonsense. I felt comfortable around them, there was nothing threatening in their good-natured banter, but no chance whatsoever of anything more than playful friendship, in spite of one or two clumsy and slightly embarrassing overtures from me. And I suppose that was the reason Pete decided it was time I was introduced to Martin.

It could have been excruciating, but it wasn't. Far from it. He had us all in helpless laughter many times, with his quick one-liners and wicked impersonations, but he was also kind and thoughtful, always ready to help with cooking or keeping the cottage fairly clean – and he did direct a lot of attention my way.

The first few days of our fortnight in Cornwall were blisteringly hot. We explored some of the nearby towns and beaches, blasting through the leafy countryside between high hedges in Pete's sporty Audi, the sun roof down and Bruce Springsteen telling us he was born to run in the glory days, and Martin and Pete yelling out the words. And always, when there was a momentary break in the roadside vegetation, there were tantalising glimpses of a horizon in which the navy blue of the sea and the sun-drenched sky were scarcely distinguishable.

We found one beach with shifting dunes and scrubby sea grass. Pete foolishly boasted about his martial arts prowess and the next thing was a photo of him, which I still have, upended and heading for the sand head first courtesy of Martin, much to his surprise. Inexplicably, Pete rapidly went off this and turned his attention to Cath. While he was distracted by the sight of Pete flipping Cath onto her back in the sand, I deftly caught Martin with a move I'd learned in junior school − foot chop to the back of the knees, one hand in the small of the back, the other across the collar bone. He was down before he could stop me, but somehow managed to pull me down with him, and held me there, hands on my shoulders while I squealed and squirmed and loved every minute.

Then there was Tintagel. I'd always wanted to see it, so we decided we'd have a day away from the beaches and take a look. I was greatly disappointed − ruined by commercialism, with tat shops selling Guinevere mugs and Merlin tea towels. But we wanted to see the castle at the end of the rocky promontory, even though it meant parking in King Arthur's Car Park. We'd bought a large frozen chicken for dinner that night, not at all sure it would thaw in time. Martin decided to help it along by sticking it up the back of his t-shirt and capering around on the car park wall with a funny, lop-sided gait, pretending to be Lawrence Olivier playing Richard the Third. Quite undaunted by the bemused looks of other holiday-makers, he declaimed the opening lines and I told them to humour him because he wasn't let out very often.

Another day we headed off to a surfing beach for some serious swimming. Pete had done an Army scuba diving course and had packed a couple of masks, but the rest of us weren't keen, although we were going to swim. I wasn't happy about the exposure of wobbly bits − Cath looked great in her bikini and I just felt like the Fat Friend, but nobody seemed to notice or care. For all my apparent confidence, I was still very self-conscious about my body. I did a personal best haring down to the sea and throwing myself in, but my anxiety about Martin seeing how fat I was caused me to totally miss

Pete's warning about a strong current. There was a heart-stopping moment when my feet failed to touch the bottom and I felt the sea dragging me out and away. I tried to yell but got a mouth full of sea water, and then a very welcome arm came out of nowhere, round my shoulders and under my chin, and I was pulled back to the shallows, spluttering. Martin.

"Bloody hell, Allie, listen next time before you launch into that sea!" Then he looked at my face, and saw the treacherous tears just threatening. He pulled me towards him and into a wet, semi-naked bear hug, whispering, "Sorry for shouting. Just stay safe for me. Ok?"

Later we walked back to the car, sticky with salt and ready for home and the fight for the shower. Pete and Martin were clowning around in front, and Cath turned to me.

"Well?"

"Pete was right about Martin. No need to ask how you're getting on!"

We both grinned.

"Actually," she said, "I was wondering… would you mind if we went out on our own tonight? Pete says we need to talk about something. There's some of that chicken left, and some salad and half a bottle of white… is that ok?"

I didn't hesitate.

"Go on then – you young 'uns go out and enjoy yourselves and we'll make do with left-overs."

But she knew why I was smiling.

Chapter Seven
2016

I didn't sleep much, that Tuesday night. I couldn't imagine how I was going to handle our meeting, how I could keep it professional in the teeth of churning emotions. I must have nodded off eventually, but when the alarm went at 6.30, I surfaced feeling sick and raw-eyed.

At least I didn't have to face him first thing. I was on duty every Wednesday morning and break that year in the Sixth Form block, which was a completely separate building, a good two hundred yards away from the main school, further down the hill towards the Lancashire road. It was much newer than the rest of the school, designed specifically for Sixth Form teaching just before the education budget cuts took hold, and was entirely free of younger kids. The idea was to make it more like a Sixth Form college, to encourage our students to stay with us rather than move to real colleges in neighbouring towns – and on the whole we succeeded.

When the bell went for lessons, the first task of my day was to be in my room, handing out timetables to the Year Twelve half of my tutor group and making sure there were no subject clashes. Year Thirteen students had been given theirs at the end of the previous year, so they wouldn't arrive till after lunch. I had eight uniform-free ex-Year 11s, several of whom I'd steered through their English GCSEs. I arrived before most of them, and opened the windows in my classroom as far as they'd go, to let in the warm September air. Joe and Hadley had already been in.

Whilst doing my utmost to avoid obvious favourites, these two were simply great. There was a very welcome cup of fresh coffee waiting for me on my desk – they'd brought ground coffee with them and persuaded Matt Haddon, our Head of Sixth Form, to fill up their large flask from the kettle in the block's tiny staff room. They'd promised to do this every day when they'd discovered, in the euphoria of their excellent GCSE results, that they would be in my tutor group.

Then the door burst open.

"Have you met the new Deputy, Miss W? Is it true he's an ex-film star?"

"Good morning and welcome back to you, too. Where on earth did you hear that, Joe?"

"Facebook."

"Well, I'm sorry to disappoint you…" (tempted as I suddenly was to lie like hell), "…but he's actually an ex-actor and stage manager who went into drama teaching. He gave us a resume of his career yesterday. Seems ok, but he doesn't look as if he'll stand for any nonsense, so you two'd better watch out in your drama lessons. I might have a word with him about you before your first session. Forewarned is forearmed."

"Miss!"

"Only kidding. Great coffee, by the way, thanks…"

The others wandered in and we got to work. It was like having two more adults in the group – Joe and Hadley were quick on the uptake and explained the mysteries of the semi-coded timetable sheets to the two boys who'd joined us from another school. It was a good atmosphere and I thought they'd all gel pretty quickly with the Year Thirteen half who were coming in later to start lessons. Break came and went, we finished off the admin and then sat around chatting before they sloped off to the communal area downstairs, where the dinner ladies would be raising the shutters of the small kitchen, ready to sell the sort of stuff they all ate for lunch. With great reluctance, I walked back up to the main school.

I wasn't teaching straight after lunch, so I spent the next forty-five minutes in the main staff room, checking through the initial submissions each faculty had already produced for the Year Seven and Eight Integrated Curriculum. At least I'd have something to go through with Martin, to bring him up to date with our progress so far.

The bell went. I stood up. This was it.

Chapter Eight
1998

By the time Cath and Pete left for their trip to the pub, the weather was turning. It was still very hot and close, but the sky was darkening and I thought I could catch a distant grumble of thunder. We ate the chicken and salad, drank the last of the good German white and opened a Cote du Rhone. We also polished off a lump of Cornish cheddar. We'd just got settled in the front room and were about to watch a film on the video player when there was an almighty flash and a clap of thunder so loud it seemed to rattle the walls of the old cottage.

The lights went out.

"Oh shit, bang goes the film… any candles?"

"Cath's left a couple of tea lights and a smelly candle on the window sill and there's matches on the shelf by the stove. I'll light them."

I paused with the unlit match in my hand and looked out of the picture window. The sea below had changed entirely – it boiled and churned in the wind that had sprung up, and flecks of foam were being flung onto the beach.

"Wow, come and look at this – it's really dramatic!"

As Martin approached the window, a branch of lightening snaked down into the sea – I imagined sizzling and sulphur as it struck – and then another clap of thunder, as if a tin tray had crashed down onto a stone floor. I involuntarily stepped back into Martin and felt his arms instantly encircle me.

"Emily Bronte would've loved this view!"

Why did I say that? He'll think I'm really weird.

"So this is the bit where I run outside and you chase after me screaming over your shoulder to your aging servant, 'Nelly, I *am* Heathcliff!', is it?"

So he's read Wuthering Heights, *then, even if he doesn't remember it completely accurately.*

"Please don't – you'd be soaked in no time."

I turned to face him and his mouth met mine. After that, I forgot all about the climate, and the darkness; my world was reduced to pure sensation, and the shedding of clothing, the smooth hardness of his muscles under the tee shirt, his hands on me, his mouth on my neck—

"Hang on a minute," I gasped. "Upstairs?"

When we staggered into his bedroom we had more space, somehow, to unpeel our various layers. There was no hesitation, no embarrassment. We fell onto the bed, then he paused for a second. His hand was stroking the top of my thigh, but he said, "Look. I'm really sorry but I don't have any condoms, and we can't risk you getting pregnant. But there's other things we could do. How about this...? Or this...? Are you ok? Shall I stop?"

"No!"

So he didn't. Later I tried a couple of things I'd read about in *Cosmopolitan*, which seemed to do the trick for him. Then he had a go at something else involving several fingers, making me clench and buck beneath him again and again. Then it was over and we lay, sticky and panting and gazing at each other and smiling stupidly.

"I've never done that before with anyone."

I felt I had to say it, but I wasn't expecting his reply.

"No," he said, "neither have I. Again?"

***

Much later, we slept, then I woke to listen to his steady breathing. I put my hand on his chest to feel the slow throb of his heart, and, nestling into his side, slept again.

The next time I woke it was light and the seagulls had started their raucous shrieking. I ran the back of my hand up his arm, but he didn't stir, and I thought, what if he's really awake and too embarrassed to face me? What if he's cringing inside and wishing it had never happened? I slid carefully out of bed, gathered up my clothes and crept into my room next door. I fished clean stuff out of the wardrobe then headed for the bathroom. No-one else was stirring, so I had a much-needed pee, then a long refreshing shower, before dressing and going quietly downstairs and out into the fresh air of the cool morning.

I made for the beach, but the tide was in and I couldn't get anywhere near what I now thought of as our rocks, so I had to make do with walking around the bay on the soft, shifting sand above the tideline. I walked for about ten minutes, then came across a wooden bench carefully placed to admire the view. I settled there, sitting sideways, hugging my knees. Last night kept replaying in my head – what we'd done, what he'd said and, more objectively, how thoughtful he'd been. I still could hardly believe how uninhibited it was, how desire had stopped my fear and made me want to give pleasure as well as take it. Gradually, the steady rolling sea worked its magic and I felt calmer and a little more confident – and absolutely starving.

As I turned and stood up to head back, I saw a figure jogging over the sand. It was Pete, waving. When he got a bit closer he said, "You're in big trouble! Martin's doing his nut, worrying about where you've got to, and your flaming mother's just rung, demanding to speak to you."

"Oh for God's sake – can't she leave me alone for five minutes? What did she say?"

"Nothing. She hung up when Martin answered."

"No wonder – I told her Cath and I were going to be on our own to draw some Cornish landscapes, but I didn't give her the number."

"No, you've got Cath's mum to thank for that."

"Great. Well, I'm not going to worry about her. If she rings again I'll deny all knowledge of the first call and say she must've got the wrong number the first time."

"Good luck with that – Martin picked up the call and said, 'Good morning, you've reached the Cornish Escort Agency, what sort of man are you looking for?' Of course he didn't know it was your mother, and he used his best *carnish* accent, ooh ahh, so if he ever meets her she *might* not recognise his voice…"

"Cheers for that. I feel *so* much better now!"

There was an uneasy silence for a second when I walked into the kitchen, and a couple of sideways glances. Then Martin came up to me, touched my face briefly and said, "Sorry about your Mum, Allie."

"Oh, don't worry, she'd have no idea what you meant in any case."

Then Cath said, "Bacon butty, anyone? Celebrate our engagement?" and the atmosphere lifted, there were hugs and kisses and good wishes, and it was all lovely – until the telephone rang.

Chapter Nine
2016

I had no idea how I was going to handle this meeting. I arrived at the door to Martin's office carrying a large file containing the faculty submissions, stomach churning. The door was open and there were two chairs facing each other on the same side of his desk.

"Hiyah, Allie. White, one sugar?"

"Black, no sugar."

Don't you 'Hiyah, Allie' me like the last fifteen years never happened.

I marched in and sat down, brusque and business-like, and opened the file, laying out the various folders on his desk.

"I have actually glanced at the submissions. Brian e-mailed them to me and I've printed off enough copies so everyone can see them all – I hope that's all right with you?"

"Of course."

Damn. What were we going to talk about now?

"I haven't really been through them in any detail—"

Thank goodness.

"—but what I've picked up so far is how inventive they are, and interesting. Allie, you've inspired your colleagues with this, and they've made a pretty impressive start, haven't they? I really like the idea of six-week units, and some connection between the Year Seven and Year Eight schemes. So… where do you see this going now, and when do you want everyone to start?"

At least he's asking, not instructing – is he struggling a bit as well?

"Well, I originally thought we'd need a term to plan, but I agree, it's coming together very quickly, and I was thinking we could start after half-term, which would give us another six or seven two-hour planning meetings."

"Yeah, I was thinking along those lines myself. So let me get this straight in my head... Victorians for Year Seven and Edwardians plus World War One for Year Eight?"

In the end it was much easier than I'd anticipated. His enthusiasm was obvious and he made one great suggestion for an end-of-term celebration to pull the two eras together, which we would put to our colleagues. I began to think that perhaps keeping things on a strictly professional footing might work.

But that was all it could ever be.

Later, we convened around several tables pushed together in the Learning Resources Centre, a cavernous space in what used to be a fine wood-panelled library till it was grabbed by twentieth-century technology, then allowed to become shabby in the face of twenty-first century austerity.

Martin insisted that I should chair the meeting, and when we arrived together, I was gratified to see my friends and colleagues chatting with animation over their collections of schemes of work. Apart from Simon Benn, who arrived late and sat apart from everyone else with a face, as Martin used to say in a different life, like a forced landing.

I kicked off the proceedings.

"Hi everyone and thanks for coming, and for all your submissions, which I'm sure you'll all agree are really exciting.

"You might notice a couple of new faces – thanks for joining the group, Simon, and a warm welcome to our new Deputy, Martin Prescott Smith – I'm sure we'll value your previous experience of teaching an integrated curriculum. And on that note, Martin, would you like to give us your first impressions of progress so far?"

"Yes, thanks, Allie. As I said earlier, I think this is a great start—"

"Can I just say something before you start praising this... *stuff* to high heaven?"

"Go ahead, Mr...?"

"Benn. Second in English. There is a major problem with this project. There appears to be no reference anywhere to the National Curriculum or attainment targets. I can't imagine Ofsted will be too impressed by us turning Years Seven and Eight into a glorified primary school. Where are the standards here? Where's the academic rigour and assessment opportunities?"

"Oh for God's sake, Simon, isn't enthusiasm and real learning more important that ticking Ofsted boxes?"

This was Sean Wooler, head of Boys' PE and a part-time English teacher, a man who spoke his mind, and wasn't afraid to voice what others were merely thinking.

But nothing would be gained by open warfare at this early stage.

"Well, you've certainly got a point, Simon," I said, carefully keeping my voice level. "But of course, cross-referencing the National Curriculum and building in appropriate assessment opportunities are two of the areas we need to address in these preliminary meetings."

"Well, let's make sure we do, then."

"And of course this is where we all benefit from pooling our resources and approaches," Martin chipped in. "Don't worry too much about Ofsted, though – if we get this right, I can't see any reason why they won't approve – they certainly did at my last school. We were described as inspirational teachers."

Benn looked furious, and Martin immediately became one of the team.

We spent the next couple of hours going over a rough draft for a week's lessons in each subject, and formulating the report each faculty rep would take back to their own meetings. Then, just before we finished, Martin revealed his big idea – a Christmas show based around 'The Good Old Days' and moving seamlessly (through music hall recruitment) into some much more serious drama and poetry based on the First World War. This was very well received, and we broke up buzzing.

As we cleared up stray paper and moved tables after everyone else had gone, Martin said, "That went well, I thought – but who was that miserable old bugger? You handled him brilliantly, by the way."

I wasn't rising to any compliments.

"Simon Benn, second in the English department and secretary of the local Tory Party. We have to put up with his right-wing crap at every English meeting."

"Good God. Every school has one, but why did he stick himself on this project? He can't go sneaking back to Brian telling tales – he'll get nowhere there – and he's totally outnumbered."

"Not entirely," I said. "He's also a Governor, one of the school reps, and on the Staffing Committee. We need to watch him."

"Well, he can't be *that* powerful, or I'd never have been appointed, would I?"

Twelve months later, those words would come back to haunt us.

Chapter Ten
1998

Cath finally answered the phone.

"Hello? Oh, hello Mrs Weston. Yes, of course she is, hang on... sorry? Why are we staying *where*? Of course we aren't working in an escort agency, we're on holiday. I've no idea – maybe you got the number wrong? No, I'm not saying that, I don't think you're blind... oh, here's Allie..."

(My mother, Doris, was married to my poor dad for twenty years without children, before then choosing to adopt me when she was forty. She was used to getting her own way, and was pretty impossible if that didn't happen. Imagine a cross between Hyacinth Bouquet and the Queen in an irritable mood – not even close. She loathed Cath with a passion. When she realised that we would be together in Manchester (and Cath was at the University whilst I'd only achieved the Met, as she never ceased to remind me), she declared that I'd have to go back to school and re-take my A Levels. For once Dad had stood up to her, but I'd only been away three weeks when I got a frantic phone call from him saying she suspected she'd had a heart attack and wanted to see me. Of course I got on the next train, only to find her giving orders from her bed at home. According to my father, the doctor had rushed out to see her and assured her there was absolutely nothing wrong with her heart, or anything else as far as he could see.

She had greeted me in typical Doris fashion – I've never forgotten it.

"Let her come in," she declaimed from her bed, "and see what she's done!"

She was, to quote my friends, 'a piece of work'. But, in spite of all that, she was still my mother, and constantly unhappy with her life and her adopted daughter, who probably hadn't turned out at all as she was expecting.)

"Alison, you'll have to come home now. Daddy's very poorly."

This was a new one.

"Oh Mum, I'm sorry – what is it? What does the doctor say? He has seen the doctor, hasn't he?"

"No, but—"

Instant launch into full aggrieved victim mode. Again.

"—are you saying you don't believe me, you selfish girl? After all we've done for you? Nothing was too good for you when you were young, *nothing*, and this is the way you repay us... Swanning off on holiday and me stuck here with your father who won't go anywhere. How could you?"

"Mum, I only asked—"

"I heard what you asked, I'm not deaf."

She was, actually.

"Is Dad there? Can I have a quick word with him? Why don't you go and put the kettle on?"

"John! She wants to speak to you – *alone!*"

There was a pause, then I heard my Dad clearing his throat.

"There's nothing wrong with me, Alison – I'm just a bit tired, that's all. Your mother's annoyed because I can't face driving into town to take her shopping. I'm sorry to disturb you. Are you having a good break?"

Guilt washed over me – I should have confided in him about Pete and Martin, I think he'd have been all right about it.

"I'm fine, Dad, don't worry about me, it's a nice cottage and the views are stunning. We've had some lovely walks..."

"I'm very pleased to hear it, you'll feel better for some sea air. You can tell us all about it when you get back."

Gulp.

"Oh and Alison, just one more thing..."

"Yes Dad?"

"This young man – is he a friend of Pete's? Is he a soldier? Is he treating you well?"

I smiled to myself. Martin, standing next to me, his head close to mine, looked aghast. There was no fooling my Dad.

"Yes. I'm really happy, Dad."

"Good. See you soon." He hung up.

Martin said nothing at first, just frowned and shook his head. Then he grinned, pointed at me and said, in his best Olivier hamming it up voice, "Filial ingratitude! How sharper than a serpent's tooth it is to have a thankless child!"

"Nothing comes of nothing, speak again!" was all I could think of to counter.

"How come you can quote so much Shakespeare?" Cath said to Martin. She'd recognised the lines from *King Lear* instantly, having helped me to learn them before my A Level exam.

"Ah, well, you see, ma'am, I may have the mind of a humble grease monkey but I have the heart of a great scholar, cruelly deprived of my education by my family's poverty—"

"Bollocks!" Pete chipped in, "You left school at sixteen to join the RAF like your dad!"

"Yeah, well, how was I to know they'd turn me down twice? I wanted to do officer training but they said I was too fat at sixteen. Then, when I'd lost weight, they said my eye-sight wasn't up to it. So eventually I thought mending army helicopters was the next best thing – which of course was how I met Private Pike here."

"Oy, less of that, bit of respect for the rank if you don't mind!"

"Piss off… *Corp*!"

Pete grinned, then Martin turned to me.

"But seriously, Allie, if you think your mother's going to give you grief when you get home, I could come with you and charm her with my razor wit and ready repartee."

I was touched, but I knew he wouldn't have much leave left, and he'd told me earlier how much his family wanted to see him. They lived near Chirk in Shropshire (which explained the decoration on his Army suitcase – goodness knows how he'd got away with that!). In the end, after a phone call to her parents, we agreed the logistics of our return home. I'd take Cath's mum's car and drop Martin off at his home, staying overnight to break the journey. He'd emphasised that if my mother was difficult when I got back, he'd be at the end of the phone and happy to speak to Dad, and even to my mother if I wanted him to.

Later, when Pete and Cath had disappeared for another of their early nights, we strolled down to the sea, enjoying the soft, salty air and the slow rhythmic shuck of the waves in the dark. We stopped just before the beach ran on from the rocky track, caught in the moment, the moonlight and the stillness, watching the silver reflections in the calm water. Martin's arm was round my waist and I leaned my head into his shoulder.

After a few moments he said, "A star for every wandering bark... in this fishing-boat bobbing sea."

I moved my head to look at his face and said, "I know Cath was joking earlier, but it was a fair question. How come you can quote so easily?"

"I've always been a reader," he admitted, still resting his eyes on the ocean. "I love the music of the words in Shakespeare – I've read most of the plays and some of the lines really stuck in my memory – and some poetry – Dylan Thomas, obviously – which I like more even than novels, unless they're really powerful – Steinbeck, Orwell, you know, stuff like that. I had an inspiring English teacher who introduced me to texts way beyond what we were studying. But I couldn't get it down onto paper fast enough in exams, so my grades ended up piss-poor and they wouldn't have me in the Sixth Form."

I nodded.

"I know – that's the trouble with exams; writing about literature shouldn't be a timed memory test. I hated being under that sort of pressure myself. Unlike you, it took me ages to learn chunks of *King Lear* and quotes from *Sons and Lovers* – and I can barely remember them now.

"But go on – how did you end up in the Army?"

"So then after school I couldn't think what to do, and Dad suggested trying for the RAF – I know I joked about it earlier, but I was really bitter about failing. The Army was the next best thing, so I applied for the REME – the Royal Electrical and Mechanical Engineers. Like Pete, I fancied being a helicopter technician. At first I loved it – I've always been good at fixing things, especially motors, thanks to Dad, and basic training was a laugh. But now, I don't know... I've made Lance Corporal and they want me to go for the next rung, but I think I've got something out of my system, and I'm beginning to realise that there could be more to life than flight-testing Gazelles and repairing Lynx… you know, Army helicopters."

Then he added. "Especially if that means I can't be with the people I really care about."

He looked at me out of the corner of his eye and smiled. Something inside me leaped. I suddenly realised that this man, for all his clowning and kindness, had a depth to him that I hadn't understood.

He lifted my face up to meet his and kissed me, firmly but very slowly and gently. I didn't want the moment, or our magical holiday, to end. But this interlude – this beginning? – couldn't go on for ever. The fortnight was rapidly drawing to a close.

***

On the last day, we left first – Cath and Pete had volunteered to do a final serious cottage clean. There was a stone in my stomach at the thought of leaving; how could anything ever be so good, so new again? I wanted to believe that what I had felt so strongly on the moonlit beach might be real – and mutual – but Martin hadn't really said anything to confirm it, apart from the occasional vague reference to a shared future. I was hopeful, but I didn't want to put him on the spot or force the issue, although I felt that we were meant to be together.

I was even more sure when I met his family. They lived in a spotless, unpretentious bungalow just outside Chirk, on the English side of the Welsh border, and they took me in as if I were a long-lost daughter. Both his mum, Dora, and his dad, Den, worked in factories on the outskirts of nearby Wrexham, and his sister, Lou, was in Year Ten at the local comp. Martin's nan was just up the road, still in the house she'd lived in with her late husband, who'd been a miner. They were like no family I'd ever met before – loud, funny, rude – I could see where Martin got his sense of humour. Within a couple of hours of meeting them, I felt as if I'd known them all my life, and that this was where I wanted to be.

The first thing Den said to me when we walked in was, "Come in, love, make yourself at home. I've got the chips on, because who makes the best chips in Chirk Bank, Martin?"

"You do, Dad."

"I do, son – and don't you forget it... Come on, Lou, do your dance, do your dance... show Allie your moves!"

Dora was no fool; she saw how things were between us instantly. She hugged Martin for a very long time, then me, briefly, and she said, "Now I don't know what you two have been up to, and I don't want to know. Allie, I'm really pleased he's found you, and you'll always be welcome, but there'll be none of that carry on under this roof before you're married. Martin, while you're here you'll behave like a good Catholic boy, and Alison, you're staying with Nan. Right?"

"Right."

Catholic? Married? Hang on a minute...

"How long does it take to get a wedding organised, Mother?"

"Oh go on with you, you daft bugger, but you know what I mean, don't you?"

"Yes Mother."

She put her arm round me.

"Now then, Allie," she said, "I've been looking at some snaps from when he was a little boy. I'm sure you'd like to see them. There's a very cute one of him naked on the rug when he was six months old, and I've always told him I'd show it to the first girl he brought home."

"Mother! Don't you bloody dare!"

"*And don't you bloody swear!*" they chorused together.

Chapter Eleven
2016

In spite of Simon Benn's persistent snide remarks in our weekly Integrated Curriculum meetings, our team managed to create some effective lesson plans, one week at a time. Finally, in mid-October, after six weeks' planning, we were ready to report back to our various faculties. On that day, Martin was with the Expressive Arts teachers, so my colleagues were given their next half term's lesson plans for Years 7 and 8 by me and Simon. He had, very unwillingly, been drawn into the planning, and as a result of his constant nagging, every lesson we'd produced had been cross-referenced with National Curriculum Key Stage Three Attainment Targets. Ironically, this gave Benn and the miserable Barker very little to complain about.

As the plans were perused by my English colleagues, there was total silence and a lot of note-making about resources that could be added.

In the midst of the silent atmosphere, Muriel Lord looked up and removed her headphones. She glanced at me, then faced Brian and Simon.

"I'm not doing it!" was all she said.

"May I ask why, Muriel?"

"Because, Mr Barker, I've always taught my own lessons and I don't want to do any of this. I don't like being told what to do, and I don't like change."

She glared at Benn, who was scowling back at her.

"But Muriel," I said quietly, "you voted to go ahead with this scheme."

"Did I?"

I knew exactly what had happened, I remembered it well. We'd had a lively discussion last term about the concept of the Integrated Curriculum, but she'd taken no part in it, sitting as usual with her headphones on. When she saw Benn and Barker put their hands up to oppose it, she instantly voted in favour, as a matter of principal. She didn't realise, or care, what she'd voted for, or how she'd be affected.

I tried to reassure her. "The thing is, it's a very flexible scheme – you can put your own stamp on it. These plans are just a guideline; as long as you cover more or less the same topics, you can tweak it in any way you like."

"We've all got to do it, Muriel," said Barry. "We're going to review it at the end of this unit, but if you still refuse, it might be difficult for me to defend your approach if any parents question why their offspring aren't doing broadly the same work as their friends."

Barry Barker was defending the Integrated Curriculum because Muriel Lord was now questioning it? Unbelievable.

She said nothing but went rather pink and put her headphones back on.

The meeting ended soon after and I followed her out. When we were well clear of the classroom, I tapped her on the arm.

"What now?"

"Try not to worry about these schemes – the IC's my baby, not those muppets' and I honestly think you'll enjoy it when you get going, but if you have any questions at all, just ask. Oh, and Muriel?"

"Yes?"

"You do realise, don't you, that thanks to you Mr Barker has now publicly committed himself to supporting it? Thanks!"

Even Muriel smiled at that.

***

We would begin, as a school, to teach the Integrated Curriculum to Years 7 and 8 at the beginning of November, immediately after half-term. On the day before we broke up, Brian asked Martin and me to a progress meeting with our Head of Governors, Mary Booth. We had collaborated to produce a full record of the decisions taken during the first six weeks, and would ask faculties to log all their lesson plans for future reference, since we hoped to reduce planning next year by having them available to everyone on the school's intranet, in the newly-created IC folder.

"Can I just say," Brian launched in, almost before we'd sat down, "how delighted I am to read your report, Allie and Martin? I think this is one of the most exciting initiatives at Hebbel High for many years, and I'm sure it'll go down well with everyone concerned, and Ofsted. Don't you agree, Mary?"

"I do, and I'd like to offer the Governors' thanks to you both, and your team, for all you've done so far. And," she added, "the Governors also have a suggestion to make, which we hope you'll like. We'd like to make funds available for display boards, running at head height all the way round the school, in the dining room, the theatre and the LRC, so that each faculty can display some of the best work. I'm sure they would be an attractive asset for the school, its visitors, and Ofsted, when they come, which they no doubt will at some point."

I couldn't hide my delight. "Oh what a great idea, thank you! We did consider a request for some display space, but we thought it'd be too expensive."

"Well, it is, really, but we feel that it's important to showcase what we know will be very interesting work."

We left Brian's office together, and as I was heading towards the staff room, Martin said, "Allie, don't you think this calls for a celebration? A quick drink somewhere?"

"Yes! It's rather short notice, but I'll put an e-mail out tomorrow and invite everyone, and tell them about the display boards at the same time. We usually go to the Drover's Arms, on the main road. Is that ok?"

"Sure."

I could have been mistaken, but I thought he looked a touch disappointed.

Chapter Twelve
1998

Saying goodbye to Martin in Chirk was awful. He had a few days leave still to spend with his family; they'd very kindly asked me to stay on, but Cath's mother needed her car back, and in any case I had to prepare for my return to Manchester – the summer was drawing to a close, and Year Three at the Met loomed.

I was leaving mid-morning; Den, Dora and Lou all hugged me soundly in the kitchen and said they would look forward to my next visit soon, and Martin carried my bag to the car. He enveloped me in a great bear hug for ages, rubbing his hands up and down my back, then held me at arms' length. I tried not to cry – and failed miserably.

"Stop that, you daft beggar, or you'll have me at it too!

"Just listen a minute, I need to say a couple of things.

"First, you know I'm only in Suffolk; I'll get a long weekend at the start of next month, and I'll be on the first train to Manchester as often as I can. Second thing - and I'm not very good at this so sorry if it sounds a bit weird - but… this has been the best two weeks of my life. The fact that I know you're out there, somewhere, thinking about me is what'll get me through the next month till I can see you again. I know it's only been two weeks, but you can probably guess what I'm going to say – I love you, Alison Weston."

I couldn't speak. I wanted to, but I couldn't. With my eyes on his, I nodded, reached up and touched his face, then kissed him briefly, got in the car and drove away.

I'm not sure how I did it, but I drove up to the M6 and headed north. I drove with the radio on full blast, and once the initial pain had subsided a little, I found myself singing. At the first services I stopped and brought a Cornish postcard out of my bag. I wrote, *I feel the same. This place will always remind me of the start of our life together.* I bought a first-class stamp and posted it there and then.

Four hours later, I went straight to Cath's; she then drove me home, dropped me at the top of the drive and chose not to come in, for some reason.

Before I could knock, my mother had the front door open.

"Oh, so you're back at last. Nice of you to *drop in.* I suppose you want to put some washing in? I don't suppose you've done any for weeks."

"Hi Mum, nice to see you. How are you? How's Dad?"

"Perfectly well, thank you. We want a word, *now.*"

Here we go.

They sat in our living room in the detached bungalow my mother had designed, and into which they'd moved when I went to Manchester. My mother had folded her arms and pursed her lips; Dad was smoking, as usual.

The rant began immediately, predictable and tedious – I was utterly selfish, she'd been abandoned…

"I've had it to do all my life, and just when I thought I might be able to get a bit of a rest, or even a little holiday, off you go gallivanting with those dreadful so-called friends who only asked you to make up the numbers so they could have their sleazy little adventure – they don't really care about you. And what's this about an extra man? Who was he? Are you *pregnant?*"

Oh for God's sake – thanks for keeping Martin to yourself, Dad – ha bloody ha.

"I *said* who was he? Is he another dreadful soldier? You'll have given him plenty to talk about with his cronies in the… what do they call it… the *Naafi?* You'll never hear from him again. You know that, don't you? Oh how *could* you do this to me, after all we've done for you?"

"He's not like that. I've met his family, who are wonderful, and—"

"He's surely *not* a soldier, is he? He is, isn't he? Oh how *very* sophisticated, *what* a good match – you'll *love* being an army wife on those *dreadful* bases, in your pokey army house with the other—"

"I was a soldier when you met me."

My dad always spoke quietly, but I could tell from his tone he'd had enough of her nonsense. She paused momentarily.

"That was National Service. You weren't a *proper* soldier. *You* are a professional, a member of the Law Society, someone with a place in the world, not some uniformed *layabout*—"

"Actually, Martin's a Lance Corporal and a helicopter technician—"

"I'm not interested."

The next few days would have been excruciating, had I not received my first letter from Martin. And then another one. And there was one awaiting my return to the grubby little terraced house I shared with Cath, and another couple in Rusholme, on the outskirts of Manchester.

Those letters! I still have them, they still make me cry. Full of him – his Army life, his mates, his boredom, his longing for me, his frustration (and how he'd like to relieve it!), his next opportunity to see me, his misery at parting, the word *always* repeated over and over, and every one of them addressed to *My Darling Allie...* And if I was in any doubt about Martin's sincerity (I wasn't), reports from Pete via Cath confirmed he used to withdraw from everyone when he first got back from a visit, lying on his bed and barely speaking until he felt up to writing another letter. Reading them now, as time went on, I can sense the change in him – he was gradually becoming more reflective and thinking more seriously about his future.

As he'd said on that moonlit walk in Cornwall, he realised that he wanted to be away from the monotony of fixing engines and out in the world doing something more creative – and he wanted to be with me. The enforced separation was almost more than he could bear. He'd served nearly seven of his nine years and he'd had enough. All he thought about now was how to start the process of buying himself out – at a considerable cost, but at least he'd saved plenty of money during the last seven years. The difficulties would be in persuading the Army to let him go – and the problem of breaking the news to his parents. I realised the whole process could take some time – and he needed to pluck up the courage to make the first move.

But during the months up to Christmas in 1998 we had a different problem. We still hadn't properly slept together. It just wasn't right in my shared house in Manchester – there was too much going on, too many distractions, too many strangers. Finally, we reached a day just before Christmas in, ironically, my parents' house, in my own bedroom.

My father had put his foot down for once – he'd wanted to meet Martin and my mother had better allow it, he'd said. So, very reluctantly, she let me make up a single bed in one of our spare rooms, but she insisted on sleeping with their bedroom door open and the hall light on, as if we might somehow sleepwalk into each other's beds. I was twenty-one and Martin twenty-three, but that made no difference at all.

He was due to go home on Christmas Eve, but on the 22nd, our TV stopped working. This was a catastrophe for Doris – she couldn't bear the thought of missing all those wonderful programmes, or the Queen's Speech. An appointment was arranged and the technician was due, but she *had* to go into town to buy bread and other last-minute provisions, and she didn't drive. We would have to be left to deal with the technician, who'd promised faithfully he'd come that afternoon (although, much to her fury, he didn't turn up until Christmas Eve).

She had adopted a hideous, girly manner with a bemused Martin, so before they left, she said, "Now you will both behave yourselves while we're gone, won't you? I'm trusting you, Martin!" The giggle which followed was excruciating.

"Have no fear, Mrs Weston, your daughter's honour will be quite safe with me."

The minute their car turned away at the end of the drive we hurled ourselves onto my bed, ripping clothes in desperate desire. I was finally on the pill, no need for condoms. This was it. The expression on his face as he looked down at me was something I'll never forget – his urgent desire coupled with his anxiety about hurting me, and the way the moment carried us into a sea of tidal sensation till we cried out, both of us, and subsided together, closer than we'd ever been.

Much later, he raised himself above me, kissed my face and said quietly, "Marry me?"

Chapter Thirteen
2016

Sharing a class with Martin wasn't as difficult as I'd imagined. "Treat me as one of your trainees," he'd said at our first lesson-planning meeting, after school on the Friday of Week One. But he was being unfair to himself – he had some inventive ideas and it was clear from his comments about classroom management that discipline would be no problem.

Our Year Seven class was full of the usual mix of abilities and personalities, but a couple of characters stood out, as is always the way. For example, there was Dean Midgley, a small, very skinny boy with a foxy face and a wicked sense of humour. After a couple of drama periods with Martin, he put his hand up in the middle of an English lesson.

"Miss?"

"Yes, Dean?"

"We think he's ace, that new drama teacher who has us for English as well."

"I'm very pleased to hear that."

"Did you know 'e's a trained killer, Miss?"

"Really?"

"Yeah, 'e told us 'e'd been in the Army, so he must be, mustn't 'e, Miss? I'm gunna ask 'im to show me how to use me dad's BB gun!"

"I don't think he'll want to do that, Dean – and anyway, he was a helicopter technician – I don't think he ever saw active service…"

"How d'yuh know that, Miss?"

Oh hell.

"He mentioned it to everyone when Mr Welch introduced him."

"Did 'e tell yer 'e fell out of a nelicopter and only broke 'is wrist? D'yer like 'im, Miss?"

I could hardly explain that when we first met, Martin had been nursing a broken scaphoid bone, which made holding hands awkward (although nothing else!) And yes, he had fallen out of a helicopter and put out his hand to break his fall – but it was in the workshop being serviced at the time.

"Yuh *do* fancy 'im, don't yer, Miss? So does Kelly Ann, *and* 'e's not married – Kelly Ann asked 'im!"

"Shut it, shit face!"

"Kelly Ann! And that's enough, Dean. How are you getting on with your work? Let me look at what you've done so far, apart from these completely unnecessary drawings of guns…"

And then there was Kelly Ann Morton, with whom one did not mess. She'd strutted into the first lesson on a pair of unsuitable shoes, carrying a little square handbag, planted herself at the front of the class, looked up at me and said, "Right, where d'yer want mi to sit?"

In lessons, at first she'd been a pain, refusing to understand even the most basic instructions, until one day Dean (who knew her from primary school) said, "Oh shut yer face, Kelly Ann, yer know exactly what Miss wants yer to do, stop winding 'er up!"

I made sure they sat together after that, which worked really well – she liked Dean, that was obvious, and he patiently showed her anything a bit tricky, which meant he understood it better himself. From then on they'd been inseparable.

***

Late in September, the year's first cohort of teacher-trainees had arrived; they would be with us until Christmas. The school had a good reputation with Leeds University, and several other institutions, as an excellent venue for trainees on their PGCE courses. Training now is done on the cheap, relying on the good will of qualified teachers, who act as mentors, one per trainee, arranging their timetables, team teaching with them at first, then easing them gradually into nearly full-time teaching. But it isn't just a one-sided arrangement – host schools have the benefit of enjoying the presence of young and enthusiastic post-grads and the opportunity to cherry-pick the best for any vacancies once they've qualified. It's a lot of extra work, but it's also rewarding. And it was my responsibility, on behalf of the English faculty, to take charge of our trainees.

I'd had a profile to look over before this year's first trainee arrived. He was a mature student of thirty-two, a former Post Office employee with a good English degree from York. Apart from his enthusiasm for English, he was also a musician who played the Irish pipes, guitar and violin. I was looking forward to meeting him. But I hadn't anticipated what an imposing figure he'd be. At well over six feet tall, he towered over the other trainees. He had a broad northern Irish accent and a slightly unnerving, unwavering stare.

"So good morning, then," he said as he shook my hand after being introduced by our Training Coordinator "Do I call you Miss Weston? Or...?"

"It's Alison, but I'm known as Allie – that'll be fine. And you're Chris, I believe?"

"Known as Chris, or Mr O'Malley to the kids."

He had very blue eyes, I noticed, and there was no getting away from them. And I wasn't the only one to notice. Eleanor Constantinopolis, a modern languages, part-time English teacher, who was also on the IC committee, had noticed him too. She was quite a character herself, although she had, shall we say, a rather unfortunate reputation amongst the younger male teachers. As the irrepressible Sean had put it, after a couple of pints at the Drovers', "She'd shag anything below forty with a pulse, male or female!"

I had no evidence to support this, although I had noticed, with wry amusement, that she'd been taking a great interest in Martin for the first few weeks of term, hanging on his every word in meetings and making a point of walking along corridors in close proximity whenever possible. He didn't give out many signs that he was enjoying her attention. Serves him right, I'd thought – let him deal with her, if he can.

Chris was a natural teacher. From his first encounter with Dean and Kelly Ann, and the rest of their class, he won them over with his easy manner and unfailing good humour. I realised that I would have very little actual training to do – and he slotted into the term's Integrated Curriculum syllabus with ease. He based some of his lessons on the music of the nineteenth century, both folk and music hall, looking at the lyrics and relating them to contemporary events. He played and sang to them as well – he had a strong but not overpowering voice, and he soon had them joining in, and writing their own lyrics, for which he made up little tunes.

Once, in our weekly meeting towards the end of his time training with us, over a coffee in the staffroom, we got talking about his music.

"Would you come and hear me play some time, Mrs Chips? Sure I'd love to buy you a beer and maybe take you for a bite to eat afterwards, just to say thanks for being such a great mentor."

As luck would have it, Martin was on his way through the staffroom as Chris was speaking. I saw him hesitate just after he'd passed us, and he looked as if he was about to speak, when Eleanor popped her head round the door and called, "Oh Martin, I've had an ace idea, can I just run it past you in your office?" I noticed his eyes roll momentarily.

"Do you know what, Chris? That would be great, although we'd better wait till the very end of your practice. Have you ever played at the Laughing Boar in Queens Bridge? There's a very informal session there on the first Sunday of every month - you could just turn up and join in."

"D'you know, I might just do that," he said, "It's a date! Well not a *date*, obviously—"

"Of course not – just two colleagues enjoying a—"

"—bit of the craic?"

"Exactly!"

That evening, as I was on my way out, Martin collared me.

"You're not really going out with that trainee, are you?"

"Not till I've written his report, no, of course not, and even then, we're only going for an early curry after the session at the pub's over."

"Session?"

"Yeah, we're having a contest to see who can knock back the most shots in an hour. Music session, obviously – you know he plays several instruments, don't you?"

"Right. I see."

"But in any case, what do *you* care who I see outside school? He's a perfectly nice bloke and I enjoy his company – and you have no right to turn into Doris all of a sudden. Just leave it, ok?"

After six weeks, there was a Year Seven parents' evening, to check how they'd settled in. Before they moved up to the Learning Resources Centre to talk to us, Brian spoke to all the parents in the theatre to explain how the Integrated Curriculum would work, since it would begin after half term, and by the time they got to us, most of them were pretty enthusiastic. Martin, Chris and I sat together on the mezzanine with other colleagues and saw a steady stream until around 8pm, when we thought we'd finished. Then Barry Barker came panting up the stairs.

"Not so fast," he puffed, "you've got another one to see. A dreadful little woman with a chav bag and a daughter. You'll have to wait."

Five minutes later, Kelly Ann (high heels and a little handbag) appeared at the top of the stairs, followed by a similarly-sized woman with higher heels – and a little bag. They could have been sisters. I recognised her immediately – she worked in the canteen. They plonked themselves on the seats opposite us.

"Now then," said the older one, presumably Kelly Ann's mother, "She likes you, Miss Weston, and I know *you're* a student, Mr O'Malley, but…" (turning to Martin) "…'oo the 'ell're *you?*"

I could see his jaw twitching as he tried to stay serious. Chris just smiled broadly.

"Actually," he said, "I'm Mr Prescott Smith. I share your daughter's class with Miss Weston – and I'm the new Deputy Head!"

"Oh my God!"

After they'd tootled away, we all looked at each other.

"Your face!" I said to Martin.

"I know, that was certainly a moment… we won't forget that in a hurry, will we?" He smiled at me and I felt a split-second, involuntary lurch.

The trainees finished their teaching practice at the end of November, so on the first Sunday in December Chris picked me up in his ancient Beetle, the back seat filled with various black instrument cases. We chugged down to the small town and parked outside the pub. It was a great venue for music – a former machine tools factory that had been completely restored, but it still retained its great iron pillars. The bar ran the full length of the wall to the left of the door. It was fairly full, but not exactly heaving with drinkers.

It took Chris a while to get his pipes in tune, but when everyone was ready, he took a seat in a circle of about ten people, whilst I sat at a small table behind, enjoying the music. I've always loved folk – it can be raw, poignant or bawdy, but there's something genuine about it, although some of it was modern and some of it decades, if not centuries old. I was just enjoying Chris taking the lead on a lovely, lilting air called, I think, 'Reach out Your Hand', when Martin and Eleanor walked in, arm in arm.

How did I feel? Surprised, I suppose, and yes, if I'm honest, just a bit of a pang – but I wasn't about to rush out sobbing. I waved them over and Martin pulled up an extra chair.

"Are you on your own?" was the first thing Eleanor said.

"No," I said, "I'm with Chris."

"*Really*? I wouldn't have thought he was your type. But he certainly is a bit of eye candy, isn't he?"

"Oh come on, Eleanor, that's a bit sexist, isn't it? Would you be happy if someone said that about you?"

She probably would, actually.

"Chris is good company and very talented – let's leave it at that."

"I'm sure he fancies you though – I've seen the way he looks at you, I'm sure he'd like to—"

"For God's sake shut it, Eleanor. Can't you see Allie's embarrassed?"

"Oh, *I've* got nothing to be embarrassed about, Martin. Eleanor's just being provocative. As usual," I added.

At the end of the session, Chris came over, shook Martin's hand and was immediately enveloped in one of Eleanor's notorious hugs. Like a Trump handshake, they were (apparently) extremely long, drawn-out and featured an uncomfortable grip. Still, he didn't seem to mind.

Needless to say, madam had already decided she needed a curry as well, so we all trooped across the road to the restaurant. She walked on ahead with Chris, holding on to his arm this time, leaving me with Martin.

I was annoyed. "Can't you take her somewhere else? There's nothing between me and Chris, but this is supposed to be his treat for my being his mentor and she's just taking over."

"I didn't want to bring her here, really, or anywhere else for that matter. She just sort of latched on to me... I didn't feel as if I could refuse. Get me out of this, Allie, *please!*"

I expect that's what happened last time too... the man who couldn't say no.

What could I do? I was really annoyed with everyone – my pleasant afternoon had been ruined. But finally, as the great meal drew to a close, and there was ominous talk of adjourning elsewhere for a drink, I had a brainwave.

"Chris, would you mind very much if I didn't go on anywhere else tonight? I don't want to spoil your evening, but there's a lot to be done for the show next week and I really need some time at home to get on with it."

Eleanor looked at me.

"Oh no! Don't be a party pooper! I was going to suggest we all came back to mine for another little drinky poo – we could have *such* a nice time together!"

Ye gods! What on earth was she suggesting?

Martin instantly shot to his feet. "I'll take Allie home, if that's ok with you, Chris? Then..." (to Eleanor) "...you two can have a 'nice time' without us getting in the way. How does that sound?"

"Like a damn fine plan," Chris drawled, gazing at Ms Constantinopolis with twinkling eyes and barely disguised evil intentions. I went about as far off him as it's possible to go, the randy worm. Boy, was he going to be in trouble if his wife in York ever found out about this.

"Well, thanks for the curry," I said to Chris, as Martin threw some notes onto the table for his meal, "and good luck in your second practice, Chris. I hope they put you a bit nearer home next time. You must miss those kids of yours."

***

In his car on the way home, Martin said, "Nice exit, Miss Weston! I owe you one for that. Are you sure you don't fancy a quick drink?"

"No thanks. I'm not in the mood. Why did you bring Eleanor in the first place? You know what she's like!"

"It seemed like a good opportunity to make sure you were ok."

"*Seriously?* How *dare* you! Who do you think you are? Stop this car, I'll catch a bus."

"Nope. I'm just winding you up actually – I did fancy her a bit, I suppose, if I'm honest, but Christ, she's unbelievable! Was she really suggesting what I thought she was suggesting?"

"I've no idea. Turn right here, please, if you must, then right again at the top of the hill."

"Well, I shan't be seeing her again, if that makes you feel any better."

I fumed in silence for five minutes, before we reached the bus layby near my cottage. As I opened his car's door, I turned to Martin and said coldly, "I really don't care what you do, Martin. Thanks for the lift."

"Really? Look, I could murder a coffee…"

Oh no, no way. I shook my head vigorously.

"You've got to be joking. See you tomorrow – oh and Martin? Please stop it, stop pretending you care. I can't and I *won't* take any steps towards going back to what we had. I couldn't bear the thought of being hurt like that again. I'm serious. I'll be your colleague, of course – but that's all. I mean it."

He looked at me out of the corner of an infuriatingly amused eye.

"If you say so."

***

There was a buzz throughout Hebble High in the weeks leading up to Christmas. After a slow start, the kids had suddenly got the hang of the Integrated Curriculum and they launched themselves into it with far more enthusiasm than we could normally inspire in the dark November days. The display boards suddenly bloomed with colourful, lively work – all related to the different interpretations of the topics. I particularly liked the Kitchener-style posters produced by the Year Eight art groups, incorporating portraits of their friends, or the Victorian diaries Year Seven had written, from different perspectives – a chimney-sweep, a mill-owner or the Queen herself. The Year Seven group I shared with Martin had loved *A Christmas Carol* and had great fun dramatising it, before going on to film some of their scenes in the Theatre, after making their own costumes in needlework lessons.

I knew it was going well when I noticed some sixteen year-olds reading some stories on display from another Year Seven class. When I asked them what they thought, one of them said, "This is fantastic – why did *we* never do it?" Wow.

***

The week before we broke up for Christmas, Hebble High's version of *The Good Old Days* played on four nights to a packed theatre. It was the culmination of half a term's integrated work, containing input from the drama, dance, music and art departments, as well as contributions from the Modern Foreign Languages faculty, English and one great act co-ordinated and rehearsed in PE lessons. In creating the programme, the links between the popular Victorian and Edwardian music halls and the Great War became chillingly apparent, and it was topical as well, since that year was slap in the middle of the hundredth anniversary of the War.

Brian had willingly agreed to wield the gavel and demonstrate his skill with alliterative pseudo-Edwardian vocabulary as Master of Ceremonies. He looked fine in a large frock coat with a fancy waistcoat stretched across his generous stomach, a cravat and a stick-on handlebar moustache. There were two front rows of kids in costumes designed by themselves and made by our tireless needlework teacher and her GCSE and A Level students. They had also made the performers' outfits, wherever possible, adapting them from the rather shabby stock of costumes accumulated from previous productions. Some of the parents had even got into the spirit of it and hired fancy dress for themselves. All the music was provided by the Junior Orchestra, although the soloist in the second half was a very proficient Year Ten girl. The lighting and special effects, although directed by Martin from the control box behind the seats, were operated by Joe and Hadley.

The show opened with "The highly harmonious, heavenly syncopated Hebble Singers, joined by… *yourselves!*"

Twenty of our best young singers gave a rousing chorus of 'Down at the old Bull and Bush'. They were followed by a comic juggler (a Year Seven boy who could almost juggle!), a troupe of Year Seven acrobats ("The fearlessly flying, fabulous foursome from Fartown!") a duo of dreadful comedians ("I say, I say, I say, my wife's gone to the Caribbean. Jamaica? No. she went of her own accord!" and so on). Next, Melissa Moore, our Year Eight budding superstar, took the stage dressed as a gentleman, complete with top hat and cane, and strutted her stuff like Vesta Tilley, singing about being Berlington Bertie from Bowe – a nod towards diversity.

The second half began with the choir assembled in front of the curtain. They launched into the deceptively cheerful theme song from *Oh What a Lovely War!* and *We don't want to lose you, but we think you ought to go*.... Then a table was brought on, and two young men in uniform sat down behind it. Two of the choir remained on stage encouraging the lads to join up, and the boys from the front two rows came up on stage, paused before the table and then disappeared behind the curtain. Melissa Moore stepped forward, the lights were dimmed and, under a spotlight and with no accompaniment, she sang 'The Londonderry Air':

"Oh Danny boy, the pipes, the pipes are calling,
From glen to glen, and o'er the mountainside.
The summer's gone, and all the leaves are falling,
'Tis you, 'tis you, must go and I must bide…"

I still can't hear that without crying.

Next, the lights went out, the curtains came back and the stage was lit with a dim grey light. Contemporary film of battle, soldiers and casualties played on the backcloth, and a group of uniformed dancers contorted and fell in front of it while our Year Ten flautist played the tune of 'Danny Boy' again, very softly.

The choir came back, dressed in simple grey, and sang 'Ich Hatte Einen Kameraden' in German, to make the point that the Germans suffered too, followed by a powerful rendition by a Year Seven girl of Siegfried Sassoon's 'Blighters', that hard-hitting poem aimed at the mindless masses who laughed and joked in the music halls whilst the riddled corpses piled up on the Western Front.

The film behind the stage changed to footage of real troops trying to keep warm in winter trenches, whilst "Exposure" by Wilfred Owen was recited by a Year Seven boy, the troops explaining that they had to be there, in that cold, because

"...we believe not otherwise can kind fires burn;
Nor ever sun smile true on child, or field or fruit. .."

The show ended with a very quiet rendering of 'Keep the Home Fires Burning', with the whole cast on stage.

After the curtain came down, if the applause was loud enough (and it always was), the encore was a much more up-tempo 'It's a Long Way to Tipperary' and 'Pack Up Your Troubles in Your Old Kit Bag', with Brian and the whole cast, plus the audience joining in – some even waving little Union Jacks in the manner of patriotic Edwardians supporting their fighting boys.

It was a resounding success. Cath and Pete, who were in the audience on the last night, and were going to the pub with Martin afterwards, pronounced it by far the best school show they'd ever seen. The local paper agreed with them, and we had a fantastic write-up by one of our elected councillors (himself a former pupil) in his weekly column.

A few days later we were contacted by a journalist from *The Teacher* magazine. She came along and interviewed many of us, asking probing and informed questions about the show and how it finished off this particular unit of the Integrated Curriculum. After Christmas, we found ourselves featured on the cover of the January issue, with a double-page spread inside.

We had no inkling at the time, however, of just how appropriate the sombre tone of the show's second half was to prove.

Chapter Fourteen
1999

My darling Allie,

Firstly, apologies for not writing yesterday, but I just couldn't do it, you were so fresh in my mind and I was so hurt at leaving you, that I doubt whether I could have put anything coherent down. This time was, as far as I'm concerned, the worst parting so far.

I can't go on like this...

I felt exactly the same. The euphoria of making a decision about the rest of our lives in the tender moments at Christmas was speedily followed by a dose of cold reality when Martin went back to Wattisham Airfield, near Ipswich, where he and Pete were stationed. Nor had we told anyone about our engagement until Martin confided in Pete. His reaction was: "Brilliant, mate, I'm really pleased for you both – but what did Doris say?"

So we had to tell our parents. Martin told me Dora and Den had written to him, after he'd rung them, to say they were delighted, there would be champagne when we next came down and Lou was keen to be a bridesmaid. When I rang Mum and Dad, Doris put the phone down on me and, according to Dad later, took to her bed for a week. But when she realised her histrionics wouldn't alter anything, she took charge and pressed us for a date.

We decided our wedding would be in the summer of 2000, the second Saturday in August. So, without any consultation, she booked the church where I'd been christened, and the reception, and ordered the invitations. We didn't care – it was really happening, and it seemed that she'd accepted it.

I was studying for my finals throughout that spring, so Martin cut down his visits to give me time to concentrate on my work, but missing him made it very difficult to do anything. Then in the middle of April, a large postcard of *The Death of Ophelia* by Millais arrived. On the back he'd written:

Allie darling,

I just want you to know that I'm still missing you, thinking about, and loving you. I'm renegotiating my leave for the first two weeks in May; I can't wait any longer, I've decided to buy myself out.

All my love,
Martin

In his next letter he described how bleak an army future looked to him. He'd signed on at seventeen for nine years, which would mean, if he stayed in, that he'd be twenty-six when he finally left, without any idea of what he was going to do next. He'd realised, he wrote, that he hated the Army – the boredom, the discipline he, as a Lance Corporal, had to help to enforce, and most of all the way it was keeping us apart. He was determined, finally, to start the process of extricating himself from all that, but he had no idea what he wanted to do next.

Neither had I, although I had a vague feeling that I might be able to teach, and I tentatively suggested it for Martin as well, eliciting a very dusty response. However, when he was told by his Commanding Officer that his application might have more chance if he had a place on a course, he contacted the Manchester Metropolitan University School of Education and was almost instantly accepted as a mature student (which he found very funny; he proudly considered himself to be the most immature person he knew). He would train to teach primary school kids and include as much drama as he possibly could.

My finals came and went at the end of April: afterwards we had a blissful two weeks touring Wales. His family loved us unconditionally as a couple and there *was* champagne, and a lot of laughter, before we set off in his mum's car. Nothing that had happened to us – enforced separation, dealing with my mother, the pain of frequent partings – had done anything to diminish our feelings for each other, feelings that were passionately expressed in bed, in secluded spots in the Welsh hills and once, hilariously but very awkwardly, in his mum's little car. We had no doubts; we discussed where we'd live, where we'd work, how many children we'd have, and their names, how our parents would take to being grandparents...

When we finally returned to Manchester, a letter was waiting to tell me I'd been accepted onto the post-graduate teacher training course at the University of Manchester. So in September we would be learning to teach at the same time, and living together.

After overcoming several hurdles put in his way by an Army that was most reluctant to release a valuable technician, Martin's discharge papers finally came through at the end of August. He was still in Suffolk, but he wrote to me on the anniversary of the day we'd met, recalling the first time he saw me, the fun we'd had on the beach, that storm the first night we spent together. I don't think I'd ever missed him, or needed his touch, more than when I read that letter.

A week later he was on the doorstep with a suitcase.

Chapter Fifteen
2017

In spite of its crumbling corridors and leaking ceilings, school was a vibrant place in the first weeks of the spring term. The new integrated curriculum topics didn't inspire me so much, since they were headed by the Geography Department and involved science and maths far more. But my colleagues knew their jobs, so that Years Seven and Eight had heated debates about climate control and the ruining of the planet with plastics, they looked at over-population and statistical projections, they investigated the diets of people in the developing world. The display boards blossomed with a crop of maps and statistics and flow charts; in English, we looked at the language of weather forecasting with some filming experience and the pupils made animations about the fate of orangutans in Borneo and the rapidly diminishing bee population all round the world. They also wrote passionate letters to MPs and the CEOs of multi-national companies, some of whom even replied.

Three weeks into the term, Ofsted came in to do a three-day inspection. We were ready for them, and so were the kids and parents. Everything proceeded calmly; the kids were on their best behaviour, keen to show the pride they took in Hebble High and their achievements.

On the Monday of the following week, Brian stood up to address us in the staff room: "This isn't official yet, so don't breathe a word, but I'm delighted and not at all surprised to read in the report that we've been judged to be... an *outstanding* school!"

To be fair, it wasn't just the Integrated Curriculum that had pulled us up from the previous assessment of "Good with outstanding features" – those excellent exam results in 2016, coupled with a lot of ongoing hard work with our exam streams, were also partly responsible. But the most noticeable thing, I think, for Ofsted inspectors was the atmosphere in the school, and the way all the kids seemed to be so involved in their learning. In spite of the plaster dropping from the ceilings, the buckets under dripping leaks and the poorly decorated classrooms and corridors, Hebble High was a good place to be at the beginning of 2017.

The weeks before half term were bitterly cold. My car needed defrosting every morning and the roads were treacherous, particularly the steep hill onto the main road that led to school. One Wednesday, which for once was bright with a watery winter sun, Brian set off to inspect a potential new site for Year Eight Camp, in the Lake District. Early that evening, I was huddled close to the stove in my living room when my phone bleeped. It was a text from Martin:

Allie, I have to see you now, something terrible's happened.

I replied instantly – *In all evening, come when you can. Drive carefully.*

Fifteen minutes later, I went to the door to answer his knock and found him ashen-faced and red-eyed on the doorstep. I stood aside for him to come in; he went straight into the living room, dropped his jacket on a chair and turned to me.

"There's no easy way to tell you this. There was a dreadful accident this afternoon on the A65, just outside Kirkby Lonsdale. Brian was killed instantly."

***

People deal with shock and grief in different ways. For me, life takes on a sense of unreality, the world spins in slow motion and I lose the ability to speak. I just stared at Martin, remembering Brian introducing us at the beginning of the year, in the Christmas show, laughing and singing on stage, and in the staff room triumphantly announcing the Ofsted verdict only two days ago. How could this big, vibrant bear of a man be dead? How would we manage without him? Without thinking, I moved to Martin. He buried his face in my hair and we clung together, crying together for the loss of a man we'd liked and respected so much. And it felt right.

After a while, we moved apart and sat down facing each other at the dining table.

"Allie, I really need your help." His voice was hoarse and quiet, I could barely hear him.

"Anything – just tell me what I can do."

He told me that Carol Carter, the other Deputy Head, was staying with Brian's wife until their children arrived home from university in Bristol and Aberdeen – that would take at least twenty-four hours. She'd rung Martin to tell him, and then asked him to organise telling the staff and the kids. She thought it was important they heard it officially from us as soon as possible, rather than seeing some lurid tweet or a Facebook rumour.

"I don't know where to start – I've never had to do anything like this before. How can I do it? I can't think."

I knew. We had a protocol in place for the closure of the school in the event of heavy snow. Deputies rang heads of faculties, they rang heads of departments who rang their teams. Teachers then contacted their teaching assistants. It was simple and it worked. I explained it to him, and he remembered he had the relevant faculty heads' numbers stored in his phone.

"Are you up to it? Should we split them between us?"

"Yes, I think I can do it, but I could do with a stiff drink first."

I poured him a drop of brandy I found in the bottom of a kitchen cupboard. He pulled a face and then said, "Right. Let's get on with it."

It didn't take too long – there were eight faculties, so we took four each.

Then we had to think about telling the kids.

"Announce to the staff first thing tomorrow that the morning's timetable is suspended, and ask form tutors to stay with their forms. Then call them into the theatre, one year group at a time. If you tell the sixth form first, I'm sure they'll help get everyone into the theatre quietly, and out and away."

"Thank you," he whispered, and took my hand again. I didn't pull away.

"Don't go home tonight – I don't want to worry about you driving down that icy hill. I've got a spare room – I'll make up the bed settee for you."

And it was true – in that bleakest of moments, I realised that I would be devastated if anything happened to Martin. In spite of myself.

He nodded. I poured him another brandy, and I had one as well this time. Then I remembered where I'd seen that sadness on his face once before.

Chapter Sixteen
2000

Living together was much easier than I'd anticipated, although I learned more about Martin in the first week than I had in the previous year. As well as reading constantly, he also had a huge music collection and we shared a love of some of it – Fairport Convention, Dylan, Springsteen and the Doors. I had to endure Led Zeppelin, ZZ Top and other heavy metal from time to time, although he did wear earphones when he really wanted it loud.

We were above all such good friends, and we were both very involved with the business of learning to teach. It was such a relief, too, to be in each other's company without constantly remembering we only had a few days left together. We lived quite well, for students – Martin had saved up quite a sum whilst in the Army, more than the three thousand it had cost to buy himself out, enough to help with food and rent, and tide us over till his student loan came through. He'd even bought an old car that we shared. From Manchester it was easy to nip down to Chirk to see his parents and Lou. At the end of every visit, Dora sent us back with bags full of groceries and her baking. Life was good, but it didn't last long.

After a few weeks, I saw a side to Martin's character that I didn't recognise. He was becoming more and more exasperated by the course he was doing – not the teaching, he liked that, especially anything involving drama – but the increasing demands of essays, tedious reading of educational theory and being forced to mix with the other trainees, many of whom were giggly eighteen-year-old girls, was leaving him tetchy and cynical. I wasn't used to this, and I didn't much like it because I knew he was unhappy. Something had to change.

One night we were at the theatre, of all places, watching a production of *A Midsummer Night's Dream*, when I suddenly had an idea. At the interval I said, "Why don't you look into getting a transfer into the School of Theatre?"

He didn't say very much, but when we were back in our little terraced house, he said, "Do you really think they'd take me? At the School of Theatre?"

"I do, my lord... for are you not he that did discomfort the good burghers of Tintagel by informing them that now was the winter of your discontent made glorious summer by this son of York, all the while with a frozen chicken making your crook back?"

"Indeed I am, good my lady, indeed I am..."

Richard the Third didn't get a look-in for his audition. Instead he chose Macbeth's famous soliloquy in Act 5 (*Tomorrow and tomorrow and tomorrow creeps in this petty pace from day to day until the last syllable of recorded time, and all our yesterdays have lighted fools the way to dusty death...*), along with a few minutes of *Under Milk Wood*.

Getting on to drama courses is tremendously difficult for school leavers, but the interview panel must have recognised the innate potential in Martin, combined with his age and experience. His auditions went well, and they were clearly impressed by his knowledge of drama, his enthusiasm for Shakespeare and his prolific ability to quote and make suggestions about the works in performance. Not only was he offered a place, but they actually agreed to let him start after Easter as a late entrant on the First Year, rather than making him wait till the following September.

His parents were appalled. As far as they were concerned, he'd thrown away a good career in the Army to go into a poorly paid and less promising profession, and then ditched that as well for something even more precarious. But they didn't complain or blame me for long, because very soon afterwards, Dora had a terrible accident at work.

It was a heat-sealing machine that caused her to nearly lose the first three fingers of her right hand. It had jammed, halting the production line of cheese slabs being securely wrapped. She'd made the fatal mistake of trying to pull out the offending plastic without switching the machine off, since employees were encouraged to maximise production and there were penalties for stopping the conveyor belts. The heavy and red hot metal crashed down, trapping her hand underneath. She was rushed to hospital in Liverpool, where she stayed for several weeks whilst plastic surgeons tried to repair the damage and restore some semblance of fingers by fusing the back of her right hand to her abdomen to encourage the flesh to regrow. It must have been incredibly painful and uncomfortable.

Being Dora, she was remarkably stoical, always pleased to see us when we visited, always trying to make the best of it – even forcing herself to write haltingly with her left hand, and always looking forward to the time when she could return home. But all the family was affected – Den was exhausted by an eighty mile round-trip to see her most evenings after work, the hospital being the only one in the north-west equipped to offer the plastic surgery she needed. Lou was upset because her GCSEs were looming and Den made her stay at home during the week to study – and Martin fretted and worried about them all.

Dora was sure she'd be up and about and able to attend our wedding in August. In the event, it wasn't an issue.

One evening at the end of April, my mother rang, something she never normally did.

"I'm ringing to say your father's very ill," she said with no preamble. "You'll have to abandon the wedding."

"Can I speak to him, please?"

"No. He's in hospital."

"Oh God, what's wrong with him? Shall we come to you? Is there anything I can do?"

"No, he doesn't want visitors. I can't talk about it. I've cancelled the church and the reception and sent the invitations back."

With that, she put the phone down.

In desperation and scarcely knowing what to believe, I rang my godmother, an old but very steady and sensible friend of my mother's. She confirmed that Dad been in hospital for a week (a *week?*), but Doris had refused to tell even her what was wrong. I realise now that it was the beginning of the prostate cancer which would kill him a few years later – but not once did my mother tell me about it. I finally discovered what had happened from a cousin, years after they were both dead.

In a few short days, all our plans had collapsed. We toyed with the idea of nipping down to the register office and marrying quietly – Pete and Cath kindly offered their flat in Halifax for a bit of a party afterwards – but Martin's mum was very keen for us to have a church wedding, even if I flatly refused a Catholic mass. And, on top of that, I was worried about my poor Dad, and I wanted him to be there. Martin agreed – he couldn't disappoint Dora, but his parents were in no position financially to help us organise anything. We decided we'd wait, at least until Dad came out of hospital, then try to talk it over with all our parents, somehow in the same room if we could.

But we were together, and we soldiered on. I qualified as a teacher and began the long search for my first job, while Martin threw himself with energy and determination into his new role as a drama student. Finally, after several failed interviews, I applied for a job in a difficult area on the outskirts of Halifax – and that time I got it. I would start as a fully-qualified English teacher at the beginning of September.

That summer was our last happy time together. We found a job working side-by-side in one of the few remaining wool-sorting mills in Bradford, which was pretty well-paid with plenty of overtime, and we still had energy for intimate moments or socialising with Pete and Cath, and Alec, one of Pete's school friends, who was absolutely shameless, very funny and got on really well with Martin. But my career was fast approaching, and Martin's return to the School of Theatre. The day on which we should have been married was uneventful; Martin spent it under the car and I went shopping, trying not to think about what we could have been doing.

When we took our holiday job we'd moved into a flat in Halifax, in a house owned by Cath's parents. It had a kitchen, living-room and two bedrooms, but we shared the bathroom with everyone else in the bed-sits downstairs. It wasn't ideal, but it was ours – and Cath and Pete were in the basement flat, for which I would be extremely glad a few months later.

Martin bought another cheap car to drive to Manchester each morning, and handed his first car over to me. He said I shouldn't have to face a long journey on public transport after those hard days at school, especially in the approaching winter. I was grateful for that – I was expecting a lot of extra work in my first year of teaching, along with heavy bags full of books ready for marking that I'd need to take home. Having a car would make my life so much easier.

***

My first job was a nightmare. The school was allegedly a comprehensive, but the presence of two selective grammar schools in nearby Halifax meant that it was effectively a secondary modern, and it had no sixth-form. It was newly-built and well-equipped, but on an estate of desperately bad housing. I had never experienced such poverty, or such alienation. The kids were inevitably hostile and took a delight in being utterly impossible – as a newly-qualified and very insecure young teacher, I was fair game. I was miserable, but I am stubborn by nature, and when Dora said to me, "I know you won't let those little buggers beat you," I knew I had to keep going.

That remark was made from her hospital bed. Her fingers had healed to a certain extent, but she'd started feeling exhausted and lost her appetite, so she'd gone in for tests. They revealed she had ovarian cancer, and had probably had it, with no symptoms, for some time. An exploratory operation had confirmed that it had spread, and there was no guarantee that any treatment could help her. But she refused to despair, always insisting that she would be home soon. She was forty-five years old.

A few days after we'd last seen her, at the end of October, Martin appeared in school. He looked as if something had bleached all the colour from his face.

"I have to go home – please come with me. Mum's *died*."

Chapter Seventeen

2017

Brian's funeral took place the week after his death. Marian, his widow, wanted his school to play as great a part as possible, but we had 1,200 pupils and they couldn't all be there. Neither could all his staff, much as we wanted to be. In the end it was resolved; Martin and Carol would go, along with a dozen other staff representing everyone who worked at Hebble High, and the Head Boy and Head Girl.

On the day of the funeral, which was as crisp and sunny as the day he'd died, Brian's cortege crept along the school's front drive in full view of all the pupils, assembled on the large area of grass in front and standing, without being asked, in complete silence, many of them crying. All the staff, in black, lined the drive or stood on the grass with their form groups.

The cars stopped to enable the mourners to slip in, and at that moment, Melissa Moore, with her fine, powerful voice, began to sing 'Keep the Home Fires Burning'. No-one had asked her to, it was entirely unexpected – but within seconds she was joined by other members of our Junior Choir. They must have planned it on their own. After a few seconds, the voices of all the pupils swelled and carried on the winter air as they too joined in, saying goodbye.

I was standing on the drive next to Martin, although I could scarcely see for tears. I wasn't going to the funeral, much as I'd wanted to, but as he was getting in next to Martin, Sean paused and said, "Allie, you go. I'll cover your lessons. Martin needs you."

Surprised, I nodded and smiled briefly, squeezing Sean's arm. Then I took his place in the car and held Martin's hand for the next hour, as I had at his mother's funeral, all those years ago.

Chapter Eighteen
2001

Losing his mum obviously affected Martin deeply, but after the first few weeks, and a dreadful, bleak Christmas, he hardly mentioned her. Looking back, I realise now that his world had been totally rocked; he was probably aware of the passage of time, and the need not to waste it, in ways I could never have predicted, or helped him to accept. On top of that, he was struggling with his new life as a budding actor and trainee stage manager.

The demands of year two of the drama degree course steadily increased over the winter. Martin was attending practical sessions in stagecraft, stage management and acting by day, and then participating in constant productions or rehearsals in the evenings. Sometimes he didn't get home till after ten; he barely had time to eat and snatch a few hours' sleep before it was time to start off again. We knew it was an impossible and dangerous schedule and so, reluctantly, we decided that he needed a flat in Manchester for the weekdays.

"It won't be for ever, love," he'd said as he left with his week's clothes at the beginning of the spring term. "It's just a place to sleep till the end of the course, then we'll be together again. I've got to give this my best shot – you do understand, don't you? It'll be Friday before you know it, and I'll be so pleased to see you..."

For a while it seemed to work, although the evenings were long and lonely, and I counted the days towards the weekends. Then one Friday he said he had to work taking down scenery after a production and wasn't expecting to finish till eleven at the earliest, so it made sense to stay over and come back on the Saturday. This became a regular pattern, but he was arriving later and later on Saturdays.

He'd usually text to let me know, but occasionally he forgot, and then I worried constantly till I heard his key in the door.

One Saturday in March at about 4pm, I heard him come in. I was pleased; this was earlier than usual. I was making a curry, I remember it clearly, and the pungent scents of garlic and onions hung in the air. He put his coat on the back of the door, then turned to me.

"Just stop what you're doing, please, Allie – I need to say something."

I stopped and smiled expectantly, but he looked serious.

"I'm really sorry, but I can't do this any longer. I want to be in Manchester all the time – there's so much happening and... well... I don't... I don't think I love you anymore. Not like I used to."

"What? What do you mean?"

"I don't know – it's hard to explain... I suppose I've just moved into a different world... different people... and you don't belong there."

"I don't understand. I don't believe you!"

It was a crazy response, the first thing that came into my head. This was *Martin*, it couldn't be real. I had the absurd idea that he might be rehearsing the line for some ghastly play, to observe my reaction, but of course he wasn't. He shook his head, but he looked wretched. Slowly I dissolved in front of him – my legs seemed to stop working, and I would have fallen if he hadn't rushed forward, caught me and held me. I howled then – a cry I hardly knew I was making.

"Oh God, Allie, don't, please don't. I hate hurting you, I'm so, so sorry—"

"Please don't leave me, I can't bear it, don't leave me alone!"

We clung together, and we slept together that night. How could he leave me, I reasoned, if he could still behave like that in bed?

Finally, after much pressure from me, he agreed to stay till after the Easter holidays, which were tortuous. We went down to Shropshire and Martin told his Dad and Lou, whilst I broke the news to Nanny and she cried too, saying it was almost like losing Dora all over again. Then the two weeks were up and we went back. I never saw any of them after that, my lovely, warm, welcoming second family. We still hadn't told Pete and Cath.

The following Monday, Martin loaded a lot of his stuff into his car. He said he'd be back the following Saturday to pick up some more, but of course he never came. That Saturday night, Pete popped in to ask if we wanted to go to the pictures, and found me in a sobbing heap at the kitchen table. Between gasps, I told him.

"Bloody hell," he said, "I never thought he'd do that. What the fuck's he playing at?"

It was, I thought dimly, a very good question.

Chapter Nineteen

February, 2017

I was in trouble. Owning and maintaining a house and a car, with all the extra expenses, plus the coal I used to keep my stove going, petrol and the smart clothes and shoes I needed for school, stretched my money to the limit. I'd never had any ambition to move up the pay structure into the management of the school – I enjoyed the classroom too much for that. Consequently, my salary was modest by most professional standards – many single teachers on my pay grade struggled, especially if they had families to feed. At least I had no-one depending on me. But, on top of all my normal outgoings, I'd had a couple of burst pipes to pay for the previous winter, which had both increased my household insurance premiums and put my account permanently into the red. Then my car needed a new radiator and work on the brakes to pass its MOT. I'd been forced to take out a substantial loan, secured on my house at a colossal rate of interest and repayable over only four years. What with all that, plus my student loan, I only just managed to pay everything each month, although there wasn't much left for food, and nothing at all for socialising. Some weeks I was forced to live on baked beans, bread and instant soup – thank goodness for cut-price stores.

Two days after Brian's funeral, the starter motor failed on my car. This was catastrophic – it was the middle of February, there was a week before I next got paid and replacing the part, plus the cost of labour, would virtually clean out my account. But I had to have a car – my cottage was way beyond walking distance to the nearest supermarket or even local shops - and they were too expensive in any case. I rang the garage and they agreed to come out and pick up the car; I would leave the keys under the dustbin. I caught the school bus and arrived just in time to register my sixth-formers before the beginning of school. Getting home would be more problematic – it was Wednesday and there was our Integrated Curriculum meeting after school, so I'd be too late for the return school bus.

It was bitterly cold and the sky was grey, heavy with incipient snow. As I walked up to school at lunchtime from the Sixth Form block, the first flakes were swirling and dancing in the wind. Martin was waiting for me in the staff room.

"Listen, I'm sorry but I'm going to have to miss our meeting today," he said. "Carol and I have to talk to the Local Authority rep this afternoon about the running of the school until a new head can be appointed. We've got a lot to get through."

"No problem – that comes first. Will you make the IC meeting?"

"I doubt it, but I'll try."

I used the extra time to catch up on marking the books I'd need for the next day – at least that meant I wouldn't have to lug them home on the bus. Martin didn't turn up to the meeting. The Learning Resources Centre had no windows on the lower floor, so we didn't notice how bad the snow was getting, but later, when I went into the staff room to pick up my coat, I was horrified to see that it was settling and drifting in the school quadrangle below. On top of that, I was feeling really light-headed; I'd had nothing to eat since a meagre tea the day before. I sat down for a minute on an upright chair and put my head down. I didn't hear Martin come in.

"Hey Allie, how did it g— are you ok? What's wrong? Are you not feeling too good?"

"I'm fine, don't worry," I said. I stood up, the room slid out of focus, went dark and I passed out.

When I came round, I was lying across three soft low chairs that were pushed together – Martin must have lifted me from the floor, I suppose. He was kneeling by my head, dabbing my forehead with a wet paper towel. It was freezing. I groaned and pushed him away before struggling into a sitting position.

"For God's sake, what the hell's all this about? Are you ill? You've looked pretty pale recently and I can see you've lost weight. You're not anorexic are you? Talk to me!"

It was too much, I couldn't bear his urgent tone and I equally couldn't stand his pity.

"Sorry, sorry, I don't want to upset you. I'm just worried about you, that's all. Can I do anything to help?"

"I'm ok, I'm ok, stop fussing. I've been so busy today I didn't have time to eat. I'm sure that's all that's wrong. There is something you can do, though. Could you run me home? I'm carless today while it has its starter-motor replaced."

"Of course I will – and we need to get going before we get snowed in – it's coming down at a hell of a rate."

I stood up hurriedly and instantly felt faint again. He was ready for it this time, and his arm went directly round my waist, steadying me. And for a split second I was back in Cornwall again, out of my depth.

His car was parked at the front of school – a great heavy grey thing with four-wheel drive, "…and we'll probably need it tonight!" There were bulging bags of shopping and laundry on the front seat, which he unceremoniously flung into the back.

Getting down the hill to the main road was interesting, but Martin had always been a good driver and he was concentrating furiously, correcting skids and using the gears instead of braking. At the bottom, we slid sideways into the main road, which was mercifully empty. The going got slightly better – at least it was level – although the twin tyre tracks in the middle of the road were rapidly disappearing. The wind had got up and was blowing the snow horizontally into our headlights; drifts were starting to form at the sides of the road.

After a couple of miles, we turned left off that road and up the steep hill that leads to the road across the valley, and my cottage. It was very slippery and the wheels spun a few times, but Martin assured me the tyres could cope. The windscreen wipers were struggling though – there was so much snow. When we turned right to cross the valley, the drifting was much worse, as the wind drove the snow – already it was approaching the level of the stone walls at each side of the road, which was narrow in any case. The car ground gallantly on, acting like a snow-plough, Martin grimly determined to keep us going as far as my cottage. Eventually, we skidded to a stop in the empty bus layby at the end of the terrace, where there was room for two cars to park.

We'd made it.

As I got out of the car the wind hit me, pushing me back, and the snow, smashing into my face, felt granular and unforgiving.

"You might as well grab your stuff out of the car," I yelled over the wind. "You aren't going anywhere else tonight." He didn't object.

Together, we floundered the final hundred yards towards the sanctuary of my home. It looks nothing from the road – a mid-terrace, with a few steps leading down to the front door, and a stone coal bunker with a dustbin on top, bounded by a few feet of wooden fencing and a gate. Tonight no steps were visible, just a treacherous slope of drifted snow. Gingerly, I made my way down, leaving footprints for Martin, but when I got to the door, my ungloved hand was shaking so much I could barely get the key into the lock. Behind me, Martin reached over and put his hand over mine and together we fitted the key and turned it. The door opened inwards and we almost fell down the remaining step inside, slamming it behind us and finding ourselves instantly in the quiet warmth of the kitchen, which settled over us like a calm blanket of welcome.

It's a small, galley kitchen with the Belfast sink under the window to the left and my washing machine next to it, and the hob, oven, microwave and fridge/freezer take up most of the wall opposite. From the kitchen there's a door into the shower room near the staircase; at the other end, opposite the outside door, there's a pine stable door that leads down another step into the living room. This is an unexpectedly large space with a long picture window opposite the door, and a deep, pine window sill under the small mullioned windows. The dining room table sits under the window, so that as I work or eat I can look at the open view at the front of the house, across the fields to the hillside beyond. To the left of the table are two alcoves with the chimney breast between them, where a stone lintel bridges the chimney gap. On the matching stone hearth below sits my trusty little Norwegian stove. It isn't particularly pretty, being a tall, dark green oblong, but it's built for very cold climates and it chugs away for hours if the vent at the bottom is closed. When it's open, the coal burns so fiercely that it can make the stove glow red-hot.

The first thing I did after I'd ditched my sopping coat was to open that vent and heap on some more coal from the scuttle I'd filled that morning. Martin followed me in, drying his hair on a towel, and stood in front of it. The last time he'd been here was two weeks previously, the day Brian had died. Together we soaked in the heat, not speaking.

Finally I said, "You know where the spare bedroom is – do you want to take that bag of laundry up? I'm assuming it's clean?"

"It is – I picked it up this morning after I'd been shopping. Are you sure you're ok with me staying again?"

"Of course I am – I'm hardly going to throw you out into the blizzard like Captain Oates, am I? And, to be honest, I don't know what I'd have done without you tonight – I wouldn't have stood a chance of getting home."

"My pleasure, ma'am."

"Oh get on, you daft bugger."

He looked at me. "D'you know, you sounded just like Mum when you said that!"

"Did I? Sorry…"

"No, I liked it."

When he came down, wearing a pair of slightly crumpled jeans and a sweater, I was loading his copious food shopping into the fridge, filling every shelf and a whole half of my virtually empty cupboard. He glanced in and saw the bare spaces.

"Christ, Allie, where's your food? What would you have eaten this weekend? No wonder you passed out! I hope this isn't another of your stupid diets?"

"No, it's not that. I'm skint."

"How come?"

"Well, it's a long story, but basically running a house and a car plus paying back the loan I had to take last year to mend the roof takes up most of my salary – I only have a couple of hundred left for everything else. And now I've got to pay this car bill—"

"Why the hell didn't you come to me? I could've helped – I could at least have repaired your car – I haven't lost all my Army skills."

"Oh yeah, like I'm going to come whining to you and asking for a sub every month – or moaning on about my car! It's taken me this long to get used to working with you – I'm hardly going to say "Please, Mr Ex-Fiance, I know I've cold-shouldered you but can you stick a starter-motor in my car so I don't have to pay for it?", am I?"

"I thought we were getting on pretty well?"

"Of course we are, professionally – you're a great colleague, but that's different. I couldn't have gone to Brian either – I'd be so embarrassed. It's entirely my fault that I'm in this mess. I should've sold up and moved into a rented place, but I just couldn't face it. I love this cottage."

"You always were a stubborn bugger, Allie. But we can sort it together, if you'll let me give you a hand. I hate to see you living like this."

Excuse me? Better ignore that – dangerous ground. Stop it, Allie – remember what he did to you last time.

"Let's talk about that later when we've warmed up and eaten. But I tell you one thing, young woman... If I don't eat soon, *you'll* be picking *me* off the floor. Now ged outta mahh kitchen and let El Supremo rustle you up a spag bol like you've never tasted before!"

"Oh God, I hope not!" I said – but I left him to it, retreated to the living room and collapsed onto my squishy old settee opposite the stove. That remark took me back to the old Martin, clowning around and impersonating and making me laugh helplessly. Back when we were young.

I thought about the last time I'd been alone with him (apart from that awful night when Brian died), fifteen years ago. I made myself go over those grim days before he finally left, and how I'd felt, and how horrified I'd been when he landed at Hebble last September. But no matter what, my stomach kept churning – he clearly cared still. I should have been starving, but my mind was far from food.

Mind you, when it arrived, it was very good – and so was his Malbec, and the stilton he'd bought, both of which we nearly demolished. It reminded me of another dinner we'd shared, before the Cornish weather turned wild. Throughout this meal, the snow continued to fall, and the wind howled and blew the icy flakes against the window.

At around nine, Martin's phone rang. It was Carol, confirming that school was now closed until after half-term, since the forecast was so grim, and she'd rung all the heads of faculty to set the Snow Protocol in motion. And I realised, with mixed feelings, that Martin could be with me for several days.

Later, we pulled the settee closer to the stove. We finished off the Malbec, then a great wine-induced weariness came over me, and I found my head sinking onto Martin's shoulder. He moved his arm from the back of the settee and pulled me closer. This was enough – I was warm and secure, I had no energy for anything else – I just needed to sleep. Financial analysis would have to wait.

"Bed time?"

"Yes, I think so – I'll get you a sheet and a quilt cover, and a couple of pillows."

He sighed, stood up and went into the bathroom.

A few hours later I woke up with a simultaneously bursting bladder and a raging thirst. Pulling my old dressing gown round me, I pushed my feet into slippers and headed for the stairs. Martin had left his door open, and I saw he'd opened out the bed settee into a double bed and was curled up near the wall, snoring gently.

On the way back, on a crazy impulse, I went into his room and slipped under the duvet – but he didn't stir. I lay awake for a while, enjoying the warmth of him, listening to him breathing, then I nodded off. When I next woke, a cold white light was filtering through the curtains, and it sounded as if it was still snowing. Martin slept on, but he'd turned over at some point, and now his arm was draped across my stomach. *Missed your chance*, I thought, and I slowly eased out from under him. I'd reached the door when he said sleepily, "Allie...?" I was back in my own, now-freezing bed and feigning sleep when I think he put his head round my door. Then he too went down to the bathroom. I slept again.

Several hours later, when I'd had my shower and was putting the kettle on, he came down looking bleary-eyed, his hair tousled.

"Allie, did you...?"

"What?"

"I thought during the night you... I thought we... no, I must have been dreaming."

"Was it a nice dream?"

"The best." He smiled at me.

"Well, let's hope you have it again tonight, then."

"I doubt I'd be that lucky, two nights in a row."

Chapter Twenty

There was no point trying to dig ourselves out. The snow kept on coming down; the wind had dropped, but it was deadly cold and the lying snow was frozen hard. What we needed to do, though, was get to the coal bunker outside the door. But the door was frozen shut – at least until I had the bright idea of training my hairdryer, on the hottest setting, up and down the jamb. Eventually, we managed to pull it open, to be then faced with three feet of frozen snow. Martin had to chip into it with the coal shovel, inch by icy inch. My job was to pour kettlefuls of hot water over it and keep him supplied with hot drinks. Two hours later, he reached the bunker, and we could finally fill up the coal scuttle, open the fire vent and set it roaring again.

"There is something really satisfying," he said, thawing out in front of the blazing stove, "about getting fuel with your bare hands. I expect that's how a peasant would feel after chopping down a few trees!"

"What a load of total crap – you're such a bourgeois romantic."

"Oy, I'll have you know my granddad was a miner – he used to do that every day for a living!"

"And…? So you're genetically programmed to chip away at an icy wall? Come on!"

"I'm genetically programmed to chip away at *your* icy wall, Ice Maiden…"

"Oh get away with you, it's like living in a surreal *Last of the Summer Wine* episode!"

"Well, show us your wrinkled stockings, then, Norah Bat— ouch!"

I'd flicked him soundly with a wet towel.

"Tell you what, though," I said, "there are a couple of things we can do to while away the time…"

"Oh yeah?"

He moved very close and put his hands on either side of me, resting on the table. I traced the contour of his face with my fingertip, very lightly.

"The first thing we need to do…"

"Mmm?"

"Is… eat a bacon butty."

"Oh God, yes, *yes!*"

"And then…"

"What… *what*? "

"Scrabble!"

So that's what we did.

***

Later, we warmed up the rest of the spaghetti sauce, cooked more pasta and opened another bottle of red. Then we sat together on the settee – I'd gone to sit apart from him but was immediately instructed to "Cwtch up" – he used to say that to me fifteen years ago. It was bitterly cold again, the watery winter sun had disappeared and the icy night held everything in its grip. I didn't need an excuse for a cuddle.

"I've been thinking," Martin said after a while, "about what we can do to sort out your money problems."

We?

"But I am a bit mystified – didn't you buy this house outright after your mother died? Why did you need a mortgage at all?"

"Actually, Mark and I bought it after we were married. His parents gave us the deposit as a wedding present."

"Who's Mark? *Married?* When? You've never mentioned that before. Where is he? What happened?"

"I don't like talking about it. It was another painful episode that put me off men for ten years."

"Tell me, please."

I sighed. "Well, after you… after we split up, I was in a terrible state for ages. Pete and Cath were wonderful, they really tried to look after me, but they were working hard and they had their own lives to lead. And Alec – remember him?"

Martin nodded. "I certainly do. At school with Pete. Great bloke."

"Well, he came round quite a lot, too – we went to the pub together, or out to gigs. He was another good friend, but a brother, not a boyfriend. In fact," I smiled at the memory, "he even asked me to help him with his computer-dating profile. Never was a man so deluded! He suggested that he could describe himself as an international man of mystery, with craggy good looks, a steely jaw and piercing blue eyes. What a buffoon! The truth was a little different, and he didn't get many takers. After a while, his mum and brother moved to Whitby and he followed. Then he met Sally over there and got married. We still talk occasionally, or text, but not so much, obviously. So after a year or so, I began to feel really lonely. I thought I'd have a go at computer dating as well. I met some very interesting men, but no-one special. Then I met Mark."

"What was he like?"

"Dark, brooding, obsessional – and for a while he was obsessed with me. I thought this was it – we were married six months after meeting, and then we found this cottage. He was just phenomenal, he made me so happy; I forgot all about you – sorry."

"Don't be – why wouldn't you? But what happened?"

"Well... he'd been quieter, not his usual sardonic self, but I thought he was just a bit down about his job – he'd apparently been working very long hours. Of course, even after my previous experience, I never doubted him, and he never said anything was wrong."

Martin looked down at me and briefly tightened his grip on my shoulder.

"Then one Sunday morning I woke up to find him packing a case. He said he'd met somebody at work and he had to be with her. So he left, and I haven't seen him since."

"Bastard." He squeezed my shoulder again and pulled me closer to him. I resisted. I wanted to talk.

"Not really – just honest, I suppose... that seems to be the effect I have on men. I was devastated at the time, though. I really missed him, and it took me ages to stop loving him. Anyway, after a while he said through his solicitor that he didn't want me to lose my home, so he'd signed it over to me. I *believe* it's called an amicable divorce.

"And, after that, I decided enough was enough, I wasn't going to risk that happening a third time."

I looked directly at him and he had the grace to close his eyes and whisper, "I don't blame you."

"—so I threw myself into my work. I did an MA in Educational Studies and that's where I came across the Integrated Curriculum. Then you appeared."

He sighed heavily.

"Ok, but that still doesn't explain why you've got this bloody mortgage. Why didn't you pay it off when Doris died?"

"Because I haven't inherited a penny yet. She put it all into a trust that will pay out when I'm forty. My dad's partner, who was her executor, said she didn't want me to, and I quote, *fritter it away.*"

"That's awful."

"I suppose so, but she thought she was doing the right thing. As always, I suspect. She had very inflexible ideas about how people should behave, and I must have been a real shock to her ordered world. I was really angry and hurt when the solicitor told me, but I've seen her differently since she died – I suppose I've mellowed a bit as I've got older. She must have been very unhappy. But I just wish she could have unbent a bit – she never even tried to hug me, and she didn't offer me a word of comfort when you and I split up, even though I was in such a state. She just said it was for the best. I don't think we ever talked about anything serious because she knew I couldn't agree with her *Daily Express* view of the world. Do you know, we never had a conversation about anything apart from her until the day she died?"

"Christ – I don't remember her being so bad."

"Oh come on - you must remember that time just before you came out of the Army? You'd been staying with us and we were having tea before you went back. She asked you what you wanted to do with your life and you said you fancied possibly working in television – and she said, 'Do you mean repairing them, dear?' Surely you haven't forgotten that?"

"I had, actually."

"Amazing."

I paused, momentarily irritated with him, as if he was taking Doris's side against me. I wasn't going to let him wriggle away from the past so easily.

"But what about you? I've told you my life story, but what were you up to for fifteen years? And before you start, let me just tell you I know about Lisette."

"Really? How?"

"Because, ironically, just after Mark and I split up, she rang and asked if you were with me. She must have traced the number somehow."

"Christ – what did she say?"

"Plenty! She started with, 'He's done the same thing to me as he did to you.' I didn't know what she was talking about at first, then the penny dropped. How naive I'd been – it would've been far better if you'd just told me you'd met someone else, then I wouldn't have spent the next few months thinking you might come back. But she didn't stop there. She really dished out some poison about you, and angry as I was, I felt very irritated with her. What business of mine was it? In the end, I just said, 'Well, *we* never had any problems in *that* department!' and I hung up. How long were you together?"

"I don't know… about three or four years, I suppose, but she was so clingy. When the novelty had worn off, there wasn't much left for me, but I just stuck around because I couldn't think of a decent way out. If I'm honest, I couldn't face hurting her the way I must have hurt you. But we really had nothing in common, and the final straw came when she wanted to get married and have kids. In the end, just as she said, I left one day and didn't go back. But I did write to her. That must have been when she rang you. I'm not proud of myself."

"No. Then what?"

"Then I met an actress – a really beautiful woman, and that was good for a while. But… I don't know, I just couldn't seem to settle. And the theatre was pissing me off too. Bolton Octagon was pleasant enough, but I wanted more than pantomime. I landed one decent role as Rosencrantz in *Hamlet* at the National, but after that, nothing. So I decided to try my hand at stage management – I was trained for that as well as acting, of course. That was much better for a while – I liked the life, always moving from one venue to another, working with a great bunch of young people. I think I was used to a nomadic life – you remember Dad was in the RAF when I was young?"

I nodded.

"Then I applied for a job in Singapore, working on the fireworks for Chinese New Year. I made some great contacts, and was offered a job at the Esplanade Theatre, running a twelve-month course for new stage managers from the Far East. That was brilliant – I realised that I really loved teaching older people, and it seemed I was quite good at it. So when I came back to the UK, I applied for a drama PGCE and was given a placement at a secondary school in Derby, and suddenly, after the first week, I knew I'd been right, and I'd found something I could stick at. I was lucky; they offered me a job as soon as my PGCE ended. I've never looked back... although, if I'm honest, I do miss the adrenaline rush of live theatre."

Typical, I thought uncharitably. *This man always wants what he can't have.*

"And what about your beautiful actress? Do you still see her?"

"No. I did, for a while when I started teaching, but she made it pretty clear that she expected me to come back to the stage, one way or another. And I couldn't do it. So we drifted apart. Then I saw the Hebble job, and I really wanted it."

"Weren't you worried about me working in the same school?"

"Not when I saw your picture on the web site, and your name – Miss Weston, not Mrs Somebody Else..."

So that was it. My simmering temper flared.

"I see. So you thought I wouldn't mind and it might be worth a try, did you? What made you think I might have the slightest interest in you, after all this time with not so much as a Christmas card? How did you know I wasn't married? I never changed my name, even when I was.

"And talking of name changing – why on earth do you use all three of your names now? I know you always signed your letters MPS, but you were plain old Lance Corporal Smith when we first met. Why the pretentious extra name?"

"That's an easy one to answer." He was smiling at me now, his eyes twinkling disarmingly. "Martin Smith was a bit too everyday for working in the theatre – who'd remember that name? But Prescott Smith sounded a lot more... professional, somehow..."

He paused and looked thoughtful again.

"As for bowling up at Hebble, it *was* the job at first, Allie – it had a great reputation, your school, and the facilities were exceptional, for drama at least. I thought I'd fit in. I didn't think working in the same place would be too difficult in such a big school, and I certainly had no inkling you'd be running the IC project. But that first day... God, I thought I'd made a terrible mistake. You were very good though, the way you reacted – you should be on the stage, never mind me. But after that... I couldn't stop thinking about you. I still can't."

"Oh yeah? Really? So let's just get this straight. You ditched me because something better came along. Then you left her because you got bored. Then you met someone else but you moved on and spent a year abroad. Now you've come back into teaching and landed a good job, which just *happens* to be in the same school as me, and suddenly you can't stop thinking about me? And you expect me to believe that? I've had fifteen miserable years to come to terms with losing you, and I'm not about to put myself through that again!"

I was shouting by then, but even as I yelled at him, part of me was thinking, *he wants to be near me – and I'm glad*! But I was determined to keep him at arm's length till I was sure.

He shook his head slowly.

"You have every right to be angry – and yeah, put like that, it *does* look as if I can't stick at anything, I agree. But Allie, I promise you, *I promise you*, it's not like that this time. Leaving you was the worst mistake I've ever made, but I suppose I've got something out of my system – maybe I've grown up in the last fifteen years, I don't know. But one thing I do know, without any doubt, is that I love you. And that's all I can say, and you have to believe me."

He turned me towards him then, and kissed me – a proper, sweet, slow kiss, before I could speak or pull away.

That was the moment. I could have slapped his face and told him to get lost. I could have repeated my determination to keep our relationship on a professional level. I could have stuck to my principles. But I didn't do any of that. Do I regret it now, as I write, after everything that has subsequently happened? Not for the minutest split second. I was prepared, instantly, to risk everything – my life, happiness, peace of mind – for this love he seemed to be offering. Would I do the same thing again if I had the chance? Unquestionably.

He suddenly stood up and went over to his laptop, left on a shelf in the alcove. He fiddled with it for a minute, then music filled the room. It was Carlos Santana playing 'Samba Pa Ti'. Music to make love to, he used to say when we were young. He held out his hand, and then, because I hesitated, pulled me to him and held me up against him, pressed closely so I couldn't escape, even if the tiniest part of me had wanted to. As the languorous notes filled the air we swayed together slowly, and the pain of fifteen years without him fell away, along with all my anger and all my resistance.

It was nothing like the first time. This was gentle, tentative, as we slowly found our way around each other again. This time we stayed downstairs, on the rug in front of the glowing embers in the stove, quietly shedding our clothes one piece at a time. We touched, discovered, remembered... and, when I finally felt him move inside me, it was like coming home out of the cold, all over again.

***

That night, and every night afterwards until half term ended, we slept together in my bed. By the time we were ready to sleep, we were always exhausted – but there is something very special about sharing a bed with a person you love. It isn't just about the sex, either, it's the trust involved in surrendering to sleep, or waking to hear the rhythmic breathing next to you. These are our most intimate moments, surrounded by the darkness.

The first Friday dawned grey and sullen – the clean light of the snow was being replaced by something less cold and sharp. The temperature was rising, and it was time to dig ourselves out.

As we were drinking the first of many coffees on that rather damp morning, Martin said, "We never finished that conversation last night."

"Really? I thought it finished rather well."

"I wouldn't argue with that... but we were talking about your finances."

"Oh God. Look, I've tried to cut down on everything – I really don't think I can ditch anything else—"

"Of course you can't. So… I've had a big idea. How would you feel if, purely as a financial arrangement, you understand, you took a lodger?"

"Not good. It would interfere with my life and the house is so sma— oh. You mean you, don't you?"

"Erm… well, I hadn't thought about *me*, exactly… but if you're offering…" He grinned at me. "Of course I mean me, you idiot. Why would I want my woman to share our space with anyone else?"

"Just hang on with your liberal misuse of possessive pronouns for a minute, sunshine. I am *not your* woman, and since when was this your space as well as mine?"

"Oh, I think you'll find you are and it is!"

Blimey, this is moving fast.

"Unless, of course, you'd rather I just left and we forget these two days ever happened? Your call, Allie my love."

"Don't be soft. Of course I don't want you to leave."

"Well, I'm very glad to hear that. So I'll get on to my landlord and hand in my notice, shall I?"

"Go on then…"

By the end of the week, he had moved in.

Chapter Twenty-One

I saw very little of Martin at school as the Spring Term progressed. He was busy every day with school business, seeing parents, dealing with minor crises. He and Carol made a great team – her experience and knowledge of the school combined with his energy and creativity. Thanks to their dedication and sensitivity, Hebble High kept going doggedly. The kids, resilient as they were, didn't forget their old Head – they often said things like "Mr Welch would like this, wouldn't he, Miss?" Marian Welch funded a series of prizes in his name, to be awarded at our speech days, and we had a large framed photo of him in the foyer.

But, much as we missed Brian, we needed a new Head. Martin felt it was far too soon in his career to apply, and in any case, he hadn't done the specialist training, so he wasn't qualified. Carol, conversely, felt she was too old – and she'd never wanted to be a Head in any case. Our local authority advertised the post and Carol and Martin were co-opted onto the Governors' Staffing Committee, in an advisory capacity only – they'd have no say in the final choice. The closing date arrived and the shortlisting for candidates began.

Once they'd whittled it down to four, staff members were invited to meet the candidates one evening after school. They were a varied bunch; a young newly-qualified man who talked well but didn't have much of a clue about the school, a very pleasant woman from a school in Cheshire, a completely ghastly oaf from Sheffield (who'd horrified Yvonne and Linda in the office by bursting in and saying "Now then, loves, where's bogs? I'm bustin' for a slash!" He might as well have gone home at that point, according to them.). Finally, there was Dr Sharp, a thin-faced little man with horn-rimmed spectacles, to whom most of us took an instant dislike.

There was a good take-up of the invitation to meet them in the Learning Resources Centre, which was packed. We shuffled from one candidate to another, listening and questioning; we'd compare notes in the staff room the next morning.

Going home in the car, Martin said, "Well? What did you think?"

"I liked Mrs Slatterthwaite. She seemed pretty well up on the school, she was aware of the possible effects of what she called 'regime change', and how it would need a delicate touch, and how important continuity would be for everyone."

"Yep, she said something similar in her application, and she has an impressive CV. She gets my vote too – not that I've got one, of course."

"What about the Head from the nineteenth century?"

"No chance – very authoritarian. Awful in every way. He'd be so wrong for the school, the kids and the parents."

It was an opinion generally shared, as we discovered the next morning.

The interview process lasted two days. On Day One, teachers or students were asked to give each candidate a guided tour. I was allotted to Mrs Slatterthwaite, while Joe and Hadley escorted Dr Sharp.

"Call me Karen, please," was the first thing she said. "And you are…?"

"Alison Weston. Allie."

"Oh *really*? I'm so pleased to meet you – I saw the article in *The Teacher* about your Integrated Curriculum and that wonderful school show. I'm keen to introduce the IC to my school, if I don't get this job. Do you think it would work for the older ones as well? Would you be prepared to come down to Cheshire and do a training day on it? We'd pay you, of course."

Talk about obsequious, was my first thought, but as we strolled round, I got the distinct feeling that she meant it. We had a long discussion about Government interference in education, inspired by the parlous state of some of our corridors and floors.

"We were promised a re-build under the last Labour government as part of the Building Schools for the Future programme," I told her, "but of course all that was scrapped when this lot got in…"

"But education *is* political, in the widest sense," was the last thing she said to me. "We need to be clear, as a society, what type of students we're creating – ones who can reason and think critically, or robots who train their memories and obey orders."

We exchanged e-mail addresses and agreed to keep in touch. I was fulsome in my praise when I wrote my brief notes for the Staffing Committee.

That afternoon, another Wednesday, I walked down to the Sixth Form Block for a chat, and a coffee, with Joe and Hadley. They'd grown about two feet over the year, and were rapidly changing into the fine, thoughtful young men they'd become. *What a privilege it is*, I thought sentimentally, as I watched them carefully brewing their coffee in the Sixth Form Block staff room and handing me a cup, *to have any influence, no matter how small, on the lives of our future citizens*. I hoped these two would always be my surrogate sons.

"How did you get on this morning?"

A look was exchanged between them. It was enough.

"That bad? Really?"

"You know who we were showing round, don't you? He was—"

"—dire!"

Like Cath and me all those years ago, I thought – same wavelength, same unfinished sentences.

"Dare I ask why?"

"He did nothing but criticise. The first thing he asked us was why we were allowed to attend school looking so scruffy, and whether there'd ever been a uniform in the Sixth Form. Then he moaned on about the colour of the walls, and all that wonderful work displayed everywhere – he said there was no exam work on display, or examples of Upper School essays. Oh, and he really objected to the GCSE and A Level art because it had a bit of nudity, and someone had designed a corset in needlework—"

"—like one of those really sexy ones in that old film—"

"—Moulin Rouge. It was awful. Keep us away from him if he ever comes back."

"Will do," I laughed.

The following day, the candidates gave presentations to the Governors about their visions for the school, had lunch with Carol and Martin, then went to their formal interviews in alphabetical order.

Martin and Carol were allowed to watch them, but not participate, and then had to leave before the final discussions began between the Staffing Committee and the Local Authority representatives.

The announcement we were expecting the following morning never came – nor on the next morning, or the next. By the end of the term, we were still in the dark. Then Easter came, with the national exams to follow soon afterwards.

Martin and I spent a pleasant fortnight together, over the holidays, still revelling in the novelty of being a couple again. Of course we argued from time to time about trivial things – he *would* keep talking through *Question Time* and he mocked *East Enders* mercilessly. I hate heavy metal, so the first time he played Deep Purple full blast I went out and bought him new headphones. But these were such tiny niggles – and every row brought a spectacular reconciliation, leaving us relaxed and peaceful. We had no way of knowing how long this would last – was it the beginning, or in ten years would it just be another memory? But hey, there was these moments, and the sharing – so, as Martin said, why worry?

The Summer Term rolled in, and all the stress of GCSE and A-Level preparation, extra notes, revision classes. Many of the students at both levels felt unbearably pressured, no matter how often we told them that it wouldn't be the end of the world if they didn't reach the grades they wanted. The media are constantly banging on about how easy it is to achieve top grades, but all teachers know they're wrong – it takes a lot of dedication and hard work by everyone involved.

Half term came and went and still there was no news about our new Head. Finally, the Chair of the Governors, Mary Booth, came to speak to us. All she said was that they'd whittled it down to two candidates, but "other issues" meant that it was taking an unprecedented time to reach a decision. Her last comment was that we'd be told on the first day of next term. None of us could work out what was going on, and Simon Benn, in his role as staff representative on the governing body, was unable, or more likely unwilling, to enlighten us.

On the last day of term, I was due to teach our shared Year Seven class for the final time – timetable issues meant that Rosemary would be taking them over in September. Martin was free during that lesson, so he said he'd try and pop in. I'd planned to watch a bit of Shrek 3 with them, as a treat. A couple of minutes before I expected the mob to arrive from their science lesson, Dean burst through the door, panting.

"Hiyah, Miss! We've just 'ad a great lesson in science and I wanted to tell yer about it!"

Without pausing for a response from me, he dashed on. "Sir was showing us what a yooman brain looks like and then Kelly Ann says, 'Sir, what do thoughts look like?' So then he starts telling us about electrical activity and sinuses—"

"Synapses?"

"—yeah, that's them – and then he goes on to conscious and subconscious and ego and id and a man called Sickman Frod who lived in Vienna (that's the capital of Austria, I knew that) and Miss, it were *ace!* Could I be a teacher, d'yuh think?"

He paused for breath, and I couldn't help smiling.

"Yes! You've been a teacher all year…"

"Ave I, Miss?"

"Of course – look how you helped Kelly Ann get the hang of speech marks and all the rest of it!"

"Don't mention 'er, Miss – I think she's packed me in. Sir started telling us Sickman Frod thought dreams were the royal road to the subconscious – imagine that! – and I said to 'er in the corridor afterwards 'I know what you were dreaming about last night', so she 'it me with 'er 'andbag and it broke. She were right mad. But she's made a nice surprise for you—"

Before I could process so much of the Integrated Curriculum in action, the door burst open and a hoard of excited kids poured in. Last came Kelly Ann, carrying two large plastic food boxes with her broken bag perched precariously on top. She was followed by Martin, who stood in the doorway with his arms folded. The class was instantly quiet. Kelly Ann stayed by my desk, not taking her seat like the rest.

"I thought we could eat these while we watch t'film," she said, theatrically whipping the lids off the boxes to reveal a large number of chocolate butterfly buns, sparkling with silver balls. "I made 'em last night. There's one fer you, Miss, an' you an' all, Sir."

"Tell you what," I said, "how about giving us the recipe and telling us how you did it, then we can make them at home as well, can't we? They look sensational, by the way!"

"Go on then, Miss, but yer'll 'av ter give me a minute. My recipe makes thirty-two, so I'll 'ave to divide everything by four. Will yer check me figures, Dean?"

This from a girl who could barely read and write ten months ago.

I took the register while they got their heads together – and she worked at lightning speed. Then she looked up and said, "Ready, Miss."

"The class is yours, Kelly Ann!"

"Right, ta Miss. Now listen up everyone – yer'll need a pen and a bit of paper – use the back of yer 'omework diaries. So, we need two hundred and fifty grams of butter…"

I moved to stand next to Martin while she dictated her recipe, and he smiled at me and squeezed my shoulder. Dean looked up at that moment, and the little bugger winked at me, but kept mercifully quiet. Simon Benn was scowling down the corridor and he paused for a minute outside the open door.

"Turned into a cookery lesson now, has it?"

"Public speaking," I said, "And if you play your cards right there could be a rather good bun in it for you."

"I wouldn't eat anything made by her grubby little paws," was his parting shot. I hoped she hadn't heard.

After the recipe had been successfully disseminated, Kelly Ann said, "Dean, can you give that lot out on your side of the class, and I'll do this one." As she approached us and we each took a bun – and they really did look good – she said quietly, "There *is* an extra one for Mr Benn, Miss – and tell him I always wash me 'ands before I cook anything."

Chapter Twenty-Two

The summer weeks raced – why is it that six weeks of term can seem unending when the holidays go so quickly? We packed a lot in – Cath and Pete had booked a week in a large cottage in Northumberland, near Alnwick, and invited us to join them. We were outside in the fresh sea air every day, swimming at Almouth, doing some wild scenic walks, visiting Lindisfarne then eating gargantuan portions of fish and chips in a converted boathouse in Amble. One day, the weather turned nasty, with grey clouds and a vicious wind. We got soaked and frozen walking up to Dunstanburgh Castle at Craster, so on the way back to the car park, we detoured to the pub and drank warming crab soup, sitting at a table in front of a huge picture window, looking out over the crashing breakers of the wild North Sea.

On the final day, as a treat, we booked a table at a stunning little bistro, formerly the village post office, in Warkworth. The teal and light mushroom walls, the sunburst driftwood sculpture, the slate table mats and the glittering tealights gave it a warm sophistication; the evening was punctuated by laughter, wonderful food and a choice of music that seemed completely personal. When the first chords of 'Samba Pa Ti' whispered around the room, Martin glanced at me and his eyes twinkled for a split second.

On the way home from Northumberland, we stopped off in Whitby and spent a week in an Airbnb visiting Alec and Sally, among other things. Alec was delighted to meet Martin again at last – his first comment was, "Christ, you hardly look any different from when you were twenty-one – but you've got a lot more hair than me!" Dear Alec…!

The night before term was due to begin was very different from the previous year. I had Martin beside me, for a start, and our urgent and apparently unfailing desire for each other ensured we went to bed before ten – and eventually slept very well. No anxiety about the term ahead this time.

Martin had to get up earlier that Monday because senior staff always had an hour's meeting before everyone else, to bring them up to speed with exam results and, of course, this year, to meet the new Head. We were both convinced it would be Karen Slatterthwaite and we'd even spent an evening looking at ways we could extend the Integrated Curriculum to include Year Nine and dovetail with the beginning of the GCSE courses. I just needed to log my ideas onto the file that held all the previous year's work schemes on the school system. I was feeling relaxed and optimistic when I parked my car behind the school building, so I could stagger some heavy bags through the dining hall and into the staff room without having to negotiate several flights of stairs.

Before I could even enter the building, however, I came across a disconsolate figure sitting on a low wall, with what looked like a four-legged mop, its paws on his shoulders, trying to lick his face.

"Hey Dean, what's up? You're on holiday for another whole day - no need to get upset yet"

A miserable face looked up at me. "It's not that, Miss. I'm right lookin' forrard to comin' back. No, it's just that... I were walking me dog on t'front field, and I'd picked up after 'im – yuh know, Miss?"

I nodded.

"And then this man... I dun't know 'oo 'e were, never seen 'im before...'e were goin' up t'steps to t'front door so I yells, 'Eh up, Sir, welcome t'ebble 'igh, 'ope yer 'ave a right grand day!'

"'E turns to me and 'e says, 'Don't be so impotent boy, and get that thing off the school field!' That were 'orrible, weren't it, Miss? Am not powerless, am I, Miss? Why were 'e so nasty ter me?"

"Did you recognise him, Dean?" A horrible thought was crossing my mind.

"No, Miss, never seed 'im before. 'E were much bigger than that 'orrible one 'oo came for that interview."

I relaxed again.

"Oh, well, don't worry. He probably said, 'Don't be so impudent,' and he was probably just a bit wound up about his first day. Do you want me to have a word with him if I recognise him?"

"Oh thanks, Miss – I weren't being cheeky either, honest, Miss."

"*I* know that, Dean, but sometimes there's a difference between what we think we've said and what other people think they've heard."

"Is there? Ruddy 'ell – sorry Miss – it's a hard thing, in't it, Miss? Language."

"It is, Dean, it is... but don't worry. I'll sort it for you. I'm loving the dog, by the way – is it yours?"

"Yes Miss – me Mam said we could ger 'im cos I 'ad such a good report. 'Ee's a schnauzer, Miss – that's German – so I call 'im Sigmund after Freud, Siggy for short. And before yuh say owt, yeah, I know 'e were Austrian, but they use t'name i' Germany an' all – I Googled it."

"Good lad! And Dean?"

"Yes, Miss?"

"Do you remember telling me last term that you wanted to be a teacher?"

"I do, Miss, yes."

"Well, hold that dream and work hard!"

"Yeah? If you say so, Miss. See you tomorrow."

He didn't look entirely convinced, but he smiled at me, even so, before wandering off down the hill away from the school.

***

I walked into an empty staff room, apart from Yvonne Watson, one of our tirelessly helpful office staff. Like many other clerical staff in other schools, she was also the Clerk to the Governors, responsible for calling meetings – and taking the minutes.

"Quick, Allie, you've to go straight to the theatre. The meeting starts at nine."

"That's unusual, but ok, I'm on my – you know something, don't you?"

"I can't say – but Allie, you'll need to keep your wits about you."

Oh God.

"And Allie," she hissed as I walked past her, "there'll be a computer in the office waiting for you to log on, and a new pen drive. Get out of the Theatre as soon as you can. And for God's sake don't say anything to anyone – I could lose my job for doing this."

On shaking legs, I went down the stairs, turned left through the door onto the Office corridor and through the foyer into the Theatre. I was nearly the last to arrive. Martin was sitting on the front row, gazing into space – but I could see his fists were clenched and his jaw looked set. He didn't glance in my direction. There was no sign of Carol. Nor was there anyone present from the support staff, the office staff or the cleaning team.

I'd just found a seat at the end of the second row when Simon Benn pushed past me without speaking, like a man on a mission, and went to the front of the room.

"Ladies and gentlemen! Could I have your attention please? Ladies and gentlemen?" So popular was he that it took several seconds for people to even notice he was speaking.

"In my new role as *Senior* Staff Advisor to the Governing Body…"

What?

"…I've been asked to make the announcement you've all been waiting for…"

He glanced towards the Theatre door, which was opened on cue.

"It gives me great pleasure to tell you that Hebble High's future is now in *very* safe hands. We are fortunate enough to have two new and *experienced* Deputy Heads, Mrs Stella Capone and Mr Jonathan Richards, who are former as well as present colleagues of our new Headmaster – a Headmaster who is a published expert on all matters concerning education. And if that weren't sufficient, he also comes to us from a very prestigious public school. Let me introduce you to….. *Doctor Jeremiah Sharp!*"

There was a thunderous round of applause – from Simon Benn. The rest of us sat in silence and shock. When he realised no-one else was clapping, he sat down suddenly, bright red in the face. *One to us*, I thought grimly.

In they stalked – a brassy, heavily made-up woman wearing killer heels, a black suit and a leopard-skin patterned blouse, followed by a tall, very broad-shouldered man with an upright, military bearing; I immediately recognised him from Dean's description. Finally, little Dr. Sharp – dour expression on a weasel face, and a pair of rimless spectacles perched over a roman nose. He was incongruous in a flowing black gown, complete with a purple stripe under his throat.

The sidekicks sat on the low platform facing us, while Sharp went up the stairs and onto the stage, where he stood next to the lectern, which was half as tall as he was.

Then, after a pause during which his eyes raked the tiered seating opposite him, he began to speak.

"Good morning, ladies and gentlemen. I am very pleased indeed to have been called in to instigate the renaissance of this establishment – a school with so much potential for academic excellence."

He went on to tell us that this year's exam results had been only fractionally better than last year's, and that consequently the school hadn't made the expected progress. We were coasting, apparently, and hadn't applied ourselves sufficiently to raising standards. Serious measures had to be taken if we were to avoid sinking still further in the league tables.

The fact that we'd had exceptionally high results in the previous year, and had at least matched them (in the most difficult of years when the whole school community was trying to come to terms with losing Brian), counted for nothing in the relentless pressure to 'add value'.

"What I am about to say to you may not be to your liking, but unlike the previous *incumbent* of this post, I am not here to be your friend. The decisions I have made about the running of the school, and the way they will be implemented are, I can assure you, in the very best interests of this institution. It is my intention, ladies and gentlemen, to make this one of the most prestigious state schools in the country within twelve months.

"Let me begin with the organisation of the school.

"There are two major problems. Firstly, all schools are looking at their spending with a view to making prudent and necessary savings…"

Necessary because their budgets have been cut even further by a new Government funding formula, I thought.

"And secondly because this school has been the victim of some… *unwise* decisions. The school will operate in future with myself at the helm, and my two highly skilled and," he repeated, "*experienced* Deputies."

He glanced at Martin as he said that.

106

"There will be no Assistant Heads. Those in such roles formerly have been offered full-time teaching positions. Mr Prescott Smith, in view of his relatively limited knowledge of management, will take the role of Senior Teacher in charge of pastoral matters, in a provisional capacity until Christmas, when the situation will be reviewed. He has *reluctantly* accepted that position. Mrs Carter, on the other hand, has chosen to take early retirement, as have Mr Barker and Miss Lord. They will be leaving us in October. From then, Mr Benn will assume the role of Head of the English faculty for the rest of the school year.

"This streamlining will go some small way towards easing the financial crisis in which this school has been placed after its previous *profligate* spending.

"Nevertheless, further economies will have to be made. Rather than making any of you redundant – for the *present* – I have decided that we, like other establishments in the area, must abandon the luxury of teaching assistants. They are having their own meeting at the moment – they will be told to look for other jobs as they will all be leaving us at half-term. There will in future be a Special Needs Coordinator, whose role will be to identify those children incapable of pursuing a rigorously disciplined academic education. They will be withdrawn from mainstream classes and placed in remedial groups, where they will be given instruction appropriate to their needs. They will not, of course, return to ordinary classes, nor will they be expected to sit any public examinations."

That'll get our grades up, I thought bitterly.

"Furthermore, bearing in mind the need for academic rigour, I have discussed it with Mr Benn and together we have decided to put an end to the Integrated Curriculum *experiment* with immediate effect. My research shows that this project-based teaching reduces education to the level of a play school. Children need to be aware that different *disciplines* – and I use that word most deliberately – require different approaches. The examination system in this country is, quite rightly, not run on thematic lines, and I consider the experiment conducted here last year to have been at best misguided and at worst, downright negligent.

"Yes, madam? Do you wish to make a comment? Who are you?"

I was on my feet, composing myself with difficulty and trying to push aside my mounting fury in order to speak coherently. Martin turned to me then, shaking his head imperceptibly, but I ploughed on.

"I'm Alison Weston and—"

"Ah yes, I believe you were the *perpetrator* of this experiment? I don't usually encourage interruptions, but I'm interested to hear your justifications for your scheme. Speak."

"*Thank* you... I was the first to suggest the Integrated Curriculum, yes, after extensive reading and research for my MA. But it *is* supported by the whole staff, after much discussion and a secret ballot. I and the Steering Committee, *including* Mr Benn, have spent many hours of our own time planning and cross-referencing lessons and assessments with the National Curriculum to ensure that every child has been given all the required skills in every subject. And the results have been spectacular, both in achievement and motivation—"

I was gratified to see my colleagues nodding in agreement.

"I hardly think you are the one to report on the success of *your* project—"

"But have you spoken to any of the children or their parents? Have you looked at their work? Have you seen our last Ofsted—"

"That's quite enough, Miss Weston. If you wish to continue this tiresome tirade, I suggest you see me in my office after this meeting. But I might as well tell you, this subject is not up for debate. And as for you, madam, your outburst and comments have been... *noted*."

"Yes, *Doctor* Sharp," I shot back, "and so have yours. Now, if you'll excuse me, I think I'm about to be sick."

With that, I rushed out of the theatre, slamming the door shut behind me. I went straight through the foyer doors and into the General Office, where Yvonne and Linda were hovering. Yvonne looked pale.

"He's told me to delete it! All that lovely stuff you did last year!"

"Don't worry, I'll save it if I can just get it before the end of the meeting."

While I logged on to her computer, Yvonne took the new pen drive out of its packaging. I started to copy and download the Integrated Curriculum file. It was agonizingly slow. Linda stood outside the theatre, listening, waiting for the meeting to draw to a close. Eventually, I had the whole file on the pen drive. There was still no movement or sign from Linda, so, on impulse, I e-mailed Karen Slatterthwaite:

Just heard the incomprehensible news, Sorry beyond words you didn't get the job. Attached may be of interest. It's about to be deleted from our system as per the instructions of Dr. Sharp. Please send all replies to my personal e-mail – suspect school e-mails may be monitored soon.

Keep in touch,
Alison Weston

Then I attached the file, sent the message and deleted it from my messages and the 'sent' box.

"They're coming out!" Linda said, scuttling back into the office. I put the pen drive in my pocket and went next door to the ladies' loo, as Yvonne sat down to begin deleting the Integrated Curriculum folder in its entirety, as instructed.

I nearly bumped into Sharp as I came out of the Ladies – he was hovering in front of the General Office door.

"Ah, the delicate Miss Weston – I trust you are somewhat recovered from your... *indisposition*?" The tiny eyes behind the spectacles narrowed. "You're not *pregnant*, are you?"

Martin was just passing at this point – the expression on his face nearly made me laugh out loud. He'd had a vasectomy ten years previously.

"No!" I said, "But even if I was, it'd be no-one's business but my own, until I chose to make it public."

"My office, *now*. Yvonne, have you deleted that folder as I instructed?"

"Yes, Sir," she replied, blushing and looking down. *Well-played, my friend*, I thought.

"Doctor Sharp? If you're speaking to Miss Weston about the Integrated Curriculum, perhaps I might join you? I was employed to assist in its implementation, after all."

Good move, Martin, I thought – *a witness.*

"That will not be necessary. What I have to say to Miss Weston is for her ears alone."

"No," I said firmly. "Mr Prescott Smith and I have no secrets from each other. Please speak to us both, or I'll be forced to reschedule this meeting with a union representative present."

"As you wish."

He turned on his heel and instead of admitting us both, he slammed the door in my face.

***

Later that morning, in a break between meetings, I helped Martin clear out his former office. We said very little. Then I went with him, plus the box of his belongings, to the Expressive Art Faculty's HQ, a room behind the sound and lighting box at the back of the theatre. Only then did we speak properly.

"Christ, Allie, I can't decide whether you're very brave or a total idiot," was his opening gambit, "but I've never felt more like cheering in my life than when you dashed out and slammed that door. Nobody messes with my woman, eh?"

"Too bloody right," I said, letting the possessive pronoun go, for once. "I've already e-mailed Karen Slatterthwaite and attached the folder and— "I waved the pen-drive at him, "—I have a copy here. Why can't we just go on teaching these lessons without so much song and dance? How would he know?"

"He'd know, because after you left, he announced that we'd all be required to log our plans daily on line, for him and our Heads of Department to check. There'll be spot inspections by him and his 'team', as he put it, to check we're following the plans we post. I'm sorry, love – it looks like the end of the line for the IC, for the time being at least. People are scared of losing their jobs."

"We'll see. But I'm so sorry, Martin – I never even asked you about what's happened to you. Can he do that?"

"I'm not sure – I'll take advice from the union. He can't alter my salary for at least a term, I don't think – I need to check. But in any case, I don't want to continue as a member of the Management Team under him. You haven't heard what else he's decided."

"Go on."

"He's introducing very stringent uniform rules, along with a uniform for the Sixth Form. He's re-structuring the school day to shorten the lunch break, introducing a compulsory homework lesson, and instructing that more written homework is set. He's introducing streaming in all subjects, and full two-hour examinations for every subject apart from PE and Expressive Arts at the end of every school year. He's banned all extra-curricular activities, including School Camp and school shows, and no mobile phones will be allowed in school. We've been instructed to have no direct contact with parents – everything is to go through him or his Deputies. And – this is the worst one of all – he's requested a snap Ofsted inspection, to, as he put it, 'shake us out of our smug attitude'!"

"Can he do that, as well?"

"He can, according to him."

A couple of hours later, I learned from Yvonne that the e-mail to Mrs Slatterthwaite had bounced back to us, along with a message from her previous school to say she had taken up a temporary headship elsewhere, and they were not at liberty to reveal the name of the school. That was the death knell for the Integrated Curriculum.

Chapter Twenty-Three

Staff outrage at the new regime was as nothing compared to the kids' reaction when they were told about the phone ban, new uniform rules, extra homework, shorter lunch break and the dismantling of the after-school clubs they loved. Parents complained immediately, there were letters in the local paper – and a few were even written in support of the new regime. The new Year Eights were disgusted at the abandonment of the Integrated Curriculum, but there was nothing to be done about any of it. Or so we thought.

Years Twelve and Thirteen set about protesting their imposed uniform – black trousers (not jeans), black shoes (not trainers), a white shirt and a school tie. Joe and Hadley led the protest, which was very dignified and restrained. Joe wrote a letter in his elegant, measured prose, setting out a very strong case for the retention of their individuality, as expressed through a personal choice of inoffensive attire. He mentioned that the local sixth-form colleges did not require any sort of uniform, and that the lack of conformity amongst the students had no apparent ill-effects on their performance, since their results had been impressive for several consecutive years. He ended by adding that it would be a great shame if the school were to lose vast numbers at the end of Year Eleven - particularly as the Sixth Form attracted so much funding.

The two of them then set about collecting signatures from every single sixth-former – over two hundred in all – and hand-delivered the letter to Dr Sharp.

That Wednesday there was an assembly in the Sixth Form block as usual – except that this time the Head himself marched in, resplendent in his usual attire of purple-striped gown.

I heard someone mutter, "Oo does 'e think 'e is... fookin' Batman?" I thought it was a pupil, but I couldn't be certain.

"Thank you so much for your *petition,*" he began after being introduced to the entire Sixth Form, who waited silently, all eyes on him. "I'm sorry to tell you that your crude attempts to manipulate me into giving way on this issue have fallen on stony ground. What you fail to realise is that when one has had so much *adult* experience, one sees things a little more logically.

"What you are clearly too young to understand is that there is much empirical evidence to suggest that a uniform increases loyalty toward an institution, and a desire to enhance its reputation within the community. *I'm* proud to be the Headmaster of Hebble High School, and I'm very disappointed that you are *rejecting* your Alma Mater in this selfish way.

"As for your crude threat that pupils may go to other institutions next year, I'm afraid that counts for nothing, since there will *be* no Sixth Form at this school in future. Year Twelve will finish their studies here; the following Year Eleven will compete for places in the new College being prepared in Halifax, where they may well come across some of their teachers, who *may* also have been redeployed. Good day to you."

He swept out. Matt Haddon, white-faced, dismissed the students and they began to disperse, in no hurry to go to their lessons after that bombshell. Joe and Hadley came straight to me.

"Did you know about this?"

"I certainly didn't, Joe – it's the first I've heard about it."

"It isn't our fault, is it, Allie? For stirring him up with that letter?" Hadley sounded anxious. They now both used my first name out of lessons, but never in front of their classmates.

"Of course not! It won't just be us losing our Sixth Form – this must be a Local Authority decision. It'll be all over the paper on Friday."

"Would you like us to get Mr Prescott Smith?" said Joe. "You look really upset."

They clearly knew about Martin and me, somehow, but had said nothing to anyone. I was touched.

"No, I'll be all right in a minute. Joe, could you tell everyone to… er… just read the next chapter and make some notes on how Hardy makes Troy seem an attractive character to Bathsheba when they first meet?"

113

"Course I will – you take your time."

"Thanks lads."

That was nearly the last straw – they were so thoughtful, those two. Hadley went and brewed some more coffee – he was a scientist, so he had no lessons till after break. I went into the loo, splashed my face with cold water then grabbed the coffee before I went into the classroom.

Joe, bless his heart, was leading a discussion on the literary genius of Thomas Hardy. I caught a glimpse of the wonderful lecturer he would be one day, and I felt tearful again that the loss of this successful Sixth Form, with its bright, energetic students, would be such a devaluation of the education we could provide. Not only that, but these older students were role models for the younger ones, and they often got involved with mentoring them, in some cases helping them to avoid some of the pitfalls of being a teenager at war with authority. All that would be lost.

"Why is this happening?" I said to Matt Haddon at break. We were on duty together, but the Block was very quiet.

"Because the LEA can't provide the funding for individual Sixth Forms anymore." he said. "Their budget has been cut so much that they in turn have to make draconian cuts in order to fulfil their legal obligations."

"But isn't it going to cost a fortune to build a specialist college?"

"No. They're converting the old council offices, patching them up so they're just about sound. I've been doing some research this morning because I'll need to apply for a job there – there'll be nothing left for me here. This building will house much younger kids – we're going to be what's called a "through school", educating them from nursery to GCSEs. That's the plan, and that's where Sharp fits in. Apparently he was previously employed as Head of some prep school down south – a feeder school for Winchcester."

Chapter Twenty-Four

On the third Monday after the start of term, the Head announced that Ofsted had given him notice of an inspection, to last three days, beginning the following Wednesday.

The changes in the school were already taking their toll on morale. All the brightly coloured walls had been replaced over the summer with a light, uniform grey. The pin boards around the school had remained empty, but now we were instructed to fill them with models of good practice in our subjects – which meant examination answers and essays, annotated to show the criteria for different levels or grades. Brian's photograph had been removed from the foyer and given to his widow; all that remained was a small plaque which read "In memory of Brian Welch, Head of Hebble High School, 1991-2017."

The school was completely silent. The classrooms were completely silent. The children marched like robots from one lesson to another, patrolled by every available teacher, instructed to hand out an immediate detention to anyone speaking. Lessons consisted of teaching from the front of the class only, to the prescribed and published lesson plan. No room for spontaneity, no room even for group work. All the classes were streamed and friendship groups separated. Dean and Kelly Ann, along with three others from their class, had been withdrawn from lessons with their friends and placed in different remedial groups, taken by Mrs Capone and Mr Richards.

Dean was the more upset – his aspiration to become a teacher seemed to have been ruined, but the thing which upset him the most, he told Martin (to whom he'd been referred after pleading to be allowed to go back to his usual class), was that he'd no longer be able to help Kelly Ann. Martin discussed his case with Mr Richards, who only said, "Ah yes, the revolting specimen who shouted abuse at me on my first morning. He belongs nowhere else." How futile of Martin to describe Dean's innocent intentions that morning, the progress he'd made the previous year or his ambition to take his GCSEs. He'd been labelled, and that, it seemed, was that.

On the Monday of our inspection week, I cut through the theatre on my way to the staffroom. It was break, and I'd taken a shortcut to avoid the lines of silent, resentful children in the corridors. As I opened the door to the foyer, I heard a man's voice raised in anger. He was standing, red-faced, in front of the window into the General Office, shouting through the grill at Yvonne and Linda.

"I don't care! I need to see this so-called Head Teacher *today*!"

I heard Yvonne say, "I'm really sorry, Mr Midgley, but Doctor Sharp never sees anyone without an appointment."

Then I realised who it was. Dean's dad, Bob Midgley. I would have recognised him in any case. Like his son, he was small and wiry, with a pleasant, open face that I'd last encountered when he shook my hand after the show last Christmas. Now he was florid and clearly furious.

"Miss Weston! Can you get me in to see Sharp? I'm sorry to come bursting in like this, but I'm that mad about what's happened to our Dean. Although he'd be upset if he knew I was here."

"Hello, Mr Midgley. I'm sorry you feel like that."

But not at all surprised.

"Can I help at all?"

"Not unless you can explain to me why Dean's been put in that numpty class, after he did so well last year. I don't suppose you were responsible, were you? After what you said to him about being a teacher a couple of weeks ago?"

"Well no—" I began, just as the door burst open from the senior staff corridor, and Wing Commander Richards (as we called him) stalked out.

"May I be of assistance, Sir?"

"Who are you? Are you Sharp?"

"No, I am Mr Richards, Deputy Head. And to whom do I have the privilege of speaking?"

"I'm Dean Midgley's father."

"Are you indeed? Ah yes, Dean – a difficult child, I'm sure you'll agree. Are you here to make an appointment to discuss his behaviour?"

"No! I'm here to discuss yours, and the changes Sharp's trying to make to this school. Are you *determined* to ruin it? And Dean's *not* difficult, he's just bored and frustrated because you've stopped educating him. "

"Very well – I can see that we need to discuss school policy at some length. Yvonne, could you look at my diary and tell me when I have a spare appointment? And that will be all, Miss Weston."

"I want her at the meeting. Miss Weston knows Dean, and she knows what he's capable of."

"I'm sure she does. But we have a policy of leaving parental meetings to senior members of staff. *Junior* teachers are needed in the classrooms."

"That's ridiculous – or are you scared they might tell you a few home truths about the crap job you're doing?"

"Mr Midgley, if you're going to resort to abusive language, I shall have to ask you to leave. And I'll thank you not to embarrass Miss Weston by attempting to contact her in future."

"Right," Mr Midgley said grimly.

"Finally, if you really don't like this new, better-disciplined, better organised establishment, you are of course perfectly at liberty to seek a place for Dean at another school."

"You haven't heard the last of this, Richards."

With that he turned on his heel and stomped out through the main entrance door.

But any attempts on his behalf to expose the shortcomings of the new regime, or muster the support of other sympathetic parents, were rapidly overtaken by a much more controversial episode for the school.

*****

I was uneasy on the first morning of the inspection. I'd heard a whisper on the corridor of the Sixth Form block that there was going to be trouble, that the students were going to take the opportunity the inspection offered to make their feelings known. They were intending to protest. Nevertheless, I was taken by surprise, and I must admit mildly amused, by the appearance of the sixth formers that day. Those who could afford them had hired dinner jackets, bow ties and red cumberbunds, or very formal evening gowns. The rest wore their normal attire of jeans and sweatshirts. Apart from that, the three inspection days passed without incident in the Block. It was a point wittily made, I thought – a harmless reproach for being patronised by Dr Sharp in that dreadful assembly.

Elsewhere in the school, things started badly and then deteriorated. On the Wednesday, before lessons, there was a Year Eleven assembly in the theatre, to be given by Dr Sharp and observed by two inspectors. The pupils filed in and took their seats in silence to await the arrival of the Great Man. As the door to the theatre opened, one of them, lost in the tiered seating, blew a brief whistle. A great chanting started up immediately – "Jerry, Jerry, Jerry!" as if Dr Jeremiah Sharp was Jeremy Kyle. Form tutors were helpless to stop it, their voices lost beneath two hundred chanting teenagers.

Dr Sharp strode onto the stage dark-faced. But standing by the lectern glowering did no good at all – still the chanting continued. Finally, after several minutes with no sign of it abating, Dr Sharp turned on his heel and walked out. As soon as the doors closed behind him, the whistle blew again and the theatre returned to complete silence. There were three inspectors sitting at the side – they scribbled furiously before, during and after the disruption. As the bell for lessons went, Year Eleven left the theatre, again in an orderly manner. Not a word had been spoken by any of the pupils to each other from start to finish.

Every single inspected lesson over the next three days was subjected to some form of bad behaviour. It was as if the presence of a stranger in the room acted as a catalyst. Kelly Ann's group, in the capable hands of Mrs Capone, seemed cowed into submission, till she told them to draw a picture of something they'd made at home, then describe it. Kelly Ann drew herself talking to the class about her baking the year before. When one of the inspectors asked her if she hadn't understood, or hadn't been listening to instructions, her response was to yell, "Oh shut yer stupid face, yer fat mare!" This was particularly inappropriate since the inspector was rather broad in the beam – and she didn't take it well. Kelly Ann was immediately suspended, and eventually permanently transferred to the Pupil Referral Unit in the nearest town. In subsequent months and years she was to do rather well under the calm guidance of the excellent Head there, in a system far more reminiscent of the old Hebble High. But she'd left behind all her friends.

Dean caused no trouble, but another child in his remedial group threw himself to the floor at an inspector's feet screaming, "I'm so fuckin' bored! Why can't we do summat good like we did last year?" Mr Richards lost it completely, dragged the unfortunate child (who was on the autistic spectrum) to his feet and threw him bodily out into the corridor. The rest of the lesson was apparently punctuated by the child running up and down the corridor, banging on doors and shouting obscenities. More frantic writing from the inspector.

I fared no better. My lesson was invaded by a grim-faced type in a suit. I had been instructed to teach my Year Nine group about colons and semi-colons using some work sheets. As they came in, one of them whispered, "Sorry about this, Miss…" just as a screaming fight broke out in the middle of the room, complete with hair-pulling, punching and furniture being thrown about, whilst the rest of the group yelled encouragement.

I was on the point of wading in to try and separate them when Benn, of all people, burst through the door. He stood at the front expecting their violence to cease, but no-one took a blind bit of notice, so he walked out and left me to it, speedily followed by the inspector. As the door closed behind them, the fighting stopped as if a switch had been flipped and the kids started picking up chairs and setting the room to rights. Five minutes later, when Sharp burst in, they were sitting angelically working. A tribute to Martin's role-playing drama lessons, clearly.

If the disruption in lessons was bad, the behaviour in the corridors and dining room was frightening. The little automatons marching in silence down the corridors at the change of lessons the previous week had been replaced by a howling, shrieking rampage of children, hurling themselves down stairs, pushing and shoving, shouting and swearing. Little ones were knocked down and forced to cower in corners, completely bewildered by their new and terrifying school.

In the dining room, food was thrown, water spilled, tables left uncleared – all taking place within a deafening wall of noise. Outside was little better – there was open warfare between different year groups on the front field, a spate of minor injuries and the chief inspector's car anointed with white eraser fluid from an open bottle thrown during a fight, which she didn't find until it had baked solid in the late September sunshine.

Previously, when the school had been inspected, we were all in it together. Kids were on their best behaviour because, underneath all their bravado, the majority of them had wanted the school to be seen in a good light. But this time the reverse seemed to be true – rendered powerless by the myriad rules imposed upon them, for no apparent reason, they used the inspection as an opportunity to give full vent to their fury.

By the end of school on the Friday we were worn out, totally demoralised and without even the energy to be angry at the appalling spectacle we had witnessed over the last three days. I could not imagine what Sharp would say to the inspectors before they left to prepare their report in a nearby hotel, and I shuddered to think what that report would contain.

Chapter Twenty-Five

Monday morning. Staff room briefing. Dr Sharp, his face contorted with rage, brandished the report, screaming at his staff like a man demented. He hoped we were satisfied by the results of our half-hearted discipline, our shoddy teaching and our inability to instil any sort of pride for their school into these most despicable pupils. He was ashamed to be associated with us. Someone amongst us must have coordinated this, because it was far too well-organised to have genuinely come from *these* children. He said he was gathering evidence which pointed to certain individual rabble rousers, and they would be dealt with most severely... blah blah blah.

I thought to myself, that'll teach you to call in the inspectors after three weeks of term, after you'd changed so much. So much for making this the most prestigious state school in the country, I thought. You've guaranteed that it could become one of the most notorious, once the media get hold of this report. But I remained silent.

He finished his rant by saying, "Once I have obtained incontrovertible evidence about the ringleaders of this... *riot*, they can expect to be expunged from the institution. I *will not have* my authority undermined in this appalling manner!"

We all looked at each other after he and his deputies had left the staffroom. His accusations were inconceivable – who in their right minds would have encouraged such behaviour? Sean, as usual, voiced what many of us were thinking.

"It's all face-saving bluff. One of *us* has to be responsible, in his mind, because he can't stand the thought that it might all be *his* fault."

Later that day, the report was published and posted on the school's web site, as required by law. It was perfectly fair – the inspectors had noted that their presence in assemblies, corridors or classrooms seemed to have acted as a trigger for the disruption; they noted the instant silence in the moments after they'd left. They were critical of the type of teaching we were instructed to offer, saying it was indeed boring and old-fashioned. They were also disparaging about the management style of the senior staff, and the lack of input from teachers or parents in the running of the school. However, they were fulsome in their praise of the Sixth Form and its approach, as well as its polite and civilised students who were so very responsive in lessons. They made no mention of the somewhat bizarre attire favoured by the senior pupils.

They concluded that it was astonishing that a school with such a glowing inspection report only eight months previously could have descended into such chaos so rapidly. Because of the sixth-form atmosphere and the superb examination results obtained by students over recent years, they placed us into the "Satisfactory" category, only one up from "Special Measures".

We had narrowly escaped a whole year of regular inspections, and, if we'd failed to make the required changes, the subsequent replacement of the Senior Management Team.

Some of my colleagues felt that was rather a pity.

Chapter Twenty-Six

The next morning, before lessons began, I received a message saying I would be required to attend an interview with the Head in his office immediately after break.

"Don't worry, Allie," said Rosemary, as she poured me a cup of strong Blue Mountain from her large cafetiere (the coffee machine, the biscuits and the free drinks had been dispensed with, since they were now apparently too expensive – the coffee machine having been placed, according to Yvonne, in Capone's office). "He'll be talking to everyone, I expect, about last week. He knows who you are, so it's you first, probably."

"Even so," said Martin, taking the next cup, "watch what you say, and if it starts getting unpleasant, tell him you want a union rep present. That seemed to throw him last time."

"Yeah, will do," I said, uneasy in spite of their reassurances and advice.

***

"Ah, Miss Weston... do come in."

Sharp had his back to me. He was staring out of the window at the scene on the front field, where pupils were gathering for their PE lesson and a game of football was about to begin. I caught a glimpse of Sean getting them organised into teams before blowing his whistle. There was no sign of any misbehaviour.

"Sit down, please."

He turned and indicated a chair directly opposite his own. There was a heavy desk between us, with a neat pile of paper in the middle.

"What is your opinion of the events of last week?"

I sighed. "Well, I have to say, Doctor Sharp, considering all my fifteen years' experience at this school, the behaviour was completely unprecedented, and utterly appalling."

"Really? And do you believe... in your *experienced* mind, that it was spontaneous?"

"I don't know, honestly," I replied. "I suppose there *might* have been some degree of collusion at first, maybe amongst the older kids – the Sixth Form had obviously planned their costume hiring, for example – but then I got the impression it developed a momentum of its own. Of course, it's very easy for every pupil to communicate using social media. What do you think?"

There was a pause, during which he stared at me through those rimless spectacles with an intensity intended to make me very uncomfortable. It didn't.

"So you admit, do you, Miss Weston, that the campaign was initially *organised*?"

"That's not what I said, because I don't know for certain. I was speculating on the way it *seemed* to me."

A pause. More fixed staring.

"You asked me what I think, did you not?"

"I did."

"Well, *this* is what I think..."

He was speaking so softly I could barely hear him.

"I think that it was very *carefully* orchestrated, by a calculating and disruptive brain, belonging to a person who has a grudge against me and my team. I think, Miss Weston..." (and now the volume was rising) "...I think this whole episode was a product of *your* warped and twisted mind! I think—" (his voice had risen to screaming pitch and he must have been clearly audible the length of the corridor outside, and in the General Office) "you *manipulated* some of your acolytes into doing your dirty work for you. You are a disgrace to the teaching profession!"

His hysteria didn't intimidate me as much as he'd no doubt intended. I'd been harangued and yelled at by Doris for the best part of thirty years; I was more than capable of dealing with this onslaught. I looked directly at him.

"So let me just get this straight," I began calmly. "You seriously think that I would set out to make this school look ridiculous in the eyes of the parents, Ofsted and possibly the press, because you made us abandon the Integrated Curriculum? In spite of the fact that I dislike everything you stand for—"

"Ah yes, *now* we're getting to the truth of the matter!"

"In spite of that fact, I have not and I *will not* do anything to undermine you in the eyes of our pupils. I have remained professional at all times, I have *never* expressed a hostile view to them, and I never will. This school and Brian's memory are far too important to me."

"I put it to you, madam—"

(For pity's sake, where does he think he is? The Old Bailey?)

"—I put it to you that you are a *filthy liar!* You have been seen to be as thick as thieves with some of the more disreputable elements in the Sixth Form. You've even been seen *drinking coffee* with them!"

"Oh for goodness sake! The two boys in question have known me since they were eleven years old. I steered them through their English GCSEs and I know their parents. They're in my tutor group and they make me a drink every morning. This is just too daft to laugh at!"

That seemed to be the final nail in my coffin.

"*Get out*, Miss Weston! I am suspending you until such time as an enquiry into your conduct reveals what you've done. Then you will surely be found guilty of gross professional misconduct and dismissed from the profession in disgrace. You will go to the staffroom, pick up your coat and leave this place immediately. You will have no contact with any other member of staff or pupil until this matter is concluded and you are no longer employed by this or any other school."

"Oh this is ridiculous. You don't have any evidence, and you know you don't, because none exists. I am completely innocent and you're making a big mistake."

"Is that a threat, Miss Weston? Are you now *threatening* me?"

It occurred to me that was for the benefit of the ears of potential witnesses – for all I knew, there were people recording this from the corridor.

"Don't be ridiculous," I said again, equally loudly, just in case, "of *course* I'm not threatening you. But you can't seriously think that I, along with two of the brightest and most loyal pupils Hebble

High's ever had, could possibly... *possibly* be responsible for instigating the awful events of last week? If I'd even *suggested* it to them (which of course I didn't), they'd have told me, quite rightly, not to be so stupid."

He seemed to waver a little at that, but then his door opened and the enormous head and shoulders of Mr Richards peered round.

"Are you quite all right, Doctor Sharp? Is this woman causing you any trouble? Can I be of any assistance?"

"Thank you Mr Richards. Miss Weston is leaving the building now. Kindly escort her to her car, and do not allow her to speak to anyone at all."

"Hang on a minute—"

"Good bye, Miss Weston."

Suddenly I realised there was no point in arguing any more. I was done here.

Outside in the corridor I caught a glimpse of Yvonne and Linda looking horrified. Then we were through the door and out into the main part of the school. We nearly bumped into Joe, on his way to the Theatre for a drama lesson.

"I've got an essay on Hardy for you, Miss W—" He stopped abruptly. "Are you ok? What's going on?"

"Hand it to Mr Haddon," Richards said. "He'll arrange to have it marked."

"But he isn't an English— what's going on?" he said again.

"PS Joe," I said. Light dawned – Prescott Smith. He nodded and hurried away.

Numbly I climbed the stairs, went into the staff room, got my coat and bag and left. Richards walked with me to my car and stood watching as I unlocked it. As I got in, I thought I heard him mutter, "Good riddance", but I couldn't be certain.

Chapter Twenty-Seven

I don't remember driving home. I don't remember unlocking the door and going into the cottage. I don't remember anything of that because all I could think, over and over again, was that this could be the end of my career as a teacher. There was no proof that I had acted unprofessionally in any way – and there was no proof that I hadn't, either. But gradually, as the shock wore off, my hopelessness receded, and I remembered Martin's suggestion. I had to contact my union and get some outside help and legal advice.

The number was on the back of my membership card. I rang and spoke to a very assured and friendly young man who said he couldn't get to me straight away – my heart sank – but would six pm be convenient? He asked me if I would be all right till then. Did I have a friend who could come and spend some time with me? I assured him I was quite composed and that my partner would be home as soon as he could. When I mentioned Martin's name he seemed to know him, and it occurred to me that Martin had probably already spoken to him about his own problem with Sharp, his demotion and public humiliation in that first staff meeting only a few weeks ago.

I made myself a cup of tea and started turning the day over - what had just happened? Was it in any way my fault? Then my phone rang, and it was Martin.

"Where are you? Are you all right? What the fuck's happened? Joe said you'd been sacked!"

"Not yet," I said wearily, and I explained, trying to stay calm.

"I'm coming home," he said.

"No, hang on – are you teaching this afternoon? Because if you are, I'll be fine till the end of school."

"Well yes, but... are you sure? I hate to think of you on your own."

"Of course I am. Don't leave the premises if you've got classes. I'll see you around three thirty."

"Really?"

"I'll be fine, love."

"I'll see you soon then."

***

An hour later there was a knock on the door. It was Joe and Hadley, carrying a large bunch of chrysanthemums.

"These are for you. Can we come in? There's something we need to tell you."

I glanced up the street, which was deserted, then I let them in.

"Thank you! But why are you here?"

"Mr PS said you'd been suspended. We feel terrible. All the Sixth Form have said they feel terrible because you've done nothing wrong. And we can prove it."

"How?"

"Because we know who was behind what happened. We all were."

"*What?*"

"Everyone was so pissed off at the way Sharp spoke to us about that stupid uniform stuff that we decided we'd teach him a lesson. The evening dress stuff was just a smokescreen. Loads of us have younger brothers and sisters lower down the school who were very happy to help. We thought if we were all in on it, he couldn't suspend the whole Sixth Form—"

"I wouldn't bet on it!"

"—so we set up a Facebook page, Help Hebble High, and it's all on there. Each comment is dated but anonymous. We're prepared to go to Sharp and tell him, but not to name anyone. We've all agreed on that."

I couldn't help but be impressed – and equally horrified.

"No! You two *must not* go and see him. Stick together as a Sixth Form – if he thinks he can make an example of any individuals, he will – and you'll be excluded, then expelled. Don't let this ruin your references, and maybe your chances of getting into uni. Say nothing, and I'll pass on your evidence to my union rep. I'm sure there'll be

128

repercussions for the whole Sixth Form – but you know that would be fair, don't you? What you instigated was really stupid, it could easily have escalated into something even worse and someone could have been seriously hurt or even killed."

"But they weren't, and we don't want you to lose *your* job either!"

"That's not the point – they *could* have been. Then how would you have felt? There'd have been no chance to put that right, would there?

"But look, don't worry about me. The union rep is coming to see me this evening, and I'm certain he'll sort it, especially using what you've given me. Your intervention has been really helpful, and I can't thank you enough. But it *definitely* isn't right that you two should be the scapegoats for this mess."

They looked miserable, but they both nodded. Sometimes they make it easy to forget they're still only seventeen, I thought, but I suspected they'd learned a tough lesson through all this about actions and consequences.

"Tell you what," I said, "Let me show you how decent coffee ought to be made. Martin'll be back any minute, gasping for caffeine."

***

Martin was amazed but clearly pleased to walk in and find us laughing about something. When I explained why they'd come to see me, he immediately repeated, without any input from me, virtually word for word what I'd said to them about avoiding any pointless confessions. I hugged my boys briefly before they left, and Martin shook their hands.

After they'd gone it was my turn for a much longer embrace.

"Christ, what a day you've had," he said. "But why didn't you stop the meeting and insist on the union coming in before it went any further?"

"It just happened so fast. I thought he was changing his mind and then that oaf Richards stuck his head round the door and that was it. Too late.

"But I have rung the rep; he'll be here around six."

He duly arrived, a pleasant, youngish man who certainly seemed to know his stuff. He recorded my statement and questioned me closely about the way my interview had been conducted; he was particularly interested in the shouting and name calling, asking me to be absolutely certain that Sharp had called me a 'filthy liar with a warped and twisted mind', and 'a disgrace to the teaching profession'. Then he took a quick look at the Facebook page and noted down the details.

"Quite frankly, Alison," he said before he left, "I can't think he's got a leg to stand on. I've got so much damning evidence here that if this ever went to a tribunal, he's the one who'd come out of it the worst. The Facebook page is the clincher – the dates and the comments exonerate you completely, in my opinion, plus the fact that he can't have any idea it exists… so far. I'll let our legal section look at it, and let you know what they say. But if I were you, I'd be wanting compensation for the way you've been treated. At the very least, I'll get him to agree to a couple of weeks' leave."

"I'd take the leave, but I wouldn't want anything from the school," I said firmly. Then I had an afterthought.

"Although a full apology in front of the staff at morning briefing would be gratifying. I might not be there to hear it, but Martin will."

Chapter Twenty-Eight

I didn't hear anything for a few days from the union, but the following Tuesday, the rep rang. Sharp had been persuaded that any further action would be both futile and damaging to the school's reputation. Since that was already in tatters after the Ofsted fiasco (and the published report, which had made front-page news in the local paper), he'd reluctantly agreed to my leave being extended to half term on full pay, and a public apology. The union had done a good job.

"But," the rep went on, "there's something distinctly fishy about his appointment in the first place. Why would the Governors appoint a southern prep school head over the other shortlisted candidate, who had so much relevant experience? And why was he allowed to bring his Deputies with him? This has opened a whole can of worms. I know it's been awful for you, but some good may come of it. What we really need, in an ideal world," he added, "is someone to take this on and run with it. We're uncovering some pretty interesting evidence. Anyhow, that's our problem. Enjoy the rest of your time off, Alison, and good luck for your return. If you have the slightest concerns about the way you're dealt with, don't hesitate to get in touch. You know where I am."

The next morning, Martin reported later, there was a sensational announcement from Dr Sharp in morning briefing. Thanks to the Deputies' diligence, and a commendable act of disclosure on Miss Weston's behalf, he declaimed, an underground organisation of dissent and disobedience had been unearthed. It originated with our appallingly disloyal Sixth Form, he'd continued, who fortunately wouldn't be with us for much longer. None of them had had the courage to confess their responsibility, so Dr Sharp had decided to punish them all.

There would be no more food served in the Sixth Form Block – they could come and queue for their meals with the younger ones – and no study periods off the premises would be allowed in the future. They would henceforth be expected to be seen working in their free periods, and to facilitate that, all the low tables and comfy chairs had been removed and replaced by desks and tables. Since no members of staff were *apparently* involved in the Ofsted disruption, he added, and in light of my action, putting the school's interests first, he'd decided to *allow* me to return after half term.

Martin was so furious he had to leave the staffroom at that point. His loyalty to me, and his knowledge about what had really happened, had made the whole farce utterly unbearable.

He was still fuming when he arrived home, hours later.

"So much spin he should be in the Cabinet, the lying, sanctimonious little *sod*! And those two odious cronies, plus the smirking Benn – I can't stand it, Allie. I can't look at them without an overwhelming desire to cause them great pain! In fact—" he took a deep breath and looked at me properly, "—I've been thinking, I want to go back into the theatre. This morning's been the clincher. There's nothing in that school for me anymore. I can't stand reading another page of some stupid outdated play or showing the little ones how to be trees. It's bloody ridiculous!"

I really hadn't seen that coming.

"How long have you felt like this? I knew you were very upset about the beginning of term – who wouldn't be? – but I didn't realise you felt so strongly. Do you really want to give up teaching completely? I thought you loved it?"

"I love some aspects of it, and I'm trying to think of ways to combine it with the theatre. Something like that course I created in Singapore, possibly, but obviously in the UK – if such a thing exists. That'll take some time and research. But I've got to get away from Sharp and all he stands for; it's just wrong, Allie.

"You've had enough to contend with recently," he added, more calmly. "But now that's over, we both need to have a think about our next moves."

Cold prickles of pure fear began to creep up my arms and legs. This was beginning to sound depressingly familiar.

Seeing the expression on my face he said, "Oh now hang on a minute, this isn't like... before. I'm not saying I want to leave you, of course I don't – whatever we decide, we do it together – we're a team.

"Listen, I've been thinking. I might see if there's anything going at Theatre Clwyd – I know a couple of people there – just to tide us over. We could maybe stay with Lou and her girls – she's got a spare room now that Dad's gone. You'd easily find some supply work until you could get a full-time job. Say you'll come with me?"

"I'll think about it," I said. "If you'd asked me that last year, nothing would have shifted me from Hebble. But my school's gone, hasn't it? At least until there's some drastic change of direction. And I doubt it'll ever be the same again."

At that moment I realised that I couldn't go back either.

***

Later, I sat alone in front of the dying embers of the stove. Martin for once had gone up to bed by himself. This was so difficult; being in Wales with him could mean possibly abandoning my teaching career, or once more losing the man I would love till my dying breath. But the school I believed in was steadily disappearing, and there was little I could do about that. *If only Brian hadn't died*, I thought to myself...

I'd been a teacher for the best part of seventeen years, fifteen of them at Hebble. I thought fondly of the pupils who'd passed through its doors during my time there, and the great things some of them were doing with their lives. All the doctors and dentists, the vets, the nurses, psychologists, physiotherapists and midwives, the famous actors, the economic journalist, the town councillors and the Parliamentary candidate, to say nothing of the lawyers, the teachers, the restaurant owner, the soldiers and the rock musician... and all the rest who'd moved away and lost touch with their home town. I thought of Joe and Hadley – I hoped we'd always be friends – and all the Deans and Kelly Anns who were being so sadly let down by the changes to their education instigated by our dreadful government. I thought of what a privilege it was to be a teacher, to touch the lives of children and to give them something positive, no matter how small, which might improve their futures in some way. They deserved better than the likes of Doctor Sharp. Then my thoughts drifted to the comments made by the union rep. And I made up my mind.

***

The following week, Martin resigned from Hebble High, with effect from November 1st. With some misgivings, I rang Yvonne in the office and had a long and reassuring chat. Then I wrote my letter to Sharp, copy to the new Chair of Governors, whom I'd never met, and another copy to the union rep. I would leave on the same date as Martin. There would be no ceremony, no gift presentation – we wanted nothing and absolutely no fuss.

That weekend Martin took a call from an old friend who was on the recruitment team at Theatre Clwyd. They remembered his name – he'd been in rep with one of the leading lights on the management committee. He was instantly offered the job of Assistant Stage Manager for a play due to run for three weeks before Christmas. They wanted him to start at the beginning of November. I heard him accept it on the spot. In the meantime, I'd been making a few calls of my own while he was at work, fixing up my future as well.

When we sat down to work out our finances, we realised that things would be pretty tight, but Martin's salary and savings would be enough to pay Lou something towards her bills – she wouldn't hear of any rent – and help with the food shopping. We wouldn't have time to sell my cottage before we left, but I still had to somehow pay the mortgage, so we decided we'd let it for the time being.

We put it in the hands of a small local estate agent, the same firm who'd sold it to Mark and me around twelve years ago. They came out to look round, waxed lyrical about its condition and the views and suggested a rent far higher than we'd thought possible – enough, astonishingly, to overpay the mortgage by a few hundred each month. In fact, they said, they already had some prospective tenants in mind. They turned out to be an Indian couple who'd come to the country to work in the local hospital – he was a consultant neurologist, his wife an anaesthetist. The tenants were also keen to take the furniture, so that was another problem solved.

The days seemed to race by – it would be the end of my life in this dear little cottage as well as the end of my teaching, at least for the immediate future.

The day before we were leaving, Martin shuttled boxes full of our books, cds and clothes; we could do without them until we were settled, keeping them at Cath and Pete's place. They'd just finished converting an old iron foundry into eleven spectacularly modern flats and had agreed, after a little gentle bribery (food was involved!) and Martin's persuasive charms, to store our boxes in their empty, unconverted basement till we found a permanent place to live. By the time the last box left, the cottage looked like a holiday home – clean, nicely furnished, but completely impersonal.

Then I got busy. It was around seven on a chilly, late October evening. When I'd finished, I went outside for a moment. The sun had set hours ago, and the darkness outside at the back of the house was completely still. In the distance, an owl called mournfully, and I heard a fox bark twice. I breathed in the clear, frosty night air, with its autumn tang of decay, the green smell of the grass in the field in front of me, the quiet movements of the cattle grazing there... Then I turned away, went back inside and locked the front door.

The back door slammed and Martin came in, yelling cheerfully, "Hiya! I'm just getting a shower before we eat!" as he disappeared into the bathroom. I put coal on the stove and turned it down – it would burn all through the chilly night – and then set our meal on the table: cold chicken, a salad, some good bread and a lump of Cornish cheddar. I opened the Cote du Rhone to let it breathe, but left the Piesporter in the fridge. Then I lit some mildly-scented candles, filling the room with the salty tang of the sea. There was music ready to go on my laptop, but that would have to wait till after dinner.

"Blimey!" was all he said for a minute when he came in. Then, "This looks vaguely familiar... I'm starving, what's for dinner? Oh yes, of course!"

So we ate, and we drank the half bottle of Piesporter. Then we drank the Cote du Rhone.

"Miss Weston," he said, after the cheese was gone, "am I right in thinking you may have nefarious designs on my body tonight?"

"Nah...why on earth would you think that?" And I picked up our plates and glasses and dumped them in the kitchen. When I came back for the empty bottles, he grabbed my wrist.

"This isn't the first time you've taken advantage of an innocent boy in this wanton way, is it?"

"That's not how I remember it."

"How convenient – but I think retribution is finally due. Come to your lord and master!"

"In your dreams!"

He made his move suddenly, before I had time to wriggle away, an exact replica of the way I'd caught him on the beach all those years ago – chop to the knees, hand on the back, arm across the collar bone – although that hand seemed to be a little lower than I remembered, for some reason. I didn't go down with a bump, though – he lowered me skilfully onto the rug and knelt over me, one leg on each side of mine, my hands pinned above my head. Movement was impossible.

"Aha! I've got you now, my beauty... you're helpless and at my mercy, and by the time this night ends you will beg for release from my evil power!"

He cackled demonically.

"Oh for God's sake," I said. "You were bad enough in Mother Goose. Shut up and put the music on."

Albatross first – that gentle soaring tune, with its cymbals and bass throbbing to a heartbeat, to a seductive heartbeat. Then, of course, Samba Pa Ti. By the time that was finished, I neither knew or cared about the music.

He knelt over me again, eyes half-closed and breathing deeply, and once more took my unresisting wrists, holding my arms above my head whilst he steadily unbuttoned, unzipped and unhooked. As his hands covered my body I moaned and rose to meet him.

"Oh, so you *do* want me, after all? Do you? Yes? No. Not yet, not yet, you're going to wait, I'm in charge tonight..."

It went on and on – the stroking, the touching, the teasing. I had no idea, no idea at all, that it could be like this. Eventually, when I was almost weeping with frustration, and still with my arms held, and never taking his eyes off my face, he unzipped his jeans with one hand, pulled himself free of them and was inside me in one swift move. But even then, he hardly moved, inching forward, then back, until I cried out, and I begged – yes, *I begged*. So he gave in, and it was… cataclysmic. I cried out, a long cry of love, and despair because it was over, then I sobbed in his arms.

"Bloody hell, Allie," he said, "I thought you were enjoying it – did I hurt you?"

"No, no, of course not, never. I just suddenly thought… that this is the last time we'll do this, in front of this stove, on this rug, and we've been so happy here, and I don't want to leave, not really…"

"You daft beggar," he said fondly. "It's not as if we're selling the place, is it? When we're rich and famous we can have it as a holiday cottage and escape here sometimes. Don't cry, please…"

"If you say so…"

"There is just one thing that's really worrying me, though."

"What?" I whispered.

"Can sheepskin rugs be washed?"

How could anybody not love him?

***

At first I slept, but I woke at five, as dawn crept through the sky. I went down and showered and dressed, hearing Martin's gentle snores. Then I took a card out of my bag and went to the table to write.

It had a woodcut of a fox in the foreground, and an owl in a tree overhead. In the background was a man walking out of the picture. Inside, on the left, I'd written out the final verse of 'Walking Away', C Day Lewis's wonderful poem about a father leaving his son on his first day at boarding school, which I knew Martin loved. On the opposite side I'd written, 'Martin, please forgive me. The letter explains everything. I was going to tell you last night, but I just couldn't. I'll always be… your Allie." I put my letter, also written the day before, inside the card and sealed them up.

Dearest Martin,

I'm so sorry, but I can't go with you to Wales. You're going back to a life that I can't be part of, a life I know you want very much.

I'm sure you'll make some good friends and I know you'll have a great time, and the last thing you'll need is me stuck in Lou's home, getting jealous or worrying about you when you have to work late. But there's another reason too.

I've been offered a temporary contract with the education section of The Post, on a freelance basis at first, with the possibility of a permanent position. They want me to write an expose of the appointment at Hebble High, which is looking as if it could be one of many examples of government interference in the appointment of head teachers all over the country. I have plenty of evidence, I have two whistleblowers from Hebble and a lot more that the union has uncovered. The editor thinks that at least one of the big dailies might pick it up.

I'm going to be working in Leeds for a while, at least until this is over, and perhaps permanently. They won't be paying me much, but I've been offered the loan of a flat belonging to the editor in Saltaire, which is only ten minutes by train from Leeds. I don't know anything else about it yet.

I know this will hurt you and it's breaking me, too, because I don't want to lose you, I really don't, but I have to do this – I owe it to those kids, and myself.

When you feel less angry, please get in touch if you can – you have my e-mail and I'll be waiting to hear from you, believe me.

All my love, for ever,
Allie

P.S. Remember that selfhood begins with a walking away, and love is proved in the letting go.

I had intended to leave the envelope for him to find – I'd loaded my bags into my car, which for once I'd parked outside the house, but I hesitated a moment, and I heard him coming downstairs and going into the bathroom. Then he came out.

"Ready for the off then? Blimey, you're keen. Just sloping off before doing the last bits, eh? Well, don't worry, I'll finish off while I'm waiting for the Patels to arrive."

He pulled me to him and I put my hand on that warm body for the last time.

"Oy, unhand me, wench, you'll have to wait at least a week after last night. I'm not as young as I used to be!"

It was so normal, so *Martin* that I smiled for a second.

"Right, off you go, then, I'll see you on the M6. Text me to let me know which services you stop at. Drive safely."

I touched his face lightly, whispered, "You stay safe for *me*, ok?" and put the letter and card into his hand. Then I got into my little car and drove away.

Postscript (I)

The Guardian, Thursday, November 9th 2017

Education Crisis Deepens – Tense Exchange at Prime Minister's Question Time

The row about Government intervention in the appointment of eighteen secondary school headteachers escalated in the House of Commons yesterday when the Prime Minister appeared reluctant to give a direct answer to a question posed by the Shadow Education Secretary. When asked if she was aware that the Department of Education had written to the Chairs of Governors in the eighteen schools, offering them extra funding for improvements to the fabric of the schools in return for appointing a DfE-approved candidate, the PM replied that, unlike the Opposition, her Government would always take decisions which were "in the best interests of all pupils in Britain's schools." When pressed, she insisted that decisions about the appointment of head teachers were always left to the schools' governing bodies, with some advice if necessary from the local authorities concerned.

In a moment of high drama, the PM was then presented with a copy of a letter, apparently from the DfE, addressed to the former Chair of the governing body at Hebble High School in West Yorkshire. Receipt of the letter, the Shadow Education secretary explained to the House, had resulted in the instant resignation of the Chair and many other governors at the school. Subsequently, a highly-qualified member of a party-run education think-tank dedicated to the re-instatement of a national selective education system (and previously a head at a prestigious preparatory school in the south of

England), along with two replacement deputy heads from the same school, had been approved and appointed, with catastrophic results for Hebble High School.

The PM responded that she could not possibly comment on such a document, since its authenticity had yet to be verified to her satisfaction, to the accompaniment of loud jeering from the opposition benches.

The Guardian can today reveal that it is in receipt of a copy of this letter, along with sworn testimonies from the ex-Chair of Governors at Hebble High, along with the Clerk to the Governing Body. More incriminating documents have been obtained by the BBC, and a *Panorama* documentary, *A Comprehensive Betrayal – Government Interference in our Schools* will be broadcast on BBC1 on Monday, November 13th at 8.30pm.

Postscript (II)

From: MartinMawganporth98
To: my1PallyAllie
Subject: Triumph!
Date: November 14th, 2017

Allie, I'm so proud of you! *The Post* stuff was sensational, but this *Panorama* programme and *the Guardian* articles have been mind-boggling. Dear God, are there no depths to which this dire Government won't sink? Might this scandal be the tipping point that finally forces a General Election?

After everything you've been through, it is so good that you took the lead on revealing it all. And what horrors will you uncover next, now your job's apparently been made permanent?

My news: the run at Theatre Clwyd finishes on December 15th, but I've been offered a season at the Playhouse in good old Leeds, from January to June, with the possibility of a permanent contract. They want me to be their next Playmaker, running courses in acting and stage management for schools and colleges. I've taken it – it's exactly what I want.

So, like you, I'm going to be based in or around Leeds for the foreseeable future. Does your Saltaire flat have enough room for both of us? Could you stand having me as a lodger again?

Your call, Miss Weston. I'm waiting for your reply, and hoping…

Martin x

Part Two

Tomorrow and Tomorrow and Tomorrow

Chapter One

Leeds, Thursday,
November 30th 2017, Morning

"I'm very sorry, Miss Weston, but I'm afraid I've been instructed by our Management Board to rescind our verbal offer of a permanent position as a writer here at *The Post*."

The editor paused and glanced at me for the first time since I'd answered his summons. I'd had no clue that this was coming.

"May I ask why?"

"Frankly, I'm as shocked as you must be, but our latest sales figures are not promising and our parent company's also in trouble. There's a possibility of us having to reduce to a weekly, or even a digital-only. It's apparently just a case of last in, first out."

"And there's no room for negotiation at all? The story about the mismanagement of academy funds by private boards is just breaking…"

"No, I'm afraid not. It's yesterday's news, especially with all the on-going Brexit uproar. I'm going to have to ask you to clear your desk, please, and you needn't come in tomorrow. But I will need the keys to my flat, and all your belongings cleared out; you don't want to run up a stack of rent arrears, do you? You can hand them in at the office in the complex near the flat – they manage it for me, after all. No need to bring them here. Someone else – a friend of mine – will be moving in on Tuesday."

It was a totally unexpected double bombshell. In the space of ten minutes, I'd lost my job and my home. I had absolutely no idea where I would go, or how I would earn money. I walked out of the editor's office and up the corridor to the newsroom. As I pushed open the door I was dimly aware of the noise and the bustle – phones ringing, the lines of computers, people moving around each other with papers in their hands – but I took little in as I wandered to my desk. I'd only worked there for four weeks. Nobody spoke to me as I bundled my few possessions – pens, a scribbling pad, a small photo of Martin – into my handbag, put on my jacket and headed for the door.

Out in the cold November air of the Whitehall Road I felt no better. I couldn't think. I set off walking in the direction of the station, past the rough empty space that served as a car park and then across the busy road, as buses and lorries thundered past towards the centre of Leeds.

"Alison! Wait!"

Incredibly, the editor was running after me, his jacket and tie flapping. He wasn't a young man, and he didn't look as though he was enjoying the exercise. I stopped, wondering what new horror was about to be unleashed.

He caught up with me, red-faced and gasping. When he could finally speak, he said, "I didn't want to tell you this in there, but I think you have a right to know. What you choose to do about it is up to you. The fact is…" he lowered his voice and glanced around, "… the fact is… I've been leant on to sack you."

"By whom?"

"Our parent company. They have close links to the Government, and they weren't happy about your appointment in the first place. Trouble is, you haven't worked for us for long enough to have any rights – but you're a fine journalist, you hear what I'm saying?"

"Why are you telling me this?"

"Because, quite frankly, I'm sick of the interference. Freedom of the Press? It's a fucking joke! Sorry," he added.

"But even so… won't *you* be in trouble if I try to use it?"

"Don't care, darlin'. I'm off into the wide world at the end of the year with a fat lump sum and a healthy pension. I'll be cruising the Med this Christmas, so you do what you like, don't worry about me. In fact, if you don't run with it, I might do a spot of freelancing. I owe these bastards nothing."

"Right," I said. "Well thanks, but at the moment I'm more worried about what happens after I've handed your flat keys back."

"Oh, I'm sure you'll have plenty of friends who can let you surf their sofas for a while? Or family? And what about a boyfriend? Or do you fancy a cruise? I'm sure I could leave the wife at home!" He grinned at me lasciviously.

This was getting a bit too personal. I wasn't about to reveal that my parents and godparents had been gone for decades, my dearest and only close friends were in Bali until January and Martin – well, suffice it to say he wouldn't be able to help me. I was on my own, big time.

"Don't worry about me, it's just the shock talking. I'll be fine when I've had a chance to think. I'm bound to find somewhere."

"Well, good luck to you," he said. "And if you do change your mind about that cruise—"

I'd rather be homeless, I thought rashly. But I smiled and shook my head.

He shook my hand, turned and headed back the way he'd come. I trudged on towards the station.

***

About ten days before I lost my job, Martin had been up for a flying visit. He arrived in the small hours of one Sunday morning and, since there was no performance on Sundays or Mondays, travelled back to Wales early on the Tuesday morning.

We'd been in constant contact since his first message, three days after I'd left him to take up my job in Leeds and the flat in nearby Saltaire that went with it. His initial silence seemed ominous; I knew he'd be hurt, and I was dreading a message or a phone call ending our relationship, but I hadn't regretted my decision at the time and, although I missed him a lot, I had no intention of making the first move.

When his first e-mail arrived, he didn't mention it at all (typical Martin!), instead telling me about his sister, Lou, who was not at all well, and going back to the theatre, as well as asking about my first days on *The Post*. Then the story about the Government's interference in headteacher appointments across the country hit the national dailies, and *Panorama* waded in with their documentary, so I barely had time to read my personal messages. When his e-mail came through on the 14th, I was relieved and touched, and at that point desperate to see him. Of course, I told him in my reply, and the next thing I knew, my door buzzer was going off at 2am one Sunday morning.

"Wanted it to be a surprise," he grinned at me, sometime after I'd let him into my flat. He was holding me lightly, at arm's length; my lips felt bruised with the force of our kisses and I could hardy speak for the sheer pleasure of it.

"It certainly was – and I haven't had such a pleasant shock since that time you turned up unannounced in Manchester, still in uniform!"

"Yeah, I remember that – but it wasn't the middle of the night, was it? And you were fully-clothed then. This is much better!"

"Why?"

"Because you're all ready for... bed..." he said softly, as his hands started to sweep over me, lingering here and there.

"Oh come on! You must be exhausted. At your age, after a long night's work, then that drive – you'll be good for nothing for the next twelve hours."

"Care to take a bet on that?"

I was being manoeuvred, not resisting too seriously, in the direction of the open bedroom door.

Twelve hours later, we lay, stupefied and sated, as a weak sun shone on us over the rooftops of the Salt's Mill complex and through the flimsy curtains of the picture window at the foot of the bed. Martin's right arm was casually draped above my head, his left hand idly fiddling with my hair, and I was resting on his chest, listening to that steady heartbeat.

"I've been thinking..." he began hesitantly.

"Oh no."

"Shut up and be serious for a minute."

"Oh dear!"

"No, really. See, the thing is..."

He turned onto his side to face me, cupping the side of my face in his hand, gently forcing me to meet his eyes.

"The thing is, I can't go on like this. The last couple of weeks have been hell for me. I thought at first you were finishing us, then

I realised, when I re-read your letter, that the job was the most important thing, and I understood that, I really did, but—"

He was looking at me intently now.

"—the thing is... I want us on a permanent basis. I want to believe you're committed to us, and I want it official. What do you think?"

I breathed again.

"Martin, I meant what I said in that letter. I don't want to lose you... ever... and I can't imagine being with anyone else. But... marriage? Is that what you mean? Because if it is, we tried being engaged once before, and it didn't work out too well, did it?"

"No. But we were so young. We've both been through other stuff since then, and I know... *I know* I've found my future with you. And you're telling me you feel that too, so..."

"Yes, I want to be with you. But I'm not sure I want to be married. I'll think about it, though."

"OK. Let me know soon and put me out of my misery, please. A man can only take so much."

Joking, but more than half serious. *Lighten things up, Allie.*

"Are you threatening me, you great blundering buffoon?!"

"I'm always a threat to you, darlin'! Come 'ere!"

"No! Not again! I'm starving... and you need to keep your strength up, old man!"

With a groan, he rolled out of bed and headed for the shower, leaving me in quiet contemplation of the way our future together might be shaped.

Later, we sat in the American diner at the heart of Salt's Mill, eating burgers and enjoying the bustle and the colour, surrounded by the giant Hockney prints that covered the uneven stone walls. Then, as we waited for our coffee, another shock. The Esplanade Theatre in Singapore had been in touch and wanted Martin to take up a short contract.

"But they don't want me for long – it's just that there's a new tutor taking over the stage management course I set up, and they want me to go through it and revise it with him before the students come in. It's only for four weeks and they're offering good money, accommodation and my return air fare. I said I'd let them know on

Tuesday because I wanted to talk to you first, but – if we're going to be together—"

"We are, one way or another, I promise."

"—then we won't want to stay in that flat for ever, spectacular though it is, will we? So this could be the first step to our deposit for a permanent place. What do you think?"

"When would you start?"

"A week on Tuesday – Theatre Clwyd have very kindly said I could leave just before the end of the run. I want to take Lou away for the weekend before I go – she's had a rough time lately, with the cancer, these hospital visits, and the worry, and she's been so good about me staying with her, so this would be the last time I'd see you before I go. You do understand, don't you?"

I nodded.

"But I'll be home on December 19th, Lou will pick me up from Birmingham airport, then I'll be up here for a meeting at the Playhouse on the 21st. So we'll be together for Christmas – and for the 22nd."

"The 22nd?"

"Don't tell me you've forgotten that afternoon before Christmas at your parents' place? That afternoon when we—"

"Of course I haven't forgotten our first time – just the date, that's all."

That was true – but remembering how he'd ditched me last time, and how devastated I'd been, made me feel slightly sick... Was this another brush-off? Did he really mean what he'd said in bed earlier? I looked at him and frowned.

"I think you've got a cheek. You soften me up with soppy dates and promises, and then you hit me with this Esplanade stuff. What did you *think* I was going to say?"

He looked startled.

"I'm sorry – I just thought it would be a bit of an opportunity—"

"For you, yeah!"

"—but if you really feel strongly about it, I'll say no."

That was what I wanted to hear. He saw the twinkle in my eye.

"You monkey, you don't really want me to, do you?"

"Gotcha! Your face!"

"You'll pay for that, lady. You'll squeal as only I know how to make you…"

"Promises, promises *again*! Of *course* you should do it – but thanks for running it past me, and for being prepared to do what I wanted. I don't really deserve that after what I did to you. I'll miss you, of course, but it's only four weeks. It'll fly past. You never know, this new story I'm working on might take off as well. If it does, then I'll really be on my journalistic way."

***

Ten days later, I pondered this conversation gloomily as I sat in the train for the ten-minute journey back to Saltaire. Promotion? What a naive idiot I'd been. My life was unravelling in front of me – no home, no job and no friends available to help me out. Panic started to knot my stomach as the full implications took hold.

What the hell can I do? What options do I have?

Pete and Cath would certainly have fixed me up with something, but they were abroad till after Christmas. My parents and godmother were long gone – I had no living relatives at all with spare rooms. Martin's father had died in a care home before we were re-united and his sister Lou was going through chemo for breast cancer and had two little girls to look after – her cousin Caroline had moved into her spare room as soon as Martin had left, to give her a hand. Rosemary, my only friend at Hebble High, had gone to her house in Carcasson for Christmas and Martin was just starting a month in Singapore. I was on my own.

Chapter Two

"Between five to eight hundred pounds per month, Miss Weston, depending on the number of bedrooms you'd require. Most of our landlords require one month's rent in advance, plus a deposit of one thousand pounds. Were you looking for something bigger?"

The site office in the Victoria Mill complex in Saltaire was staffed by a woman who exuded an air of competence and brusque authority. She had my file up on the screen in front of her.

"No," I said, "I was wondering if there was anything else in my price range?"

"This flat you're in at the moment is owned by an employee on *The Post*, isn't it?"

"He's the editor actually, and he wants me out because he's got another tenant coming in."

"Yes, I've been informed today that you'll be surrendering your keys by Monday. Is that correct?"

"It is, I'm afraid. The newspaper has told me I'm no longer required."

"So you've lost your job?"

"Yes, but I'm intending to make a few phone calls and I'm confident I can start supply teaching as soon as my police check comes through – it shouldn't be more than a couple of weeks."

"I see. Well, that shouldn't be a problem, as you're already a tenant, provided you have the funds for a month's rent in advance, plus the deposit. Around fourteen hundred pounds," she added.

"Right. When do I need to let you know?"

"Monday morning would be ideal – then you could move straight in to…" She checked her screen, "Ah, no, I'm sorry, the one-bedroomed I was thinking of has just been let, not an hour ago. The best we could offer would be a two-bedroomed penthouse, but it's a lot more expensive – eight hundred a month. It's up to you, of course, but I'm guessing that would be beyond your means?"

"It would at the moment, yes."

Seeing my face, she said, quite kindly, "Look, I think your best bet is to do two things. Go and explain your circumstances to your bank and see if they'd agree to a loan to tide you over. Then make an appointment at the council's Housing Advice Centre."

"Thank you for that. I will."

A seed of hope. I did have my house in the Hebble Valley. Although it was let for twelve months, I'd been paying a mortgage on it for fifteen years – indeed, the rent would cover a sizeable over-payment each month. Surely there'd be some equity in it to set against a loan?

I walked through the mill complex, into the entrance nearest to my flat and took the lift to the second floor, where I unlocked my door. The flat was light and well-appointed – a shiny shower room to the right of the door, a medium-sized bedroom, complete with a king-sized bed and fitted wardrobe, at right-angles to the bathroom, with a large picture window. The living space had French windows onto a small balcony overlooking the quadrangle below, with its neat gardens and tubs of greenery. The kitchen at the back of the room contained a modern white sink, a huge fridge-freezer and an oven, hob and microwave. It was, by any standards, luxury accommodation – and it was beginning to feel as alien as a once-familiar hotel bedroom at the end of a holiday. I made a coffee, stood in front of the French windows and wondered gloomily where I'd be at the same time next week. But then I imagined Martin's voice telling me to stop sulking and get on with it.

I Googled the name and address of my bank, which was still in Halifax – I'd never got round to switching the account – then I made the call to arrange an appointment. Fortunately for me, as soon as I mentioned a new loan application, there'd suddenly been a cancellation. I could see someone at 10am the following day.

Next I found a teaching supply agency. This call did not go so well. Yes, they said, I was perfectly qualified for supply teaching and there were schools looking for English specialists. In order to sign up with them, I simply needed to provide a CRB check (costing £46 and taking a couple of weeks minimum to come through), plus documents showing my current address, which had to be a bank statement and a utility bill in my name. I tried two more agencies and was told exactly the same thing. The standard advice was to contact them again when I'd had a new address for a couple of months. But I needed a job immediately.

Finally, I found the address of the Bradford Housing Options Service, the nearest council department offering advice on housing queries. I spoke to a perfectly polite and apparently sympathetic man who advised me to complete an application for housing on line, then come in for a chat at 2pm the following day, on my way back from Halifax.

At 2.30, Martin Skyped me, at half-past midnight for him, and I thought he looked tired.

"How's it going?" I asked him.

"Brilliant, thanks, although the jet lag's taking its toll… and the heat, and the damned flies, Carruthers. They're driving me insane! I can't stand it, I tell you…"

I gritted my teeth through the usual eye-rolling ham actor display, which I normally found light and funny. Not today. He stopped as soon as he saw my expression.

"Sorry! They've lent me a great flat, within walking distance of the Esplanade," he babbled on, "so I don't need to spend anything on transport. I get a proper lunch in the staff canteen so I don't need to buy much apart from a few beers and snacks. And the money's incredible – I'd have to work for six months at home to earn what they're giving me here, and that's before the tax I now don't need to pay. After Christmas we can ask in the Mill, if you like, and see what the charge would be for a bigger flat – are you all right? You look proper peaky."

Big dilemma. Did I tell him? I'd already decided not to – what could he do, apart from ditch the job and come home to look after his wimpy little woman? And even if I managed to persuade him to stay there, he'd worry all the time, and I didn't want to be responsible for that. But seeing that dear, friendly face so far away, suddenly concerned for me, I was sorely tempted to burst into tears and blurt it all out.

"I'm ok. I think I must have eaten something dodgy – I'm feeling really off and I didn't sleep much last night. There is something else as well…"

I hesitated. This was the moment – but I couldn't. Call it stupidity, call it pride – but I just couldn't.

"I just miss you so much. I thought I'd be fine, but… well… that's all. Really."

"Oh, don't, love – it *will* soon pass, like I said, and believe me, I miss you, too, very much – especially at night. But listen – just remember that I'm thinking about you in every quiet moment, and this is for *us*. We'll make up for lost time at Christmas – I was thinking of taking you away somewhere for a few days, you'll deserve a break by then. If I see anything on line, I'll let you know, or if you see somewhere you fancy, you could maybe book it from your end? I'll be happy to go anywhere you like – let's have a treat for once. I'll pay you back any deposit you have to put down. Keep busy and I'll be in touch soon. It'll probably be Monday, because I've got to work over the weekend, but if I get a chance, I'll e-mail and send you some photos. Is that ok?"

Bless him, he was doing his best – and normally I'd have been completely fine – but where would I be on Monday night?

"Ok," I whispered, and I even managed a half smile. "That's a lovely idea – thanks. You look bushed, though – maybe you'd better get to bed?"

If I'd known then I wouldn't be able to see him for the next three and a half weeks, I'd have been desperate to prolong the call.

"I think you might be right, but Alison?"

"Yes?"

"You know I love you very much, don't you?"

"I know. And I love you too…"

That almost did for me. As the tears came it was a relief when he said, "Night night, God bless," like his mother used to do, and put his fingertips onto the screen before he closed it down.

Night was falling by the time I'd cried myself out, and I felt weak and drained. Wearily, I made some cheese on toast and collapsed in front of the giant, flat screen TV for a night of mindless drivel.

Chapter Three
Friday, December 1st

Of course I hadn't slept much. Before my phone alarm went off at 7am, I'd finally fallen into a fitful doze, so I felt vaguely sick and my head was pounding as I dragged myself out of bed and into the shower. There was no way I could face food, so I put the pod machine through its paces again and choked down an eye-watering espresso. Everything I did, every five-star facility I used, reminded me that this was not mine, that soon someone else would be making use of this stuff. Not helpful, I told myself, just get on with it.

The morning was crisp and clear, with a watery sun making the frost sparkle on the car windows as I walked out of the car park in the direction of Salt's Mill and the railway station. I'd decided not to drive, even though a return ticket would cost me eight pounds. At least I knew where I was going from, the stations in Bradford and Halifax, and I wouldn't have to worry about parking.

I walked down the steps opposite Salt's, over the bridge and onto the platform. As I paid for my ticket, it occurred to me that I'd better check my bank balance. Normally I would have been paid £450 on December 1st – not a fortune, but not bad since all my rent had been covered, paid directly to the editor. But as I'd only worked as a journalist for a few weeks, and I was paid a month in advance, I was pretty sure they wouldn't owe me anything else, and of course, I hadn't saved anything at all. Thank goodness Martin had paid off my bank loan when he'd moved in last year, I thought.

Arriving at Forster Square station a few minutes later, I found a cash machine and discovered that I had precisely £18 in my account – along with the fiver and some change in my purse, it was just enough to feed me over the weekend. The bright day suddenly seemed a little darker.

An hour later I walked up Horton Street in Halifax, past the glamorously-refurbished Piece Hall, and turned right along Commercial Street towards my bank. It was a large and imposing Victorian edifice, all sandstone, pillars and a revolving door, a tribute to an age when Halifax was a flourishing mill town. But the heart of the building had been ripped out, the fine old dark wood counters replaced with modern, toughened-glass barriers between the public and the staff, plus a plethora of computers and paying-in machines. The lofty ceilings, stained-glass windows and elaborate stucco mouldings remained, however, making the interior an uneasy compromise between an age of dignified integrity and the rushing onslaught of contemporary metallic consumerism.

"Good morning, Miss Weston, do come through."

My advisor for the appointment was a young man in his mid-twenties, I estimated. He was tremendously tall – well over six feet – and he towered above me, in his corporate polyester suit and tie.

"How can I help you today?" he asked, after finding me a coffee and settling me in the sensible straight chair on the opposite side of his desk. He listened intently as I explained my dilemma, nodding occasionally, frowning appropriately and scribbling notes on the pad in front of him.

"Is your cottage mortgaged through us?"

I nodded.

"And may I ask how long you've owned it? And how much was the mortgage for, initially?"

"It's been in my name since my divorce, over fifteen years ago; I think the buying price was about fifty thousand, and I estimate its worth at least ninety now, possibly a little more. I've never missed a repayment, and now that it's let, all the rent is going towards paying off the mortgage as quickly as possible."

"On the surface, that looks very promising. Clearing your loan in March has certainly helped your credit rating. Let me get your file up and we'll have a closer look. How much would you be wanting to borrow?"

"Well, I'll need enough for a month's rent in advance, and a deposit on a new flat, plus living expenses until my police check comes through and I can sign up with a supply teaching agency. I would think four thousand would be plenty. But I could probably manage with a bit less... say three?"

He was frowning more deeply as he looked at the figures on the screen, and shaking his head.

"You do realise, don't you, that you have what we call an interest-only mortgage? Which means that, although the repayments are low, they're only paying the interest on the loan, rather than reducing its capital sum. However, if the price has increased as you say, then the situation may be different. We would need to have a written valuation from a RICS qualified surveyor – although of course the fact that it's tenanted would considerably affect its value."

"So how much would that cost me? And how long would it take?"

"You'd be looking at several hundred pounds for the survey, and we could probably get everything sorted out by January 1st."

"But I need the money now!"

"Oh, I see. That is difficult... the only thing I can suggest in the short term, and it's not much, is that we divert the mortgage over-payment into your bank account each month, giving you a monthly income of about three hundred pounds. Do you want me to do that?"

I nodded, shocked into silence.

***

On the train returning to Bradford, I gloomily considered my options. If I could supplement that £300 with some sort of state benefit, to pay my rent at least, I should be able to manage, as long as I could find a cheap room somewhere – surely there'd be student flats or houses with rooms going? Not ideal, but I could cope for three weeks, till Martin got back. At least he'd have money to pay for something better. *There are people much worse off than this*, I told myself.

I got off the train at Bradford Interchange and headed down the hill towards the Housing Options Centre in Britannia House. I had an hour to kill, so I bought the cheapest sandwich I could find and wandered across the road to eat my cheese salad roll on a bench in the gardens in front of the Town Hall. I sat in the cold winter air watching scurrying crowds of Christmas shoppers making the most of their lunch hours, looking rushed and stressed. I felt strangely detached – this had nothing to do with me anymore. The only shopping I'd be doing for the next three weeks would be for the bare necessities. There'd be no presents to buy until Martin came home. I checked my phone, but there was no text or e mail from him. I'd better remember to charge it on Sunday night. I'd need to let him know that my laptop was down, so Skype wouldn't be possible – I didn't want him to suspect I'd changed my accommodation.

At ten to two, I crossed the road again. Britannia House rose before me, a four-storey light stone building with many windows, on the corner of Hall Ings and Bridge Street. The Housing Options department was on the ground floor to the right, through a double door and stretching away in front of me, its windows obscured with blue tinted glass, each window having a white design against the blue, reminiscent of three feathers. Opposite the windows was a series of doors, each with an opaque glass panel, leading into what seemed to be interview rooms. By the double entrance doors was a counter at which sat three receptionists. I approached the nearest one, a middle-aged woman in a cardigan, who looked exhausted.

"Can I help you?" Her voice wasn't exactly welcoming.

"I hope so. My name's Alison Weston and I have an appointment to see someone at 2pm."

She checked the screen of a computer in front of her. "Yes. You'll be seeing Mr Rogers, but he's still at lunch. Please take a seat and you'll be called when he's ready."

"Thank you."

I moved to the side and sat on a hard chair in front of a blue window pane. I seemed to be the only customer, although after a few minutes a woman and two little children, both under five, came in. She was red-faced and clearly tearful, the children bored and fractious, refusing to sit still. A couple of minutes later they were all called into one of the rooms by a smart young woman with a clipboard. Seconds later, I heard voices raised in anger and the wail of children. The door burst open and the woman came out; her two little ones looked frightened. She sat down heavily and took out her phone.

"No! They bloody won't! They say th've got nowt and we've ter go into an 'ostel! Cos 'e's belted me an' chucked us out and we're 'omeless... I'm so scared..."

She dissolved into loud hiccupping sobs.

"Miss Weston?"

The door to another room was being held open by a dapper little man in his fifties, wearing a dark suit, complete with sober tie fixed in place by a tie pin. Throwing the poor woman a sympathetic smile, I followed him in and sat down in front of a desk. He took his place on the other side, his computer screen open in front of him. He glanced at it, then looked up and stared at me.

"I see from the form you completed on-line recently that you consider yourself to be homeless, as of Monday. Is that correct? And why is that?"

I explained briefly.

"Am I correct in thinking, then, that you resigned from a permanent teaching post to take up the job of a freelance journalist?"

"Yes, that's right – but I was told there was a very good chance it would be made permanent, and they did actually confirm that last week."

"In writing?"

"No, verbally. Then yesterday the editor told me that they couldn't keep me on after all, because the paper is experiencing some financial difficulties. My flat in Saltaire belongs to the editor; I've agreed to move out on Monday. It would have been far too expensive for me without a job in any case. He said someone else was moving in on Tuesday."

"I see. But you also state that you own a house. Can't you move back there?"

"No, it's let for twelve months and the rent is paying my mortgage."

He was beginning to irritate me now; as if I hadn't thought of that myself!

"Have you provided a proper written tenancy agreement?"

"Yes, it's for a fixed term of twelve months and it was drawn up by the estate agent who handled the letting. My bank holds a copy of it, and they didn't query it."

"I see. And what about your own tenancy? Do you have a formal written agreement for that?"

"No, I agreed verbally with the owner that I'd stay there as long as I worked on *The Post*. I've now agreed to return the keys on Monday morning, as I said; I believe someone else is due to move in soon."

"Dear, dear, dear, that is unfortunate. You do seem to have made some foolish choices, Miss Weston, both in the surrendering of your tenancy and the quitting of your teaching job."

"It might look that way, but I had a very good reason for resigning. I left teaching because I was accused of something I hadn't done, by a new Head. I had evidence of malpractice in his appointment, which went right up to ministerial level, and I had the opportunity to make that public. It was a point of principle."

"So it was *you* who broke that story was it? Yes, I saw that *Panorama* programme myself. Rather one-sided, I thought."

My heart sank even further.

"But, in any case, Miss Weston," he went on, "it's clear that on this occasion, principles don't pay the bills, do they?"

"What do you mean?"

"I mean your principles have landed you in rather a difficult situation. The problem is that we would only have a statutory duty to house you under certain circumstances. We'd look at the question of whether you really were homeless or threatened with homelessness, and whether you would fall within one of the priority need categories, as defined by the Homeless Legislation."

Too much jargon.

"So, where do I stand then?"

He looked up at me.

"Unfortunately, in a nutshell, although it's clear that you *will* be without accommodation from Monday, you don't qualify for any sort of priority need arrangement, and therefore we have no statutory duty to house you."

"So what on earth can I do?"

"Well, I suggest that you return to your flat and put in an on-line application for whatever benefits you might be entitled to – possibly the new-style Job Seekers' Allowance. But, of course, I must warn you that new applications are taking up to eight weeks to be processed. You'd need to go to the Job Centre on Monday morning to ask for an advance payment, which would, of course, be deducted from any money you were awarded."

I explained the arrangement I'd made with the bank.

"I see. Well, that might affect their decision to advance you some money, since you are not technically destitute. I really do advise you to find some sort of work."

"But I need a permanent address before any employer will consider me! Seventy-five pounds a week isn't enough even for a room in a shared house, let alone any food. Where do I go on Monday?"

"As I said," he repeated with an air of weary patience, "*If* you'd had dependent children, or you were threatened with domestic violence, or you were vulnerable in any way, then we could possibly have offered you a place in a hostel or a women's refuge. As things stand, the best we can do is to give you a list of bed and breakfast accommodation. The cheapest, which I think is The Blenheim, is about twenty-five pounds a night."

"So are you telling me that I can have three nights a week under a roof, providing I eat nothing for the rest of the week? Seriously?"

"Do you have a car, Miss Weston?"

"Yes, but—"

He'd clearly had enough of me.

"Well, I suggest you either sell it or sleep in it. You're a resourceful person, you'll manage. Here's the list. Good luck."

End of interview.

I can't describe the depths of my frustration and anger as I walked across Bradford to Forster Square. I'd worked all my life, starting with holiday jobs, then seventeen hard years as a teacher. Perhaps I did make a mistake in walking out of my job, and letting my house, but now I felt like a criminal who was trying to obtain money I had no right to. All I needed was a little temporary help from the state, because I had nowhere else to turn, so that I could find somewhere to live and start working again. But no – I was on my own.

The shock remained with me as I got off the train in Saltaire and walked back towards my flat as the light was failing around me. The night was drawing in, and the sun had disappeared; the temperature had already dropped noticeably. The mills of Saltaire were gradually turning into dark shapes that loomed against the inky sky. But, as I turned into the iron gate, which marked the boundary of the Victoria Mill complex, I saw my small blue car, reproachfully alone in the still-deserted car park. And my spirits lifted, just a little. At least I wouldn't be out in the cold air of the street on Monday night.

Chapter Four

Monday, December 4th – Morning

The boot of my car was stuffed with a rucksack containing my clothes, my flask and a bag with all the portable food I could eat without cooking it: some bread rolls, cheese, fruit, bottled water and a box of instant soup (in the hope I could find a hot water supply). On the back seat was a large bag containing my quilt and pillows, plus a sports bag with a spare pair of jeans, a couple of jumpers and my underwear, toiletries, a couple of packs of antiseptic hand wipes and some multi-surface wipes containing bleach, along with a hot water bottle and some thick socks. I'd used up every vegetable in my kitchen, plus a bit of surplus bacon and some ketchup to make a thick vegetable soup, which I'd decanted into a wide-mouthed flask I'd bought from a cheap store on Saturday, along with a hot-water bottle. I'd put new batteries into my torch, fully charged my phone and lap top, and bought a lead, which would enable me to recharge them from the car's battery. I was as ready as I could possibly be.

I'd tried to keep busy over the weekend, packing, soup-making, cleaning, but I found it hard to sleep. The fear I'd pushed aside during the daylight hours crept back, so I lay wide awake in the crumpled bed, wondering when and where I'd be able to stretch out again, and how I'd manage in the car during these pitiless winter nights. When I did finally nod off, on the last night, I was disturbed by a dream so frightening I think I may have screamed out before I woke up, heart thudding, to a cold grey December dawn. This was it.

It took me several trips to load the little car, then I had a final check round and closed the door of my flat for the last time.

I walked around the building to the Estate Office and handed over my keys to a young man, who wasn't at all interested in anything apart from ascertaining that this was, as he put it, "An immediate express surrender of the tenancy" – at which I nodded without having the faintest idea of what it meant – and checking both keys were there. When I said I had no forwarding address as I would be living in my car from then on, he didn't comment. He simply ticked a box on a form that he then asked me to sign. My tenancy was terminated; from that moment, I was of no fixed abode.

I drove out of the car park, through the great iron gates for the last time, and turned left. Fortunately, my car was full of fuel – I'd filled up a week ago, and as I hardly used it, and it was very economical, that was one thing at least I didn't have to worry about, even though it was only a small tank. It would take me about a hundred miles. So I at least had the ability to drive to somewhere more hospitable than Saltaire or next door Shipley. For the time being, at any rate.

At the end of the street, I turned left onto the main road out of Shipley and drove away up the hill towards White Cross. My plan (oh, the middle-class smugness of it!) was to base myself in Ilkley. I would spend my days in the library, with a regular visit to a swimming pool, or a launderette, every few days. I could write in the quiet warmth of the library – I was hoping that I'd get an article, or even a book, out of this experience. Then at night I could find a quiet back street and sleep undisturbed. That was the theory, at least.

The first problem I encountered was the parking.

Ilkley is a lovely destination for Christmas shopping – a series of largely independent stores, quirky gift shops and swish watering holes and restaurants. Tasteful white lights twinkle in the trees on the Grove, and Betty's window groans with superior comestibles, seasonally displayed. But for those with little money it is a place for the pressing of noses against window panes whilst having no hope of actually buying anything.

The parking charges are far from the worst I'd ever encountered, but over two pounds for two hours was hardly practical, given my limited means. So I was obliged to drive right out of the town centre, up Cowpasture Lane, and find a place on a quiet residential street off the road leading up to Ilkley Moor, where there were no charges at all.

The houses on this cul-de-sac were all silent; large, semi-detached or detached, with bulging bay windows surrounded by soft sandstone. They were bounded by high leylandii hedges, with their characteristic green piney smell, and up their broad drives I caught glimpses of ostentatious displays of large holly wreathes or swags on carefully painted or stained front doors. There would be many lights twinkling from dusk onwards, I suspected. The houses stared at me impassively as I parked my battered little car next to the pavement between two of them and got out, into the crisp, clear air.

I put my flask of soup into my rucksack, along with my money belt, laptop and phone, hoisted it onto my back and strode purposefully away towards the road down to Ilkley and the welcome of the library. The December cold froze my breath as I walked, and there were treacherous patches of black ice lingering in the shadows at the side of the flagged footpath. The hard frost would return as soon as the sun set; the forecast on my phone predicted minus five in rural areas by midnight. I tried to push that out of my mind and concentrate on how I would spend the rest of the day, but the fear kept creeping back as I envisaged the car's windows becoming opaque under the relentless cold of the night air.

At the bottom of the hill, I turned towards the little town, along Grove Road, and came immediately to the municipal building on my left, a large no-nonsense Edwardian structure, which had clearly been stone cleaned at some point in its long history. The library occupied half of the ground floor and was reached by a communal door and lobby. I pushed open the swing doors to the left of the lobby, and was instantly absorbed by the warmth and hush.

I sat at a large wooden table close to the back, where I'd noticed a plug socket on the skirting board below a wall-length bookshelf. I bent down and connected my lap top, hoping it was allowed, and checked my e-mails. Nothing of any importance. But I wasn't in the mood for writing. I looked around, noting the neat displays of magazines and periodicals, the newspapers on some tables, and above all, shelf after shelf of books – different genres of fiction, separate shelves for non-fiction and reference, tables for displays of books by local authors. This was a proper library with very few nods to the world of information technology. Instead, it breathed different air, the air of slow but honest methodical endeavour, pervaded with the special smell of books – a library for a former age. I loved it. I felt safe here, and welcome – but not for long.

My plan was to write a piece on the reality of being a homeless woman, in the tradition, I'd rather loftily imagined, of George Orwell. But Ilkley Library in 2017 was hardly the same as being down and out in Paris and London in the Depression; I had a car to sleep in, a few pounds in my pocket and a flask of hot soup in my rucksack. Compared to many, I was lucky. I decided to start by looking up some statistics on line, and was startled to read that nearly four and a half thousand people would be sleeping on the streets in the UK every night in December.

I was so lost in my thoughts that I barely registered someone coming round from behind my table and sliding onto the seat opposite me. But I came back to reality with a start when she leaned over and whispered, "Excuse me, do you have the time, please?"

"Yes – it's twenty past two."

She was a woman of indeterminate age, but older than me – perhaps in her fifties. Her grey hair was fixed away from her face in a loose bun, and she had no make-up, nor needed any; her face had the sculpted effect of serious cheek bones. She was wearing a navy polo-necked sweater and one of those quilted sleeveless jackets in a fetching shade of mustard, the two colours effortlessly tied together by the patterned scarf tied elegantly below the polo neck, on whose edge the legend 'Chanel' was artfully displayed.

She must have seen my lap top screen, because she leaned towards me and said, "You don't want to believe all that propaganda, you know. For a lot of them, it's a lifestyle choice. Nobody has to be homeless in this day and age."

"Really? That's interesting – what makes you say that?"

"Well, it's obvious, isn't it?"

She lowered her voice and leaned over the table.

"Most of them are alcoholics or drug addicts. They beg and steal to feed their habits, you know. There are plenty of hostels and the government has provided an excellent safety net. Nobody needs to beg either – the welfare state is there to make sure of that."

"Can I just ask, because, as you probably noticed, I'm researching the subject – do you know anyone who's been made homeless? Or have you ever spoken to a homeless person?"

"I've seen them hanging around on the Grove, selling their *Big Issues* and their sob stories. Most of them park their cars around the back before they set themselves up and stick their hands out. They make me sick."

"Really? Actually, I don't think it's quite as simple as that. People lose their homes for many reasons – losing their jobs, for instance—"

"And that's another thing." She was really getting into her stride now. "There are plenty of jobs if people are prepared to get their hands dirty. But oh no, nobody wants to do an honest day's work, they all expect a huge salary for sitting in front of a computer all day—" She stopped abruptly. "What did you say you did for a living, dear?"

"I'm a journalist, and I was an English teacher. But as of today, I'm an unemployed and homeless journalist. And I can assure you it wasn't a lifestyle choice for me. Oh, and just for your information—" I was gathering my things together and bundling them away as I spoke, "—I don't qualify for any benefits or emergency housing, and I can't get another job until I have a permanent address. Now, if you'll excuse me, I have to collect my *Big Issues* and find a nice patch on the Grove – but don't worry, I won't hold out my hand in your direction."

I had the satisfaction of seeing her mouth drop open before I swept out. Suddenly I needed some purer air.

Chapter Five

Monday Evening

Already the sun was low in the sky. I headed away from the library towards the centre of the town, passing the church, which I noticed was advertising a craft fair.

I decided to have a look – it would kill a bit of time, and it was warmer inside than out. Browsing round stalls filled with a mixture of home-made crafts and junk, I came across a man who was selling framed pieces of calligraphy. There was a tiny Shakespearian sonnet, written for the marriage of one of his daughters and including the line Martin had quoted on the beach in Cornwall, half a lifetime ago. It was beautiful, written in black italics over a colour wash of blue and green, the colours of the sea. As I read it, I felt tears in my eyes – it expressed a simple sentiment with which anyone in love could identify, and I so wanted to buy it for Martin. But it was ten pounds. How could I afford that?

"Is it for someone special?" The man on the other side of the table was white-haired, with kindly eyes.

"Yes, very special, but I can't—"

"Tell you what," he said, "it's nearly Christmas and I love that sonnet too. I want it to go to someone who'll really appreciate it. Could you manage four pounds fifty?"

Of course I could. I thanked him profusely and left with my present wrapped in bubble wrap and pushed carefully to the bottom of my rucksack.

Back out into the bitter weather, feeling a little less bleak. I came to a small grassed area with a bandstand and some green municipal benches. I sat down on freezing wrought iron, and with hands that were already tingling, I pulled my flask out and poured a metal cupful of steaming vegetable soup.

Opposite me, the wide pavement of the Grove boasted a steady procession of shoppers heading towards Betty's and their afternoon tea, largely ignoring a busker playing carols on his violin, at a speed that suggested he had a certain number to get through as quickly as possible before his feet froze to the pavement. Suddenly I saw Our Lady of the Library steaming along. I'd like to report that she'd been upset by my words and placed a fiver in his hat, but she just stalked straight past him. There's no opening a closed mind.

I finished my soup and set off back to the library, striding out as briskly as I could to try and restore the feeling to my feet. Our Lady had inadvertently given me a focus – I would write a diary of my experiences for the next three weeks, but first I would e-mail *The Guardian* to see if they might be interested in it. I was hoping my name and past contributions might just do the trick for me.

The librarian smiled at me as I walked past her desk, and it occurred to me she might have overheard the exchange I'd had – and I was right. As I connected up my lap top again, she came towards me.

"I couldn't help but be impressed by your reaction to those comments," she began. "Are you *really* homeless?"

"Temporarily. My partner's away till just before Christmas, working abroad, and I lost my job and my flat at the end of last week."

"How dreadful for you. Look, I can't suggest anything much to help you, but there is a supermarket on the road out of Ilkley that stays open till nine and has a very cheap cafe. You could probably spend your evening there. They only charge about one fifty for a decent coffee. Have the first one on me."

She pressed a couple of pound coins into my hand, and went back to her desk, ignoring my whispered protests. I turned back to my writing.

"On my first day of homelessness I have encountered the best and the worst that this little town has to offer…"

Once I started writing, I was lost to the world. I began to outline the circumstances that had brought me to this library, but I had barely reached the Bradford Housing interview when the librarian coughed discreetly. I looked up and realised the tables were all empty, and the clock opposite me said six forty-five. It was time to embark on the next stage of my wandering existence.

I saved my work, packed the lap top into my rucksack and went out into the freezing night. I walked steadily up Cowpasture Lane and turned into the cul de sac. Just as I'd expected, it was full of twinkly lights celebrating a Christmas that was entirely irrelevant to me. My car's windows were white and the door opened reluctantly. I set about defrosting and scraping the top layer, then started the engine and let its heat do the rest. When I had enough clear glass to see safely, I inched the car out onto the hill and headed back down into Ilkley, towards the supermarket with the cheap cafe.

***

I parked in an unobtrusive spot in the large supermarket car park and unpacked my quilt and pillows, spreading them out as best I could on the back seat. Then I pushed the hot water bottle and my sponge bag into my rucksack and wandered into the building, past the stacked fir trees, all waiting for their final home, and the holly wreaths with their red berries and ribbons, a snip at fifteen pounds.

The place was heaving with shoppers, all no doubt stocking their freezers. I made grateful use of the free toilet at the entrance, then I had a desultory look around at the displays stacked with every fruit known to humanity, much of it out of season and so very expensive, and the chocolates and crackers, the beautifully presented poultry and game, the cheese, the crusty bread.

My stomach rumbling, I found the cafe and ordered a hot chocolate, courtesy of the generous librarian. I would drink that for pudding, after I'd surreptitiously eaten the bit of bread and cheese I'd brought with me. I had about an hour before everything closed for the night, and I had the first Poldark novel in my rucksack. Martin had bought me the entire set some time ago; I happily lost myself in the traumas and scandals of eighteenth-century Cornwall, until the cafe had emptied and the floor was being swept. Then, gritting my teeth, I went back to the counter.

"Sorry, love, we're closing," said the plump-faced woman in a blue pinny behind the till.

171

"I know, but I was just wondering… erm… could you possibly fill this hot water bottle for me? I have to sleep in my car for the first time tonight, and it would make a huge difference to me."

"Seriously?"

I nodded.

"You don't look the sort – I'd never have guessed. I shouldn't, really – health and safety, you know, but I will. Give it here."

"Thank you so much."

She disappeared into the kitchen behind the till, then reappeared with the bottle wrapped in a thick white towel.

"Bring this back to me tomorrow when you've finished with it, and if you want a hot bottle again, make sure you ask me – some of the others would say no. Oh and look here—"

She went to the display counter and took out a couple of sandwiches and a custard slice, which she put in a bag.

"These would be going to the food bank at the church in any case. You didn't look to have much of a tea. Come in about ten tomorrow and I'll do you a breakfast half price."

I was speechless and not far from tears. "Thank you so much," I whispered.

"Take care, and I hope you manage to keep warm and get some sleep."

So do I, I thought, *so do I*.

Chapter Six
Tuesday

The night had seemed interminable. I'd wrapped my bottle in the quilt and driven out onto the main road, out towards Middleton and Burley. The car seemed to warm up quite quickly, so I went round the first roundabout I came to and drove back. I found a quiet street not too far from the supermarket and parked, being careful not to block any drive or stop in front of one of the road-side terraced houses. Then I dived into the back of the car, removed my boots and my quilted, hooded jacket, took the blissfully still-hot bottle out of its towel and wrapped the quilt round me. So far so good, although I was forced to keep my knees bent and had little room to turn over.

I started reading by the light of the torch in my phone. By ten, I was starting to feel a bit sleepy, and I was just about to turn off my phone when a text came through from Martin.

- *Ok? Tried to Skype but you're off-line. Want to see you!*
- *Sorry, Wi-Fi down. All tucked up reading Poldark. Still missing you though.*
- *I should think so – me too. Let's go back to Cornwall next year. I want to see Mawgan Porth again, where it all started. Love you.*
- *Love you more.*
- *Nighty night, sleep well… xx*

Well, I hadn't really lied to him, had I? But I felt uneasy, worried about how he'd react when he did find out. It was reassuring, though, to know he was thinking about me, even though I realised I'd scarcely given him a thought all day. And I liked his suggestion of going back to the place where we began.

Eventually, I dozed and then slept, fitfully. But I could never quite relax into a deep sleep – every little noise had me listening intently, wondering if there was someone out there on the street who might try to steal or damage my car, or break into it and find me.

Towards dawn, when the car windows were fully opaque with the settled frost, I had a couple of hours of proper rest, but waking up and realising I was in the car, and outside my quilt the air was frozen, was not a pleasant experience. I was stiff and cramped and longing to stretch out properly, and I didn't relish the idea of leaving the cocoon in which I'd slept to cope with another lonely December day.

I finally plucked up enough courage and wriggled out of the quilt and into my boots, gloves and jacket. It was just after eight. With difficulty, I manoeuvred myself into the driver's seat and held my breath as I attempted to start the engine. But I needn't have worried – my faithful little car, used to being outside all year, started first time. As it warmed up, the ice inside gradually melted. After ten shivering minutes, I was able to open the door and get started with my de-icer on all the windows and mirrors. When I could actually see the road, I turned the car round slowly and drove back to the supermarket, which opened at eight-thirty.

Thank goodness for free toilets, I thought again, as I emptied my now not hot water bottle and changed into clean pants and socks in the cubicle, using my hand wipes as best I could before dressing. Then I cleaned my teeth, washed my face and hands, combed my hair and put it into a ponytail. I had promised myself I'd go swimming and take my washing to the launderette on Friday, the day my clean underwear supply was due to run out. In the meantime, today's treat was to be the half-price breakfast promised the night before.

But when I went into the cafe, I was disappointed to see no sign of the nice woman in the pinny, so I had to make do with a coffee. At least there were some fresh newspapers on a stand by the door, for the customers; I settled again near the radiator for a quiet read.

"Excuse me?" Ten minutes later, a woman I'd never seen before had appeared in front of me, holding a steaming plate. "Margaret said you'd be here first thing, so she ordered this for you, and paid for it herself. We've only just got the cookers going, so it's freshly cooked."

"Oh wow, thank you – and please tell Margaret it's a lovely surprise."

I couldn't think what else to say, but I made a mental note to come back with some flowers and a card after Christmas. That gesture meant so much – not just the full English, which was fantastic, but the fact that someone cared enough to provide it. It made me feel as if I could get through this – although it was just as well I didn't know then what was in store for me in the days to come.

The day passed uneventfully; a long morning in the library, getting on with my account of being suddenly homeless, then a brisk walk to my bench where I sat for a while eating one of last night's sandwiches and my custard slice. The fiddler was again sawing away on the other side of the road, so I wandered over and put fifty pence into his hat. I suspect he thought I was pretty mean, but he thanked me and wished me a Merry Christmas nevertheless.

The library closed at six on Tuesdays, so I passed another half-hour walking round Ilkley as the shops were shutting up and their lights were going out. I took the opportunity to check my bank balance at a cash machine on the corner opposite my park, and was very relieved to see that the three hundred pounds of surplus rent money had appeared in my current account. My plan was to draw out seventy-five pounds to last me each week, which would leave me a surplus for emergencies. I tucked the money safely into the belt I wore around my waist.

Further down the hill, on another corner, I came to a bar called The Honest Lawyer. The name appealed to me. I was cold and in need of a hot drink, so I went in.

It was surprisingly large and virtually empty, but the young man polishing glasses behind the bar called out a cheery "Hi!"

"Hi, could I have a latte, please?" I normally drink my coffee black, but I thought the milk would do me good. It would set me back three pounds, but I hadn't spent anything at all so far that day, and I just wanted to rest somewhere warm. I put the three coins on the bar.

"Sure." He put down his towel and turned to the coffee machine on the wall behind him. "Sit down and I'll fetch it to you," he said over his shoulder.

There was a low table and some soft seats to the right of the door, in front of a window looking out onto the street. I sank gratefully into one after peeling off my jacket. When the barman arrived, he was carrying a tray with a large, steaming mug, some brown sugar and, glory be, a plate of shortbread fingers.

The barman was in the mood for a chat. He was younger than me – late twenties, I guessed – and he had a pleasant open face with bright blue eyes and unfashionably floppy hair.

"Cold, isn't it? This'll warm you up, anyway – fancy a tot of something in it?"

I did, but my bank balance wouldn't run to it.

"No, it's ok, thanks – I'm keeping off alcohol for a while. But this looks perfect as it is."

"Right. Well…" He hesitated. "Enjoy. Sing out if I can get you anything else."

I smiled and nodded, and he retreated behind his bar again. Another life, another time, I thought, fancifully, and I could have been drinking tequila slammers with you by tomorrow night. But not anymore. I wondered what Martin was getting up to in the evenings, all on his own in that vibrant city. It wasn't the right time to text him, but I sent him a message anyhow, to speak to him later:

Just having a coffee in Ilkley and been almost chatted up by gorgeous barman. Don't worry – not tempted – but really missing you... xx

P.S. Hope your phone's off till the morning – sorry if I've woken you up!

Within a minute the reply came back:

I never mind you waking me up, but preferably when you're within reach. Keep your paws off the barman, Miss Weston, or I might have to come round and break his legs when I get back. Now piss off and leave me alone – it's after 4am here!

I replied with a red heart and a smiley face. Then I looked at the time – 6.45pm – and realised I needed to dash if I was going to get to the supermarket in time to get my hot water bottle filled for the night. I left, calling a thank you towards the bar but not waiting for a reply.

An hour later, I was again in the back of the car. It didn't seem quite as cold and I must have been tired because sleep came more easily. But a lot later I was woken to the car being violently rocked.

There was no frost on the windows, and I could clearly see a man's red, contorted face peering in through the windscreen.

"Move this fucking car, you dirty homeless dosser! This is a decent street – we don't want your sort here. Get going, get this heap of old rust started and go somewhere else – go on, get lost, if you don't want your windows smashing!"

I wasn't arguing. I scrambled into the front, started up and drove away.

After an aimless circuit of a silent and deserted Ilkley, I ended up parking out of sight at the back of the supermarket, in front of large garage doors. But it was a long time before I nodded off again – I was cold and shaky, and super-sensitive to the slightest noise; even the rain on the car roof and the wind moaning softly disturbed me. Finally, I fell into an uneasy sleep, full of fear and irrational conviction that the man would find me, somehow.

Chapter Seven

Wednesday

The last dream before I woke transferred itself into a horrible reality. I thought I was in the sea, and the water was slowly creeping up my body. There was no-one to pull me out this time. I sat up in a breathless panic, but instead of the reassurance of wakefulness, I was rapidly aware that my legs and feet were indeed wet. My first thought was that the car's rear window had leaked and let in the pouring rain that had been drumming on the car roof, but it was worse than that. When I pulled off the sopping quilt, I saw that my wretched hot water bottle was nearly empty, and its contents had soaked my legs and feet, my jeans, quilt and half the back seat. Fortunately, my rucksack and spare clothes had been on the floor of the car next to my head, and they were untouched, as were my boots.

I threw the rucksack into the front and again scrambled between the seats. In the passenger seat, with some difficulty, I peeled off socks and jeans, then used the towel I'd brought to dry myself. I put my wet clothes into a carrier bag and dressed myself in dry socks and my only spare jeans. But I was so cold. My phone told me it was 7.30am. Another hour before the supermarket opened. Sliding into the driver's seat, I started the car and put the heater on full blast.

I realised I would have to spend at least the morning, and a small fortune, drying out my quilt at the launderette. I thought I might as well go swimming first, then wash all my dirty clothes. Then it occurred to me that the pool might open early to accommodate keen types who wanted to exercise before work. I drove back into town, turned right towards the river and followed the sign that said 'Pool and Lido'. I was right – it would indeed have been open, had it not been closed for refurbishment.

I'd had enough of Ilkley.

By the time I reached Shipley, the town was clogged with traffic as commuters headed into Bradford. I was in no hurry, but I was perturbed to notice that the temperature was falling sharply again, and the rain was turning rapidly from sleet to snow. The thought of a night on a wet car seat did nothing to lift my spirits.

I eventually turned into Alexander Road and managed to park opposite the swimming pool and leisure centre. I dashed up the steps and into a warm, chlorinated atmosphere. I handed over £4.75, but I didn't care – I intended to make full use of all the facilities on offer. As I pulled my costume out of my rucksack in the changing room, a large piece of paper fell out. It was the list of approved accommodation I'd been handed by the unsympathetic housing advisor. I knew then exactly what I was going to do later.

After twenty long lengths, I was luxuriating under a blissfully hot shower. I'd washed my hair twice and conditioned it and the changing room had been empty the entire time. I decided to risk it, so I quickly peeled off my costume and had a proper wash. Then I wrapped my hair in my smaller towel and myself in the larger one, dried and dressed, feeling much better. The hairdryer ate money at an alarming rate – my hair was well below my chin, heavy and straight, and it took some drying. Finally, it felt finished. It fell over my face in a fragrant curtain, which I ruthlessly tied up in a ponytail at the nape of my neck. I rinsed out my costume in a washbasin and wrapped it in my hair towel, ready for the launderette.

By then I was starving. In another life I would have found a cosy little cafe and ordered a pleasant and satisfying lunch. But now I had my budget to consider. I settled for an apple, a packet of cheesy biscuits and a hot chocolate from a vending machine and sat in the small swimming pool cafe to eat. Then I went back to the car and was surprised by just how much snow had settled in the couple of hours I'd been away – a good three inches, I estimated.

Getting the car going through the accumulation was interesting, but after a few skids and slides I was under way. The snow was a brown slush once I reached the main road. I should probably have saved my money and abandoned the laundrette, but I felt it was important to wash and dry my clothes and dry my bedding. So I drove cautiously through the centre of Shipley and out onto the Leeds road.

I knew there was a laundrette housed in a small shopping complex just outside the town.

Two boring hours it took to get my stuff sorted out, and more money than I'd bargained for – the dryers were £2 a go, and my quilt needed four attempts before I was satisfied. When it was dry, I bundled it back into the large laundry bag with my pillows, folded my clothes, packed them into my rucksack and prepared for another snowy drive, this time to Bradford.

***

The Blenheim Hotel, the cheapest on the list that had fallen from my rucksack, was situated on Manningham Lane, on the right, just before the traffic lights with the junction of Marlborough Road. It was in the middle of a row of large terraced houses set back off the road in what was rather grandly called Blenheim Place. But the houses all looked dilapidated and in need of some serious renovation, and the sign above the Blenheim was illuminated by the faintest of lights. I wondered if it was a sensible move to enquire about a room, but the wet, freezing car was a poor alternative. With some trepidation, I parked in front of the building, walked up the steps to the front door and rang the bell.

At first there was no response. The daylight outside was rapidly failing and the streetlights had come on – it was just after three on one of the shortest days of the year. I rang the bell again, and noticed a light through the eye-level spy-hole on the door. There was a pause, and then the clanking of bolts being drawn back, before the door slowly opened.

"Yeah?"

On the doorstep was a scowling man of indeterminate age. He wasn't tall – much less than six feet – but his shoulders were broad and powerful, although his upper body ended in an overhanging belly. He was wearing a dirty off-white hoody and a pair of jogging pants over dirty trainers, and the hand that held the door open looked none too clean. His face was slightly distorted, somehow, but the eyes, sunk in flab though they were, looked sharp and calculating. He was looking around furtively, as though expecting someone else, then his eyes finally focused, and he stared at me intently.

"Um… I was wondering if you had a room for a couple of nights, bed and breakfast? I've got a list from the council, and the Blenheim is at the top…"

"Yuh'd better come in, quick."

I stepped hesitantly over the threshold as he locked and bolted the door behind me. In front of me was a short passage with a reception desk at the end, and another corridor running off it to my left. The walls were off-white and round the cornice the paint was flaking here and there. The carpet was thin and slightly sticky under my boots, and there was a curious smell – a mixture of stale cigarettes, cabbage and something else sweetish and foul. Under normal circumstances, I'd have made an excuse and left, but this wasn't normal – I was homeless and cold, it was snowing heavily and I had just about enough cash from this week's budget to buy a roof and a bed, at least for a couple of nights.

The man went round to the other side of the desk and tapped something into an ancient computer. I noticed a rack of keys on the wall next to a door into some kind of shabby office. There were twelve hooks, and all had keys on them.

"It's your lucky day," said the man, "I've gorra ground-floor room free for a few days. Only thing is, I've stopped doing breakfast. The owner's away and I dun't 'ave an 'ygene certificate."

I'll bet you don't, I thought.

"Ok – so how much would it be per night without breakfast?"

"I could do it for twenty quid."

"How about four nights for sixty?"

"Cash?"

I nodded.

"Go on then. It's a bargain, but I'll do it as a favour. It's this room."

He came round the desk again and unlocked the door nearest to the entrance. I followed him in.

The room was surprisingly large, with a dilapidated sliding sash window looking out over Blenheim Place, directly opposite my little car. There was a small flat screen TV mounted on the wall opposite the door, over a fireplace housing an electric fire. Opposite the window was a double bed covered by a quilted mattress protector, which did at least look clean. To the left of the door stood a small wardrobe and an upright chair, and to the right a dressing table with a swing mirror, and a kettle and cups. The furniture was solid but ancient.

"The bathroom's across the 'all. We don't run to *on sweet*."

"That's fine, I'll take it."

"That'll be sixty pounds then for four nights. You'll be leaving Sunday morning."

"That's right."

I opened the money belt I wore round my waist and handed over three twenty pound notes. He must have been able to see there wasn't much left in it.

He handed me a key ring with two keys.

"My name's Russell," he said as a parting shot, "Russell 'utchinson."

"Thank you, Mr Hutchinson. I'm just going to nip round the corner for a bit of shopping, then I'll get my stuff in. Oh, and you needn't bother to make up the bed – I've got my own bedding."

He nodded and disappeared round the desk into the office, shutting the door behind him. Fine by me – the last thing I wanted was a cosy chat over a cup of tea.

After a quick look round the room, I noticed something interesting on the inside of the door. There were two sets of holes, one just under the handle and the other just above. Someone had evidently wanted more security than the door lock offered. I didn't like the feel of the place, but I really had to risk it for a few nights. I couldn't afford anything else.

I shut the door and went quietly out into the rapidly-deepening snow. Putting my hood up, I set off to trudge to the traffic lights, then right up Marlborough Road towards the large Marlborough Superstore on the opposite side, beyond the junction with Lumb Lane.

As I slipped and struggled, trying to keep my hiking boots out of the drifts, I thought back to that night, nearly a year ago, when Martin had taken me home through the blizzard, trudged with me from the car to my cottage, and put his hand over mine when it was shaking too much to fit the key into my door. Then he'd stayed, first for a week and then until I left him eight months later. God, I missed him.

I crossed the road and went carefully over the small, icy car park towards the store. I ignored the fruit displayed under a plastic sheet outside (although the mangoes and pineapples really tempted me, despite the fact they must have been close to freezing solid), and went in. It was quite a large shop, with well-stocked shelves – familiar groceries next to more exotic items – and it smelled pleasantly of spices.

Eventually, I found some cheap coffee, lemon tea, cheap fizzy water (I didn't fancy drinking unboiled tap water from the grubby bathroom at the Blenheim), a packet of custard creams and a box of instant soup. The woman in charge was just putting some fresh hot samosas into a glass-topped counter cupboard by the till. They cost a pound each and looked pretty substantial. I asked for two, and she put them into a pale yellow polystyrene box with a little plastic bag of tomatoes and sliced onions and another with some minted yoghurt.

"Not seen you round here before, have I?"

She was quite young, in her twenties, I imagined, and had dark, kohl-rimmed eyes over a strong and intelligent face. The bright scarf covering her hair was tied in a traditional, elaborate fashion, but in contrast she was wearing black jeans, boots and a sloppy sweater that reached almost to her knees.

"No, I'm just here for a few days till I get myself sorted out. At the Blenheim," I added.

"You'll be all right there – Mr Abbas is a nice old man."

"I'm sure he is, but he's away, apparently. Some bloke called Russell Hutchinson's been left in charge."

She raised her eyebrows.

"Yes, I've heard of him. You need to watch yourself there. Look, if he gives you any problems, ring me dad. He's a taxi driver, but he – you know – *knows* people who could help." She handed me a card that had the legend, 'Akhbar Taxis - any time, 24 hrs a day, cheap rates' and a mobile number.

Blimey.

"Brilliant – that makes me feel a lot better. Cheers – and see you tomorrow."

I thought I heard her say, "With God's blessing," as I went out – but I could have been wrong.

Twenty minutes later, I was back in my room, along with my bedding from the car and my shopping-filled rucksack. There had been no sign of Hutchinson when I got back, although there was a black Mercedes with tinted windows parked next to mine, and I could hear what sounded like an argument coming from the other side of the door behind the counter. *I bet that's a dealer*, I thought to myself, remembering the sweetish smell in the hallway. Still, I'd rather he spent the evening smoking dope than bothering me.

I put on the heater, plugged my phone and lap top in to charge, made up the bed, switched on the TV and settled down to watch the six o'clock news. Then I ate my samosas, left the TV on in the background for company and put on the fleecy hooded pyjamas I'd packed but not worn before. I got into bed and spent a couple of hours reading Poldark, before I found myself struggling to make out the words.

Almost time to sleep. I took my sponge bag and towel to the bathroom, and the kettle. I used the loo, washed my hands with my soap and filled the kettle. I hadn't taken my keys, though, and when I came back, the bedroom door was wide open. "Idiot," I thought to myself, pulling it shut behind me. Then I wedged the chair under the door handle, turned the electric fire down to its lowest setting and went to bed.

I slept, grateful for my clean bedding, like a body that hadn't seen a bed or much sleep for several nights.

Chapter Eight
Thursday

The morning light, dull through the thin curtains, woke me, according to my fully-charged phone, at 8.07. But I had nothing to get up for, and I was just drifting off again when my phone bleeped to tell me there was a text. Martin.

- *Just checking to see how you are. Is your cold better? I can just picture you sitting at that little table with your coffee and toast. God, I miss you. xx*

I replied:

- *Me too. No work today – snowed in! Still in bed – wish you were here. Cold better, thanks, but feeling very washed out and tired. x*

He came straight back with:

- *Long lie-in for you, doctor's orders. You'll need your stamina in good working order for when I get home. Sleep tight – I'll text again tomorrow. xx*

I sighed and pulled the quilt over my head.

Three hours later I woke up again. I nipped out to the bathroom (locking the door behind me this time), washed, then quickly dressed and went back to my room to make some coffee.

I had a plan for the day. Manningham Library was just within walking distance, up Marlborough Road, and I wanted a quiet, uneventful day's writing. I demolished half a packet of custard creams, then pulled on my boots, scarf, coat and gloves, stuck my laptop and phone in my rucksack and set off.

As I opened the outside door, Russell Hutchinson was just lurching out of his office.

"Morning," I said breezily. He just grunted and scratched his copious belly. Nice.

I escaped without further conversation.

It was still snowing and my poor little car was virtually buried. My boots made deep imprints – at least thirty centimetres, I estimated. There was very little traffic along Manningham Lane, and Marlborough Road was silent and deserted, even though the snow had been partially cleared. I trudged up the hill, past the terraced houses on my right, their sandy stone and dilapidated windows semi-obliterated beneath the drifted snow. It took me a good twenty minutes to walk to the library, but it was well worth it – it was warm and quiet since there was virtually nobody in.

I found a large round wooden table, opened up the laptop, logged in and checked my e-mails. I was gratified to see I'd had a reply from my contact on *The Guardian* – basically they would look at my blog when I'd completed a couple of weeks' worth, and might publish it as a daily update in the tabloid section. For the first time I began to feel as if I could make something positive out of the experience of being homeless, and my spirits lifted.

By 5pm I was finished for the day. I had basically just been cataloguing my experiences since losing my job, not including anything in the way of my thoughts or reflections at this stage. I would update them every day, and aimed to start structuring them into a daily blog, ready for publication.

I set off back towards the Blenheim, calling in at the supermarket on my way. The young woman was behind the counter again as I ordered my evening meal from the various snacks on offer. Vegetable pakoras this time, and one samosa.

"Thanks," she said. "You ok?"

"No problems so far, but thanks for asking. I'm Allie, by the way."

"Sabrina Akhbar," she said. "You know you said Mr Abbas wasn't there? My dad's worried about him. He's an old man and it's not like him to go off without telling anyone. Did Hutchinson say where he'd gone?"

"No – but I could ask, if you like?"

She looked thoughtful.

"No, better not. The less you have to do with that thug, the better – I've heard he's into some very nasty… *stuff.*"

Then she looked at my purchases and said, "Hang on, I'll warm these up for you. And, erm, Mum's just made a big pot of keema and rice. Could you eat some?"

"I'm sure I could, but I've got to be careful with my cash."

"Oh, this is on us."

"Seriously? That's really kind of you, but I can't—"

"Hang on."

She disappeared into the room behind the counter. Five minutes later she was back with a sealed cool bag.

"Here you are. It's not much, but it's a bit more substantial for such a cold night. This should keep it hot. Hope you enjoy it."

"I really don't know what to say, except thank you so much."

"We've got plenty every night, and you need it. Don't give it another thought."

The kindness of strangers again. My eyes were watery as I left, overcome with the thought that I had absolutely nothing to offer in return, apart from putting this life-affirming gesture in my blog. It was about time the Pakistani community got a bit of credit for their generosity.

The night passed without incident. Next morning, I trekked through the now-frozen snow up to the library, wrote for about four to five hours then returned, seeing Sabrina on the way back. That night her dear family put hot food into my bag for me, refusing again to let me pay for anything apart from the little treats I could now afford – a few biscuits and a bar of chocolate.

Chapter Nine

Saturday

I got up and going earlier on Saturday morning. The library closed at 2pm, and an idea had formed in my head. After I'd done my four hours' writing, I continued up Marlborough Road to the branch of Barclays at the next junction. There I withdrew a hundred pounds, leaving me with one hundred and forty in my account. I called in to the supermarket as usual, but this time I arrived with a little plastic pot of hyacinths I'd bought for two pounds fifty from another, smaller grocery shop. Sabrina was delighted, and she came around the counter and gave me a hug.

When I got back to the Blenheim, Hutchinson was on the doorstep, shouting at an elderly man with a white beard. I could hear his coarse voice from a hundred yards away.

"No, I fookin' don't know where 'e is. And what's it to you, yer nosey old bastard? Just fook off and mind yer own fookin' business!" And he slammed the door in the old man's face.

As I approached, he was stumbling and slithering over the frozen snow towards me. He looked shaken.

"You staying here?"

I nodded.

"Please to be careful. He's bad man."

"Thanks, but don't worry – I'll be ok."

He shook his head and tottered away.

When I opened the outer door, Hutchinson was still behind the desk. I sensed he'd been waiting for me.

"You going tomorrow?" His usual delicate manner.

"Well actually, I was wondering…"

"Yeah?"

"Would it be possible for me to stay another week for seventy pounds?"

He looked me up and down, his little brain clearly working overtime as he calculated.

"Seventy-five for cash."

"Seventy's all I can afford. That only leaves me a couple of quid a day to feed myself."

"Go on then. Yer a lucky girl, aren't yer?"

"Thank you."

I handed over my money and went into my room, bolting the door behind me. No doubt there'd be another visit later from the Mercedes with blacked-out windows.

I ate an early meal – vegetable dopiaza, loaded with onions, and chapattis freshly made by Sabrina's mum. I saved my two samosas, hot and wrapped in tin foil, for later in the evening. It was 3pm, around 11pm in Singapore, and I wanted to speak to Martin. I didn't feel comfortable deceiving him any longer.

I tried to contact him on Skype but there was no reply, so I had to make do with texting instead, hoping he'd pick up the message and reply soon.

- *Hi Martin... now don't panic when you read this, I'm OK, but I have to tell you something.*

  Just over a week ago I lost my job and the flat that went with it. I tried sleeping in the car for a couple of nights but that didn't work out. Now I've found a cheap B and B, the Blenheim, on Blenheim Place, off Manningham Lane in Bradford. It's not the Ritz but it's only £15 a night. I'm not keen on the bloke in charge, but I'm making sure the door's locked and I've wedged a chair under it.

Within five minutes his reply pinged:
- *WHAT THE? Are you serious? Why didn't you tell me?? Why didn't you go and stay with Pete and Cath, or Lou?? I want you out of there, it's a rotten area.*
- *I'm all right, really. I've had nothing but kindness from most of the people who live round here, and the Asian supermarket up the road is run by a lovely family who give me a bit of hot food*

every night. Pete and Cath are away till January, Rosemary's in Carcasson and, even if I'd had enough for the petrol down to Wrexham, I didn't want to bother poor Lou. She's got enough on coping with being so ill, and anyway you said Cousin Caroline was staying to help with the kids. I can manage, honestly.

- *I won't rest till I know you're staying in a proper motel. Here's the plan. On Monday, I'm going to try to get permission to come home a few days sooner, but tomorrow I'll get some cash to you – send me your bank details and I'll transfer a few hundred to tide you over. In the meantime, keep that door secure and text me regularly so I know you're ok. You're your own worst enemy at times, Alison Weston.*
- *Thanks, love you too! I'll send you the bank account numbers now. But I will text regularly, I promise.*
- *Make sure you do. I'll let you know as soon as the money's in your account. Remember – stay safe for me, ok?*
- *See you soon. Love you... xx*
- *Love you more. xxx*

That was the last text conversation I had with him, although I sent him the bank numbers from my debit card.

Much later, I'd watched all that the TV had to offer, eaten my samosas and, made thirsty by the spiciness, drunk two cups of lemon tea and a whole bottle of water. I went to the bathroom, locking my bedroom and the bathroom door carefully, then I set to work with the wipes I'd brought with me and gave the whole room – bath, wash-basin and toilet – a thorough cleaning. Then I pinned my hair up, ran a hot bath and had a soak.

When I got back into my room, I put my dirty laundry into a plastic bag and pushed it into my rucksack, taking out clean clothes for the next day and laying them on the chair, which I then wedged under the door handle, as extra security. Finally, I sent a quick message to Martin:

Safely locked in for the night, all quiet here.

I put my phone and laptop on to charge and tucked myself up in bed.

I woke some time later, desperate for the loo. I swung my legs out of bed, pulled my feet into my socks and went to the door. I moved the chair to one side, took the keys out of the lock and went out, making sure to pull the door closed behind me and check it was locked. I noticed that the light was still on under the office door.

I went quietly to the bathroom, had a pee, washed my hands and came back to find my door open. Hutchinson was standing in my bedroom wearing only his filthy tracksuit bottoms. His white belly hung flaccidly over them. His face looked slack and wet, and his eyes were barely open. Of course, I thought uselessly, he'll have a pass key.

"Thought yer might like a bit o'company on this cold night. 'Spect yer were disappointed when I weren't 'ere t'other night after yer'd left yer door open fer me. So I thought, give 'er what she's askin' fer. 'Ave done yer a few favours, 'aven't I? And a man has *needs*."

Deep breath. Keep calm.

"I'm sorry, Mr... er... Russell... if I've given you the wrong impression... but I'm afraid I'm not interested. I'm spoken for, you see. He's coming home the week after next and then we'll be leaving together—"

"Oh aye? Is that what 'e's told yer? That's bollocks love, 'e in't comin' back. Yer've 'ad the push!"

"No, I'm sorry, you're wrong. Really. In fact, he's expecting me to text him regularly to say I'm ok – here, let me show you my phone—"

"Stop playin' 'ard ter get. Yer know yer want it – come 'ere."

"No, no, let me show you my phone—"

"I *said* come 'ere, bitch – stop pissin' about."

As I tried to walk past him, he barged in front of me, lunged for my phone, ripped it away from the charger and hurled it deep under the bed, swiftly followed by my lap top, even though I frantically tried to stop him. Then his fist slammed into my solar plexus so hard the breath was forced from my body. I fell backwards, gasping for air, only to be dragged onto the bed. While I still struggled to breathe, and deal with the sudden pain in my ribs, he pulled off my pyjamas.

As soon as I could, I started yelling, "Nononono, stop it, nonono, I don't want to, stop it, *stop it!*", making as much noise as I could in the vain hope there might be someone else in the building. But he was too strong, for all his flabbiness, and I felt his leg forcing mine apart. That's when I really screamed, high-pitched and right in his face, until out of the corner of my eye I was aware of his fist coming fast towards my head. Instinctively, I turned away, and the blow missed my eye by a fraction, but landed with full force on the side of my temple, just above my ear. The world exploded in silver, then went black.

When I came to myself, he was stinking and sweating on top of me and inside me, his festering breath in my face and trickles of drool dribbling down his chin as he grunted and strained. One hand was clamped on my neck, the other agonisingly pulling my hair. I lay and endured the sharp burning between my legs, silent and convinced he would kill me, either now or when he'd finished.

It seemed to go on and on, but finally his porcine grunting grew louder, then stopped with a guttural groan. His grip on my throat loosened and he rolled off me onto the other side of the bed.

"Yer'll 'ave ter do be'er than that if yer gonna make yer livin' at it. Tell yer what, we'll 'ave another go tomorrow, eh?"

Then he wiped himself on my quilt and pulled it over him. Within minutes he was snoring loudly.

I still hadn't moved as I tried to process the magnitude of what had just happened, and what he'd just said. Then, as I gradually recovered my wits, I had only one thought – *get out.*

Gradually, I inched my legs to the side of the bed and swung upright. But, as I tried to stand, the searing pain doubled me over. I was afraid he'd broken my ribs. Added to that, the whole side of my head throbbed with more terrible, shooting pain and I felt physically sick. My vision was blurred so that I could barely see.

Somehow, I managed to creep across the room, and, bent double, pick up my pyjamas, clothes, boots, rucksack and coat from the back of the door, which was still open. His snores followed me across the hall and down the corridor, the space dimly lit by a street light shining through the glass above the outside door. Very slowly and with great difficulty, I went back to the bathroom, shut and bolted the door and, with cold and shaking hands, managed to pull on my clothes, putting my pyjamas into my rucksack. I desperately wanted to wash, but I knew that would destroy evidence. Finally, after a desperate struggle, I had my boots and coat on, my scarf round my neck and gloves and car keys in my pocket.

He was still snoring as I inched back across the hall to the outside door. Which was bolted and double locked by a key I didn't have.

Ohgodohgodohgod... Stop. Think.

I inched my way to the desk, and behind it to the keyboard. It was full of room keys, but none that would let me out. As I looked round, trying to stem the rising panic, I noticed there was a shelf under the desk, and propped against it was a large baseball bat. Behind it I could see a keyring with much larger keys. Surely one of these? Gingerly, I moved the bat to one side, carefully picked up the keys and made my way back to the door, but before I could try each key, the snoring suddenly stopped and there was total silence.

I froze. Then with a gasp it started again. Carefully, I put the keys one by one into the lock until at last I came across one that turned. I undid the bolts and had the door open and was outside in a split second, barely noticing the icy air. Then, on impulse, I locked the door behind me and put the keys in my rucksack pocket. He'd probably still be snoring when the police arrived, with a bit of luck.

But I wasn't out of trouble. The snow under my boots was frozen solid and my car was covered. Even with a shovel, I'd have been hard pressed to dig it out, and as I could still barely stand upright for the pain, I couldn't possibly have got in and driven it anywhere. But I couldn't stay there either, to die of exposure on the doorstep.

Cautiously, I slithered towards the road, struggling to keep my footing, anxious not to fall and find that I couldn't get up. I was thinking that somehow I would have to try and walk up to Sabrina's shop and attempt to wake someone up to beg for help.

As I left Blenheim Place and reached Manningham Lane, a taxi came round the corner. I waved feebly and it drew to a halt and reversed towards me. It said 'Akhbar's Taxis' on the side, and I knew, with a great surge of relief and hope, that it was from Sabrina's father's firm.

The driver was a clean-shaven, dark-haired man of around fifty, wearing a thick jumper over his salwar kameeze.

"Need a ride, love?"

I must have hesitated because he said, "Are you our Sab's mate? From there?"

He gestured towards Blenheim Place. I nodded. Then I moved slowly towards the car's open door.

The street light shone full onto me, and with a sharp intake of breath he said, "Did he do this to you? Hutchinson?"

"Yes," I whispered.

"Get in quick, love," he said. "You don't want to be hanging around out here at this time of night."

I tried, but I couldn't bend to get myself onto the front car seat. He opened the back door and said, "Can you slide in and lie down on the seat? Hurry up, please."

I managed it in spite of the awful pain – the urgency in his voice was making me afraid. He closed the door behind me and did a screeching u-turn. I assumed we were going to the shop, but the car continued without stopping. Oh God, what was going on?

"Where are you taking me?" My voice was squeaky with fear.

"Hospital."

Thank goodness. I let myself relax slightly and closed my eyes against the glare of the streetlights flashing over my head.

Soon the car stopped; he got out and opened the back door. I was dimly aware of a sign in front of me saying 'A and E', and a double door leading to a brightly-lit corridor. I struggled out on rubbery legs and the taxi-driver helped me to stagger through into the safety of Bradford Royal Infirmary.

"How much do I owe you?" I whispered.

"Nothing," he said. "We've been worried about you ever since Sab told us. And we're worried about Mr Abbas too," he added.

"I'm going to ask for the police, and I'll tell them about him as well as my attack."

"Hutchinson will be long gone before they get there."

"I don't think so," I said. "I've locked him in."

My taxi-driver gave a slow smile, but he didn't respond any other way.

Chapter Ten

Sunday

Hours later, I woke in a hospital bed.

When the receptionist the previous night had seen what a state I was in, I'd jumped the queue and a nurse had come to assess me. It was difficult to explain what had happened, but as soon as I mentioned I'd been raped, as well as beaten and hit on the head, she sprang into action. A doctor was summoned, swabs were taken and I was sent for an x-ray and a head CT. When I arrived back in A and E, the police were waiting for me, but apart from the basic facts of where, when and who, I was in too much pain to give a detailed statement, so they promised to return the next day. I think I heard a whispered conversation with my nurse on the other side of the curtain.

I lay there for a while, drifting in and out of consciousness, then two porters arrived and my bed was wheeled through the hospital to a ward, whilst I clutched my clothes, boots and rucksack. I was put into a small side room, mercifully alone.

It took me a long time to feel comfortable, let alone sleep. There was constant noise from the corridor – footsteps, voices, the trundling of trolleys – and I found myself listening in trepidation for someone coming in. I was in constant pain, no matter which way I turned, and my head throbbed mercilessly. What was almost worse was the torment of knowing my only lines of contact with Martin were lying under Hutchinson's bed. I didn't even think I could remember his number, so buying a cheap phone when I got out of hospital wouldn't help me at all.

Eventually, I must have dozed, but it was fitful and, I suppose just before I woke, I was convinced that I had to lie motionless because I was back in that room, listening to my rapist snoring.

When the door finally did open, I had to choke off the scream that formed in my throat. There was a trolley with a huge teapot in the corridor, and a cheerful young woman came in, and said, in an Eastern European accent, "Goot mornink! Tea or coffee?"

She poured me a cup of tarry liquid, which she left on the table, smiling at my feeble thanks.

Later, she came back with some scrambled eggs and toast. I'd been expecting it to taste foul, but actually it was ok and quite easy to eat, when I'd finally managed to drag myself into a sitting position. Then I needed the toilet, and I didn't know how I could get myself out of that room, or where I had to go. Reluctantly, I pushed the button next to my bed to call for help. But nobody came.

Gingerly, I pulled back the thin quilt. I was wearing a flimsy hospital gown that barely covered my knees, and the shaking started as soon as my feet touched the floor. It was an irrational, consuming terror and my logical mind kept repeating 'you're ok, you're safe, no-one wants to hurt you'. But still I shook. Finally, I steeled myself and stood up. The room swayed and lurched and my head throbbed again. But I had to find the toilet.

Just as I was making my way towards the door, holding on to the side of the bed, a young nurse came in. She didn't look too pleased.

"Are you all right? You're not really supposed to get up without assistance, you know – you've had a nasty bang to your head."

"I'm sorry," I whispered. "But I really need the toilet."

"Right," she said, "come on then."

It turned out to be almost opposite my door, and as I moved, I started to feel a bit stronger.

"I think I can manage, thanks," I said.

"Good," she said. "Well, don't be long. Doctor will be coming to talk to you soon."

She bustled away.

I locked myself in, then used the toilet and washed my hands and face, drying myself as best I could on the scratchy paper towels. Then I took a deep breath, opened the door and regained the sanctuary of my room without mishap. First hurdle overcome, I told myself.

I looked at the mechanism at the side of my bed and worked out how to raise the pillow end so that I wasn't lying flat. That was much more comfortable, and I dozed again.

The doctor arrived a long time later. She was an Indian lady, quite young, with deep shadows under her eyes, but she seemed competent.

She checked my notes and then said, "So, Alison, you were admitted last night and you were given an x-ray and a head CT. Is that right?"

I nodded.

"OK. Well. I can tell you that the x-ray showed that you have no serious internal injuries, although you do have severe bruising to your abdomen, two cracked ribs and some internal scrapes and contusions, which support your having been sexually assaulted. We are concerned about the blow to your head, but you've been lucky to avoid a fractured skull or serious damage to your eye. You could easily have lost it if that fist had connected full into your face. How do you feel today?"

"Pretty shaky."

"That's not surprising. Do you have a headache?"

I nodded again.

"Is it better or worse than last night, do you think? And is your vision blurred at all? Have you been sick?"

It was too much. I dissolved into tears, and then I couldn't stop crying.

Her tone softened. "I'm sorry," she said, "I know this must be an awful experience. But I have to ask you something else as well."

I looked up.

"There's no easy way to put this, but have you considered the possibility that you might be pregnant?"

I hadn't, but now I really did feel sick. I must have looked even more stricken, because she said, "We can offer you the morning after pill in these circumstances. You don't have to decide immediately, but we do advise taking it within twenty-four hours of unprotected sex."

There was no decision to make. "Yes please," I said. Then something else occurred to me. "What if he was HIV positive?"

"Is he a drug user?"

I remembered the car with the blacked-out windows.

"I expect so."

"Right. Oh dear. Well, we'd like to keep you under observation for a couple of days, but you'll need to come back for a blood test in about three months' time, after the middle of next March. We can give you the result on that day, but until then, I strongly advise you not to have unprotected sex."

Dear God in heaven, she had to be joking. The very thought of it turned my stomach. But that was one more thing I needed to tell Martin – if I ever managed to contact him.

"Would you like me to organise some counselling for you?"

"I don't think so, thanks. I have to deal with this myself, somehow."

"All right – but if you change your mind, help is available. Just have a word with your GP."

"I will. Thank you." But my GP was far away, and might as well have been on the moon, for all the chance I had of contacting him. All the numbers I needed were of course in my phone – under the bed in the Blenheim.

When she'd gone, all I could think about was Martin. Then I remembered his meeting at Leeds Playhouse on the 21st; it was a planning session for the theatre experience days he would be teaching after Christmas, so he would certainly be there. All I had to do was to make sure I was at the theatre first thing in the morning on the 21st. But that was twelve days away. Somehow I had to survive till then.

I didn't have long to ponder before the police arrived.

A nurse brought them in – two uniformed officers, a man and a woman. It was going to be very uncomfortable, sitting in bed in my flimsy hospital gown, with my livid, bruised face, and my swollen and semi-closed eye, talking about such an intimate and horrible experience. But I knew I had to do it, and I expected them to be pretty sympathetic.

"Please don't keep Miss Weston too long," the nurse said firmly. "She's not at all well and she needs to rest."

The woman nodded. Then, as the nurse closed the door behind her, it began.

"Alison Weston?"

I nodded.

"Last night you made a very serious allegation about a sexual assault carried out on you by Russell Huchinson at the Blenheim Hotel on Manningham Lane. Is that correct? Do you still maintain that you were raped by Mr Hutchinson?"

"Of course I do," I whispered.

Could they not see the state of me? It occurred to me he might have tried to lie his way out of it, and indignation gave strength to my voice.

"Is he saying it was consensual? It's the obvious defence, of course, but I can assure you—"

"No," said the male officer. "He's not saying that. In fact, he's not saying anything at all. When an investigating officer arrived at the premises, he wasn't there."

"But that's impossible, unless he went out of the window! I locked him in when I left – look, the keys are in my rucksack."

They glanced at each other, and the man gave a slight nod to his partner.

"Miss Weston, the outer door to the property had been smashed in with considerable force, and there was a baseball bat covered in blood and a large quantity of blood on the hall carpet. Emergency DNA testing confirms it is Mr Hutchinson's. Do you have any idea how it came to be there? And when we take your fingerprints, will we find them on the bat?"

My anger boosted my strength – how dare they suggest I was anything other than the victim here?

"Yes you will – but only because it was propped against a shelf behind the counter and I had to move it to get the big outside door key. I left it there. When I crept out he was snoring in my bed. In any case," I added, "if you're familiar with him, you'll know Mr Hutchinson is a heavy, thick-set man who had no trouble overpowering me before he raped me. It's ridiculous to suggest that *I* could have attacked *him*!"

Then the female officer chipped in. "How long had you been staying at the Blenheim?"

"Since last Wednesday night."

"And were you... comfortable staying there?"

"No, I wasn't, but I had no choice. I'd spent the two previous nights in my car, but the back seat got soaked when my hot water bottle leaked, and it was so cold. I don't have much money, and the Blenheim was the cheapest on the council's list. I didn't like the look of Hutchinson, but I wedged a chair under my bedroom door handle and I thought I'd be all right, But he… he…"

"Go on."

"But last night I had to use the bathroom, and even though I locked my door when I went out, he must have had a pass key. When I came back he was standing half-naked in my room. I asked him to leave but he punched me in the stomach and winded me and then he… pulled my pyjamas off… and I couldn't breathe, and then he hit me when I started screaming and when I came round he was on top of me. He had his hand round my throat and he was pulling my hair. I was sure he was going to kill me. I just froze until he'd finished. Then he rolled off me, wiped himself on my quilt and went straight to sleep. So I got up and went to the bathroom with my stuff, got dressed and… but I couldn't find the outdoor key and I thought he'd hear me. I found it behind the desk so I opened the door, went out and locked him in."

"How did you get to the hospital?"

"A taxi picked me up."

"Did you call for the taxi?"

"No – Hutchinson had thrown my phone under the bed. It was just luck that the taxi came. It turned out the driver was related to Sabrina Akhbar from that supermarket up Marlborough Road."

Then they announced that they needed to take my rucksack and all the clothes I'd been wearing when I was admitted, as well as my pyjamas, for forensic testing.

"But they're all I've got! The rest of my stuff's locked in my car. What if the hospital discharges me?"

"Miss Weston," the male officer said, "you don't seem to understand that we suspect a second serious crime has been committed in the Blenheim Hotel. We need your things to help eliminate you from our enquiries. You surely can't object to that?"

"But… how will I…?"

"You'll be in hospital for a few days in any case," said the woman, firmly. "We'll look into bringing you some clothes from your car, but in the meantime, you will remain a person of interest in this enquiry, and you should not leave the hospital without informing us of your whereabouts. Do you understand?"

"Yes," I whispered. My head was throbbing again, and I felt wretched. "Um... is there any chance of you looking for my phone and laptop and getting them to me?"

"If we find them, you'll have to wait until forensics have finished with them. It shouldn't be more than a couple of weeks."

So poor Martin would have to remain in the dark, wondering why I hadn't been in touch, and I was left in this hospital with absolutely nothing.

Chapter Eleven
Tuesday and Wednesday

I'd had a relapse after the police had left. My head continued to throb and I was violently sick, then I sobbed for ages. I was quite unable to comprehend how, after being on the receiving end of a savage and callous attack, I was now a 'person of interest' because Hutchinson was missing and apparently in trouble. The police had seemed far more concerned about that than they were about my rape. Added to all that was the constant worry about Martin, and the feeling of total helplessness to alter anything. Never before in my life had I felt so wretched – abandoned and let down by a system that was supposed to protect me, and to offer me help and support when I needed it. I got myself into such a state that my doctor was summoned; she immediately prescribed 'something to help you sleep'. After taking that, and the morning-after pill I had earlier requested, I fell into merciful oblivion.

I barely remember the following day. I was still very dopey and disorientated; I think I woke up once in the morning to drink some water with the help of a nurse, then slept again. I came back to some sort of consciousness around tea time, when I was moved, complete with my bed, to a shared ward of four beds. At that point something happened to cheer me a little, because draped across my bed I found my padded outdoor jacket, complete with car keys and my money belt sticking out of one of its pockets – the money belt I'd removed from my rucksack to pay the taxi driver on Sunday morning. Somehow the police had overlooked it – probably, I realised, because it had been hanging on my door under the old dressing gown the hospital had lent me.

I had access to my money and my car. It was a huge relief.

I was also cheered to find a card and a bunch of very early budding daffodils by my new bed. Sabrina must have called in while I was out of it, which was really kind of her, but I was disconcerted by the message in the card:

So sorry to hear about what happened and hope you're soon on mend. Sorry too that we won't be here when you come out. Going to Pakistan for visit to do family stuff. Maybe see you when we come back to Bradford in January. Sabrina and family from shop.

On Wednesday, I woke up for the coffee trolley and ate my breakfast, followed later by pie and mash for lunch and a sandwich and, glory be, a tangerine for tea. The enforced inactivity and regular meals helped to heal my bruised body a little; some economic independence and the thought of my little car faithfully waiting for me lifted my spirits.

Later, I was beginning to feel much better. The hospital had provided me with some basic toiletries, so I showered and washed my hair before lunch, able, for the first time, to walk confidently to the bathroom without as much pain. Of course there was no hair drier, so I wrapped my hair in a towel. It would soon dry in the warm hospital air. The bruise on my face had darkened to purple – a good sign, apparently, even though I looked like I'd done a few rounds in a boxing ring.

After lunch, I had another visit from the police. It was a different female officer and she arrived carrying a black plastic bin liner. She didn't stay long, but she drew the curtains round my bed – she needn't have bothered – my fellow patients were either deaf or comatose.

"Miss Weston," she began quietly, "we've spoken to several neighbours on Blenheim Place who all confirm they heard a loud uproar, and saw Hutchinson being bundled into the back of a black car, around 3am on Sunday morning – a couple of hours after you were admitted to hospital. So you're no longer a person of interest in this enquiry. You will need to keep us informed of your whereabouts, though, as you may be required to give evidence in court."

She dumped the bin liner next to my bed. That was it – no message of sympathy, no enquiry about my health. Still, it was a huge relief – at least I hadn't been arrested.

"Erm... hang on," I said, as she turned to leave, "have you found my phone? And have you arrested Hutchinson? And have you found the Blenheim's owner, a Mr Abbas? Sabrina Akhbar from the supermarket said the community was worried about him, because they hadn't seen him for ages."

"Your phone and lap top weren't under the bed, although the chargers remained in the plug sockets by the bed. They're in the bag. As for Mr Abbas..." She leaned closer, glanced around quickly and whispered, "I might as well tell you as it'll be in the papers tomorrow. His body was found in the cellar at the Blenheim. We don't know how he died, but there wasn't any obvious sign of foul play. The post-mortem will tell us for certain, but it looked from the state of the body as if he'd been there for at least three weeks."

"Would Hutchinson have known that?"

"We have no idea, but it's possible."

"So you're telling me that Russell Hutchinson, who may be a murderer and is certainly a rapist, is out there somewhere?"

"I wouldn't worry too much," she said, rather coldly. "From the amount of blood he lost on Sunday, he won't be in any position to come looking for you. Even if he had any reason to," she added.

But he has got a reason, I thought after she'd left. *I locked him in. He'll blame me for not being able to avoid whoever bundled him into that car.*

That's when the real fear began.

Chapter Twelve
Thursday, December 14th – Morning

Another almost sleepless night. How would I avoid an encounter with that awful man? What if he was lurking near the hospital, waiting for me to come out? And even if he wasn't in any state to do that, what if he sent a complete stranger, or a relative, instead?

At around ten a nurse came in to take my temperature and blood pressure, and check my eyes weren't seeing double. Then the doctor arrived and looked at my notes.

"Well, I'm happy to tell you, Alison," she said, "that, because your body is functioning almost normally again, you're ready to be discharged. I am still a bit concerned about your concussion – ideally, I'd have liked to keep an eye on you for a little while longer – but you're quite young and strong and well-rested, and unfortunately we need this bed for a very poorly patient. However, if you have any migraine-like symptoms, or unexplained vomiting, please come straight back to A and E. Do you have someone to look after you?"

Oh Martin.

"No," I answered sadly, "and I'm homeless. But I do at least have my car, and a tiny bit of money. My partner will be back in a week. I expect I'll be ok."

I sounded more confident than I felt, but my fears were no reason to deprive a needy patient of a bed. Had I been elderly, apparently, they would have kept me in, but there simply weren't enough beds.

By 2pm, after a lunch that seemed a bit more substantial than usual, I dressed myself in my grubby clothes and pulled on my boots and jacket. In the large entrance atrium of the hospital, I found a cash machine and withdrew one hundred pounds, leaving me with just forty pounds of emergency money in my account. Martin's money hadn't yet appeared. My plan was to find a taxi to take me down to Manningham Lane, get my car started and drive into Bradford to see someone from the council in the Housing Options office.

As I left the hospital, the cold took my breath away for a moment. It was a bright, blue-skied day and it must have been milder because most of the snow had disappeared, but after four days of hospital heat it was a shock nevertheless. I looked around for a taxi but there were none, and the card Sabrina had given me was useless without my phone. In any case, I wasn't sure exactly what I would need my money for. I had vaguely wondered about finding a cheap motel, as Martin had suggested. I didn't want to hang around – my heart was thumping and I kept scanning round for anyone taking an interest in me. After a couple of minutes, I started walking down the road towards the exit, noticing grimly that I was stiff and sore as well as shaking with the cold.

There was a bus shelter not far from the main hospital entrance, on Duckworth Lane. It looked from the timetable as if I needed the 620 to take me to Manningham Lane, but I had no idea where to get off, since Manningham Lane runs all the way down to the centre of Bradford. Then a small woman in a burqa came into the shelter, accompanied by a teenage girl. I smiled at them, and then said to the girl, "Could you help me, please? I need to get to Marlborough Road."

"No problem. Get 620 and get off at mosque on the corner of Marlborough Road."

"That's great, thanks."

When the bus came, a couple of minutes later, I got on rather stiffly, handed over two pounds and sat by a window near the front. There was hardly anybody on it, but as we chugged down Duckworth Lane stopping, it seemed, every couple of minutes, it gradually filled up. After a while, I recognised the big mosque ahead, so I stood up and gingerly got off. A few steps brought me to Marlborough Road, where I turned left and headed down towards the crossroads with Manningham Lane, then round the corner towards Blenheim Place.

This was the bit I was dreading the most, but I kept repeating to myself: not long now, you'll soon be at the car, keep going.

I turned left at the lights. On the home stretch. Then I was walking into Blenheim Place and it seemed to be growing colder by the second as the sun disappeared. Around the hotel was a cordon of blue and white tape, and outside the metal-screened door, a uniformed officer was chatting to a few people. One of them, a grim-faced woman, reminded me a bit of Hutchinson. *Oh God*, I thought, *it's his family.*

Then I saw my car. Or what was left of it. The tyres were slashed, all the windows were gone and it had been burnt out. All that remained was a dull shell onto which someone had painted 'Bitch' in white letters.

The shock caused me to stop dead. Hutchinson's family hadn't noticed me – the conversation was becoming heated and there was a lot of gesticulating.

I heard the woman scream, "Where is he then? Where's our Russell? And who's that woman 'e were shacked up with?"

I wasn't hanging around. Without pausing, I turned tail, crossed Manningham Lane at the traffic lights and walked unsteadily towards the nearest bus stop. Only then did the hot tears start, and that shaking. How much did Hutchinson's family know?

Chapter Thirteen

Thursday Afternoon

Forty-five minutes later, I was back in the centre of Bradford. My walk across town took a while because I had to keep stopping for breath in the cold air, which was hurting my ribs.

Finally, the Housing Options office. Ten days and a lifetime after my previous visit, I pushed open the door. The same woman was on the reception desk, but it seemed quieter. She was drinking tea and glancing at a *Telegraph* and *Argus* next to her computer. The front page headline read, *Man's Body Found in Hotel Cellar.*

Without looking up, she said, "Yes?"

"Erm… I need some help, please. I've just been discharged from hospital and I've got nowhere to sleep tonight. Could I speak to someone?"

"Do you have an appointment?"

"No."

"Well, you'll need to make one and come back then."

"Excuse me? I don't think you fully understand. On Saturday I was beaten up and raped at the Blenheim, a hotel you sent me to – well, not you personally, of course, but it was the cheapest on the list I was given on the first—"

"Come off it. You're just trying it on because you've seen the *Telegraph*! You're the third today. You must think we're all stupid."

"No! Check if you don't believe me! My name's Alison Weston and I was here on the first of December."

She tapped away for a second, then looked up and saw me for the first time. There was no apology, she just said, "Right. Take a seat, Miss Weston. But you might have a long wait."

Back to the seats by the blue-patterned windows. Above the blue, where the glass was clear, I could see the sky darkening, and black birds wheeling around overhead – *it must be around 4pm*, I thought.

Eventually, a door opposite opened and a woman came out, followed by someone I recognised from my first encounter. My heart sank, but the dapper little man walked past me without a second glance. Thank goodness. Shortly afterwards, I was ushered into another interview room by a young woman. She sat down at her desk, indicating I should sit on the other side, and quickly scanned the screen of her lap top. Then she looked at me for a couple of seconds.

"Oh dear, you have been in the wars, haven't you? What happened?"

I went through the whole thing yet again, sparing her none of the details. When I'd finished, she passed me a tissue, shaking her head.

"On behalf of the Housing Options service, I can only apologise to you. You've been through a horrible ordeal and I'm going to see what we can do to help. Just one moment."

She began scrolling down her screen.

"Now then. Because you're now classed as a vulnerable person, we can look at getting you somewhere safer to sleep. There's a hostel place available in Wakefield, but it's a mixed hostel so you might not want to – oh, hang on, a room's just been vacated at our Women's Refuge. Would that suit you better? Of course, the cost will have to be met by you—"

"Perfect," I said, "Could I take it, please? It'll only be for a week," I added, "as my partner will be around after the 21st. He'll be able to pay for me."

"Well, let's not put a time limit on it, just in case things don't work out. At least you'll have somewhere to stay over Christmas, if the worst comes to the worst. And you'll need to fill in some forms when you get there – Eunice will talk you through it."

"Eunice?"

"The woman in charge. It's only a small place, so she runs it more or less on her own. She's wonderful, she'll look after you."

"Thank you," I whispered, but I didn't think she heard me.

She made a phone call which, after she'd described my situation, seemed to involve a lot of "Yes, that's right. Yes – yes, ok, thank you.

In about forty-five minutes or less – depends when Pat arrives and if the traffic's bad. Right."

Then she turned to me.

"OK, I've booked you in. Eunice is expecting you as soon as our taxi can get you there."

The relief was indescribable.

"I can't thank you enough."

"It's the least we can do, in the circumstances. I'm just so sorry you had to go through that to qualify for a safe place. We just don't have the resources to help everyone."

She told me to wait for about ten minutes for the taxi to arrive, and wished me good luck. Then she held the door open for me and went to speak to the receptionist.

Back into the waiting area. It was pitch dark outside now and the streetlights were coming on. After a few minutes the phone rang, then the receptionist looked at me and called, "Your taxi's on its way."

"Thank you," I said, and out I went through the double doors and onto the pavement.

A man was stumbling past on the other side of the road, bent double and moving slowly. He looked familiar. Instinctively I moved back into the doorway, but when he turned towards the building in which I was sheltering, I was in no doubt. It was Russell Hutchinson.

I don't think he saw me, and at that moment my taxi drew up, driven by an African woman this time. I dived onto the back seat as fast as my bruised body would allow, and bent down, ostensibly busying myself with my rucksack, as we sped away. The shock had made me shake uncontrollably again. Why was he hanging around there? Was he expecting me to turn up? What would he have done if he'd seen me? Why hadn't he been arrested?

"I've turned the heater up for you, chicken. You look starved," said the driver without turning round.

"Thank you," I whispered. I tried not to think about what I'd seen, but the memory of his contorted face kept floating in front of my eyes.

The drive seemed interminable, through the melee of the rush-hour traffic. Glaring headlights made it impossible to see whether we were being followed, even though I kept glancing behind. But the route out of Bradford was familiar, and my heart sank at the idea that the refuge might be somewhere in Manningham.

Eventually, we reached Manningham Lane once more and I breathed again as the taxi drove past the end of Marlborough Road. There was finally a clear stretch as we left the traffic lights. We seemed to speed up as we passed Blenheim Place, but I risked a quick glance. All was deserted, although I caught a glimpse of the wreckage of my car being winched onto some sort of breakdown truck. *End of an era*, I thought sadly, and my thoughts drifted to my cottage, my career at Hebble High, Brian's death and then, as the snow came down again onto the windscreen, that journey home with Martin last winter and the resumption of our lives together.

But before I could become tearful again, the taxi turned left into a much narrower road, then right into an avenue opposite a church, and drew up outside the back of a large detached house on our right. We'd arrived.

"Here we are. Now don't be scared – we weren't followed and you'll be safe here. Eunice is a lovely lady. No, it's all taken care of," she added, as I offered her a ten-pound note. "Courtesy of the council."

"Well, thank you very much – and… erm… have a nice Christmas."

"You too, chicken!"

I got out and opened the gate.

"Go to the side door!" my taxi driver called out of her window.

I walked round the side of the house. I could see lights blazing inside. Before I could knock, the door was flung open and a white-haired woman said, "Alison? So pleased you're here at last – thanks Pat!" and she waved at the taxi, which was just drawing away.

"Come in, come in, it's freezing out here – oh not more snow! We'll get a white Christmas yet!"

She pulled the door closed behind me, locked it with a large key and drew on two substantial bolts.

"There we are – safe as houses now! Oh, you poor love – what's happened to you? Was it your husband? Anyway, don't tell me if you don't want to. Get your coat off and I'll make you a brew, then I'll show you where you'll be sleeping."

We were in a warm kitchen; there was a permeating odour of baking and something more savoury. There were six chairs round a large oblong table in the middle, and behind that an Aga. She flipped up one of the round lids on the top and put a kettle on the hotplate. It started whistling almost immediately.

"Coffee, please," I said, as she held up a box of teabags and a jar of instant.

"I won't offer you a biscuit because supper's nearly ready. I just need to put the veg on."

I sat and sipped the scalding coffee, watching her pour boiling water onto a pan of sprouts, and place them on the hotplate. When I felt up to it, I filled her in on my recent history. She listened quietly, nodding from time to time. Finally, she told me that she too had taught in Halifax – at the very school where I had done my first couple of years – but her subject had been Home Economics.

"So of course I'm in charge of the cooking here, but I try to get everyone making things – it saddens me that so few people actually cook from scratch these days. Tonight's meal is a real group effort. The others'll be down in a minute. There are only four in at the moment, plus you – one young lady went back to live with her parents today. They're a nice crowd – as I said, everybody mucks in with cooking and cleaning, but you're excused tonight. You look dead beat."

I nodded, smiling gratefully.

"It's been a long day. I was only discharged from hospital this morning and I've barely slept since Sunday night. I just found it so noisy, and I keep having nightmares as well."

"I'm not surprised – anybody would, after what you've been through. But you'll be all right here, honestly. Everyone goes to bed pretty early and it's a quiet neighbourhood. And nobody knows this is a women's refuge – we have to keep it very low-key, so please don't mention it to anyone. Now then, let's go and look at your room if you've finished that coffee."

She held the door open for me and we went into a substantial hall with a sweeping staircase leading up to a landing.

"This is yours," she said, unlocking a door at the top of the stairs, on the right.

It was a large room with a double bed (made up, ready for me), a bay window and a pine wardrobe and dressing table. Eunice pulled on some heavy dark blue velvet curtains around the window, and switched on a lamp sitting on the small table by the bed.

It was just wonderful.

"You can dump your rucksack and unpack later if you like. The bathroom's across here," she said, going out of the room and opening another door on the opposite side of the stairs. "Towels are in the cylinder cupboard – help yourself, keep them in your bedroom and wash them when they need it. We have a machine and a drier downstairs. Here are your keys – this one for your room and these for the outside doors. Guests usually go out with someone else, and you'll need to leave a note to say where you're going, please, just in case you have any problems. Oh, and there's just one other thing. You know you'll be charged for this accommodation, don't you? Have you got an application for Housing Benefit in yet?"

Numbly, I shook my head.

"Well, not to worry," Eunice said kindly, "I've got some spares. We can look at that together when you're feeling a bit better."

While I was digesting all that, another door opened and a child peeped out, a girl of about seven, I guessed, with a cheeky face and bright yellow hair in plaits.

"Is it teatime yet, Auntie Eunice?"

"Nearly, love,"

"Can I do the big noise?"

"You can, but we need to set the table first."

"I can do that!"

She ran down the stairs and disappeared into the kitchen. Another face, a carbon copy but older, also looked out of the room and said, "Hi, you must be Alison. I'm Mags and you've just seen my daughter, Rosie."

"Hello."

We all went down together. Rosie had already laid the table for six, and the sprouts were bubbling away, steaming up the kitchen. Eunice checked them with a fork then said, "Right, Rosie, it's time."

Rosie disappeared, and from the hall came a sound I hadn't heard since my childhood, when Doris and Dad took me to small seaside hotels. It was a loud, metallic clanging, the noise made by a brass gong being hit hard with a metal drumstick.

Doors were slammed upstairs and there were heavy footsteps.

"Shut that bloody racket!" came booming from a stout, small woman with a huge stomach unflatteringly emphasised by a white sweatshirt which was several sizes too small. She had short, boyish hair and black-rimmed glasses, and she stopped dead when she saw me.

"Is this the new one? You didn't waste much time filling Barbara's room, did yer?"

"Vanessa, that's not very friendly, is it? This is Alison. She told me she used to be a teacher like me, so you'd better behave yourself!"

"Oh bloody 'ell, not another strict one. I've enough on wi' you!"

Then the last woman appeared. In contrast to Vanessa, she was one of the thinnest people I'd ever seen. Her gaunt face looked lined and wary, and she had huge shadows under her eyes.

"I'm Sharon," she announced without preamble, "and I'm trying to get clean."

I smiled and said, "Alison. Hello to you both."

"Eat eat eat!" Rosie was jumping up and down, so we all sat round the table and Eunice carefully carried over an enormous roasting tin of shepherd's pie and a bowl of sprouts, followed by six hot plates from the bottom of the Aga. She spooned out great dollops, and suddenly I was ravenously hungry.

"Ho-ho-hot!" said Rosie, blowing her fork and waving it around, "but yummy."

Vanessa was too busy shovelling food into her mouth to reply, but Sharon smiled and said it was good as she picked at her food. I can't remember ever enjoying a meal more and, unusually for me, I also managed to demolish a sizable helping of apple crumble. Then Rosie was ushered away by her mum to do some homework before bedtime. After Vanessa and Sharon had cleared away the plates and put them in the dishwasher, the four of us sat round the table.

"Oo did that to you?" Sharon asked me, nodding at the dark purple bruise on the side of my face.

"Bet it were 'er 'usband!"

"No, Vanessa, I'm not married. My partner's out of the country till next Thursday."

"So 'oo were it then? Some Paki I expect."

"No! In fact, I've had nothing but kindness and help from that community. They gave me food when I needed it and took me to hospital after—" I hesitated, "—I was raped and beaten."

"Where did it happen?" Sharon was staring at me now.

"At the Blenheim Hotel in Manningham. It was all I could afford. But it wasn't the owner, it was the vile slob who was looking after the place, a man called Russell Hutchinson – what's the matter?"

Sharon had suddenly turned white.

"Oh shit, oh no, it *is* him, Eunice. I showed you the *Telegraph*, didn't I? This morning…"

"You did, love." She turned to me. "Hutchinson was Sharon's dealer and pimp. He accused her of stealing some money from him—"

"But I never!"

"—and threatened her with a baseball bat. It was a miracle she got away."

"I kneed him in the balls, so the fat slob couldn't run. But then I kept gettin' these dodgy phone calls, so the filth sent me 'ere, 'cos there's no rehab places now. But now you're 'ere as well."

"I'm sorry," I said lamely. "Maybe I should leave?"

Sharon nodded but Eunice said firmly. "You're going nowhere, love. No-one knows where this house is, and no-one knows you're here apart from the council, do they?"

"Only the taxi driver."

"That's Pat. She's sound – she was here herself once. She understands about secrecy. Nobody needs to worry."

Later, lying in a warm, comfortable bed, my mind wouldn't switch off. Had Hutchinson stupidly upset people even more violent than him? People who had used that baseball bat on him, and were responsible for the large quantity of his blood that had soaked into the sticky carpet at the Blenheim? If that really was Hutchinson I'd seen a few hours ago, he certainly wouldn't be happy about being locked in the hotel to await their arrival, before the police could take him in for questioning. But why was he beaten up on that particular night? Had someone (Sabrina's dad or the man who took me to hospital?) tipped them off? And were these the same people who were looking for Sharon, believing she'd stolen their money? Did they believe Hutchinson? Was that why they'd let him go?

It had been so frightening, that feeling of being totally at the mercy of someone who had no self-control and certainly didn't care about me. Inevitably, my mind drifted back to the last time with Martin, and the absolute trust I had in him to stop immediately if I asked him to. I remembered the look of alarm on his face that time in the cottage, just before I left him, when I'd cried for a different reason, but he thought he might have hurt me in some way. I ached to be able to talk to him – but first I'd have to tell him what had happened, and I couldn't face doing that on the phone, even if I'd known how to get hold of him.

I lay awake for ages, turning everything over in my mind, trying to decide what I should do next. I had a week to hang on, I was warm and fed here and I couldn't face going back to the streets with virtually nothing this time. But would Hutchinson or his family be looking for me? If he had seen me, might he know where the refuge was, somehow? Was I putting the others in danger by staying?

I fell into an uneasy sleep, unable to decide what to do next.

Chapter Fourteen
Friday 15th – Monday 18th December

I was in the supermarket on Marlborough Road, with Sharon. I knew Sabrina and her family weren't there. We were looking for some stuff for a curry but we couldn't find what we needed. Suddenly, we turned a corner into another aisle and Hutchinson was standing in front of us, holding a large baseball bat.

"Two for the price of one!" He advanced towards us slowly.

"Run! Run! Get the police!" I screamed. Sharon fled, but I tripped and the last thing I saw was Hutchinson raising the bat above his head. Then there was an almighty bang. Then another, and someone was shouting.

"Alison! Alison! Are you ok? What's happening?"

I opened my eyes. I was in my bed at the refuge. No-one else was in the room.

Eunice shouted again and banged on the door. Blearily, I stumbled out of bed and opened it.

"I'm so sorry," I whispered, "I must have been having a nightmare…"

"Oh love, this has really got to you, hasn't it?"

She gave me a long hug and patted my back soothingly.

"It's ok, don't worry, there's no harm done. Look, I've brought you some coffee. I thought it was time you stirred your stumps."

"Haven't I woken everyone up?"

"No, don't fret – Rosie's gone to school, Mags is looking for work at the Job Centre in Shipley and Sharon and Vanessa have gone into town to do some Christmas shopping. Everything's fine."

"Thank goodness."

"Come down when you're ready – I could do with a hand."

"Ok."

I took the coffee, dressed (thinking my clothes could do with a wash, but I hadn't anything else to wear), then sat for a moment looking out over the white landscape, covered by a fresh fall of overnight snow. Gradually, my heart rate slowed, until I felt ready to go down and start peeling potatoes.

Eunice made pastry that day. Supper was steak pie, veg and tarte tatin, which looked complicated but turned out to be fairly straightforward. There was even enough pastry left for a batch of jam tarts ("Rosie's favourite!") Once more the spotlessly clean kitchen was filled with the smell of baking – that lady certainly knew what she was doing.

Then we sat down together with mugs of soup and I told her that I thought I'd seen Hutchinson the day before.

"I didn't mention it last night because Sharon was so upset. What do you think I should do?"

"Tell the police," she replied instantly. "They'll probably want you to make a statement."

"Will they come here?"

"No – we don't want to attract attention with a police car outside the refuge. They'll need you to go to the station at Manningham."

"I can't." An automatic response, but as soon as I'd said it, I realised it was true. I could not face the streets of Manningham, so close to Blenheim Place, where I had seen Hutchinson's family.

"I just can't," I repeated. "Maybe I could talk to them when Martin gets back next Thursday."

"That's not ideal, but if you really can't face it… and you know," Eunice added, kindly, "You can't be certain it was him. You were very tired, and sometimes the brain plays tricks."

I nodded, but privately I thought she was just saying that to make me feel better. I was fairly sure of what I'd seen.

The others came back later. Rosie skipped in with a satchel full of little cards she'd made for us all. Her mum returned, looking tired and defeated after an unproductive day on a computer at the Job Centre, then Sharon and Vanessa arrived with armfuls of carrier bags. I did vaguely wonder how they managed to afford all that stuff.

Eunice went home around 7pm. She returned quite early the next morning with a loaded car, having already stocked up with supplies for the weekend. We spent Saturday cleaning our rooms, the kitchen and the bathroom and taking it in turns to wash our clothes and dry them in the tumble drier. I washed and dried my pyjamas, slopped around in them and washed everything else I owned, then on Sunday morning, I showered, dressed in clean clothes and felt much better.

There was a treat for Rosie on Sunday. Eunice had the day off, but she called in at around eleven with a sizeable Christmas tree and a box of lights and decorations. Rosie and Vanessa then decorated it after planting it in a large pot of special compost and watering it. The hall started smelling pleasantly piney and when the lights were switched on, the tree looked festive, if a touch lopsided.

Monday and Tuesday passed without incident. The good food and comfortable house were slowly healing my body, although my ribs still felt sore and the bruise stubbornly refused to fade on my face. But I couldn't really relax; I had a mounting feeling of apprehension, and something I'd never experienced before – a total lack of confidence. I hadn't left the house once, and the thought of doing so filled me with dread. But I was forced to overcome my fear the day before I was due to go to Leeds to meet Martin.

Chapter Fifteen

Wednesday December 20th

Eunice had the afternoon off. The others were all out; I was expecting them back around seven. They'd all gone to watch Rosie in her school nativity play. Then they were staying on for the end-of term Christmas party.

At five to six, the house phone rang. Without thinking, I picked up the receiver.

"We know where you live, bitch. We're coming for you."

A gravelly voice with a Yorkshire accent, using the word that had been sprayed onto my car.

Hutchinson's family.

"Piss off, moron."

Then, as I put the phone down, I thought, half-witted idiot – they really do know you're here now.

Suddenly I felt very cold. If I stayed in the refuge and there was trouble, I could be putting all the others at risk. They didn't deserve that. And I was going to Leeds the next day – surely I could cope with going a day early, and hanging around somewhere until the morning – Leeds Station, perhaps? That was it – decision made.

I dashed upstairs and loaded my possessions into my rucksack; that didn't take long. Then I came down and checked the bus timetable, kept next to the phone. There would be a bus to Shipley at half past six. From there, I could get the train direct to Leeds. I scribbled a note: *Gone to meet Martin. Thanks for everything – I'll be in touch.* I left it on the kitchen table.

It was six twenty-five.

I let myself out of the back door, glancing around carefully to make sure there were no occupied cars near the house. The street seemed empty, so I locked up and put the keys back through the letter box. Boats well and truly burned now. Then, treading carefully because it was slippery underfoot as the sleet froze on the cold paths, I walked as quickly as I could to the end of the road, turned left past the church and slipped and slithered down to the main road, just as the bus was appearing in the distance. The bus stop was about a hundred yards away, and I risked a hazardous jog, trying to stay on my feet. The bus passed me, but it stopped almost immediately to release a couple of passengers and I just made it before the doors closed. Without hesitation, I threw myself up the steps and on. I found change in my pocket for the fare. The bus lurched forwards and I collapsed into a seat near the front by a window. I turned back for some reason, and through the window, I saw a dark car turning left in front of the church, but I couldn't see who was driving it.

The bus carried me slowly into the cold night, on a journey to Shipley, which seemed interminable. The traffic was still pretty heavy, and there were frequent bus stops. I found myself looking intently at every new passenger, but no-one showed the slightest interest in me. Nevertheless, I shook quietly for the entire journey, even though it was warm and stuffy on the bus.

Just past Bradford Grammar School and Lister Park we turned right and trundled down the hill towards the bright lights of the town centre. My plan was to get off before the terminus, because I could then walk down the hill and turn right towards the station. As I walked as briskly as I could on the slippery pavements, I noticed the green and white sign of a Subway on the next corner. A decent club sandwich would set me up for the night, and would probably be cheaper than anything I could eat in Leeds. Plus I could buy another for breakfast.

I pushed open the door and went in. The menu was enormous, displayed above the counter with every possible combination of fillings, bread and extras. I sat on one of the plastic chairs at the back of the shop to check my finances before I ordered my food. My money belt was round my waist as usual, but when I opened it, instead of the ten-pound notes I was expecting, there was a small wad of toilet paper. My debit card had also gone. I understood bitterly, then, just exactly how Sharon and Vanessa had funded their Christmas shopping.

That was the end of my evening meal, and my breakfast. I stared at my empty purse numbly, all appetite instantly gone, wondering how the hell I was going to get to Leeds.

Then I had a thought. I checked my coat pockets for more loose change and there – miracle of miracles – was the ten-pound note I had taken out to pay Pat on the night her taxi dropped me at the refuge. I breathed deeply, trying to compose myself. I knew the fare I needed was probably only about four pounds fifty, so it would be enough. I *was* going to Leeds.

There was no point in hanging about. I wanted to buy my ticket and climb onto a train, to start the journey away from all the horror and back to Martin. But first I had to get to the station. With a pounding heart I left the Subway and set off across the main road, before turning right by the familiar large M of the station sign. A mixture of freezing rain and sleet was falling, blown painfully into my still-bruised face by a sharp wind.

The narrow road to the car park and ticket office took a matter of seconds by car, but on foot I had to negotiate a dark path with a high wall on one side and a scrubby, steeply banked hedge leading to shrubby undergrowth on the other. In the past, I would have strode boldly on, unperturbed by the night, the cold, the shadows. But now I kept checking that no-one was following me, and avoiding eye contact with anyone walking towards me.

I had thought at this time on a Wednesday night it would be very quiet, but there was a surprising number of people, both on foot and in cars, all leaving the station – especially as I hadn't heard any trains. A half-empty bus passed me, taking commuters into the centre of Shipley. It seemed like a long, hard walk, but after a few minutes, I rounded the bend and saw an empty car park in front of me – empty, that is, apart from one car.

Clutching the money in my pocket, I went into the ticket office, but there was no-one in the booth. Then I noticed an elderly man in uniform sweeping out the waiting room, adjacent to where I was standing. Through the open door, I could see a second door leading, I assumed, onto the platform.

I called to him, with mounting apprehension.

"Sorry, lass, no trains now 'til tomorrow. Points are frozen all t' way down t' line. Best come back in t' mornin'."

Oh God. I couldn't go back to the refuge – someone obviously knew where it was – and I had very little money and no debit card to access any that Martin might have put into my account, even if Vanessa and Sharon hadn't spent it all on contactless purchases, which was pretty unlikely.

"Please," I said. "Please, I need to get to Leeds tonight. I've nowhere else to go. What can I do?" I was shaking again, and close to tears.

"Nay, dun't tek on, lass. Get a taxi – roads are fine."

"I've only got ten pounds, so I can't. I just can't. I don't know what to do… I haven't even got a sleeping bag."

He shook his head. "Well, I don't know, I'm sure."

I tried a new tack. "Would it… could I… possibly wait in the waiting room?"

"What – all neet?"

I held my breath.

"I'm not supposed to let anyone doss overnight, but… look. I've a granddaughter your age. I'd hate to see her in your predicament. Just stop cryin' and come in 'ere."

The Waiting Room was warm, heated by a little stove, similar to mine. Next to it was a scuttle-full of coke; to the right were Gents and Ladies toilets, and to the left, a vending machine. The room was lined with benches all along the walls; three large high windows, two on each side of the platform door and one at the car park side, were covered by grey blinds. The station master bent over, opened the stove door and loaded more coke in, so that flames leapt till he slammed the door shut. Then he went and fed some coins into the machine and put a large steaming paper cup on the bench, along with an enormous chunky KitKat.

"Now then, lass, just think on. Keep t' blinds down and t' lights off, and if yuh know what's good for yuh, keep topping up t' stove wi' coke and don't let it go aht. If I were you," he added, "I'd get them soakin' boots off, and yer jacket. Stick 'em close ter t'stove – they should be dry by mornin'. And… yuh've ter promise not to blab to anyone, else there'll be a 'ole army o'dossers 'ere tommorer."

"I promise! And thank you so much…"

"Aye, well, yuh'll be all right now. Fust train's due at six, but I doubt it'll come, and any road it dun't stop 'ere. Fust one you could catch will be at eight. Someone'll come ter open up around half-seven. I'll be lockin' t' main door terneet, but yuh can still gerrout onto t' platform - it's locked off from t'car park, so yuh'll be safe if anyone comes. Which I doubt they will. Reet?"

I nodded, grateful beyond words, yet again, for the kindness of a stranger.

After he'd locked up, and his car headlights had disappeared, I laid my coat out on the floor by the stove, took off my boots and turned them on their sides, so that the heat would dry them inside. They were proper hiking boots and they'd kept my feet mercifully dry. But I felt reluctant to turn out the lights. The clock on the platform side of the waiting room revealed that it was just after eight-thirty. Less than twelve hours to wait, I told myself, before the train.

Finally, I compromised with the lights; I checked both toilets to make sure they really were empty, then propped the door to the Ladies' open with my rucksack, leaving the lights on in there. I hoped, as I plunged the waiting room into semi-darkness, that they'd be invisible from outside. Then I settled down with my hot chocolate and KitKat, and my copy of Poldark, and read for a while by the light from the open stove door. It got so warm that I had to move myself and my gear back a couple of feet, and remove my thick jumper, rolling it up to put under my head later.

Eventually, I stopped making sense of the words, which seemed to dance in front of my eyes. I got wearily to my feet, used the toilet, washed as best I could and cleaned my teeth with my finger (as I'd left my sponge bag in the bathroom at the refuge). Then I closed the door of the stove and stretched out on the hard floor, head on my woolly jumper, with only the sonorous ticking of the clock breaking the complete silence. I closed my eyes.

***

Sometime later, I woke from a strange dream, thinking the station master had come back in and was pushing his brush across the floor. But in the half-light I could see there was no-one else in the waiting room. Then I heard it again, the noise that had woken me – a slow, low sliding, as if something – or someone – was being pulled across the platform just outside the window. I had to know what it was.

Cautiously, I approached the window onto the platform, stood on the bench, lifted the heavy blind and peered out.

I was looking straight into the eyes of a large fox, its front paws on the bin under the window. It regarded me calmly for a couple of long seconds before clearly deciding I was no threat. Then it dived back into the depths of the bin, moving it along a few inches as it struggled to extract something. I watched, completely fascinated, as it popped up out of the bin and stepped back, tipping it onto its side. Then its head darted in again, and this time came out with the red and gold box of a discarded burger. After some determined pawing, it was through the cardboard and devouring the contents. Then it went back into the bin again, but this time it apparently failed to find anything. It backed out and stood sniffing the air, one speculative paw raised. It was magnificent – long reddish winter fur, tinged with grey – an old, experienced animal, wise enough to scavenge for its supper where wasteful people dumped their leftovers. It looked up at me again, acknowledging my presence, then turned and loped steadily away across the railway line. The last glimpse I had of it was its grey-tipped tail as it dived into the bramble bushes on the far side of the tracks.

I was alone again, but moved by what I'd seen. I never cease to be amazed by the power of nature, the will to survive in the harshest conditions. How could anyone bear the thought of such a creature being illegally destroyed for sport? I knew Martin would agree with me – he was passionate about protecting animals, contributed regularly to animal welfare charities and refused to buy products with palm oil because of the destruction of the orangutans' habitat. And I wished, again, that he had been there with me to share the fox's visit – or that I'd had my phone to take a picture.

I topped up the stove, which had burned down to glowing embers, then lay down again. But sleep wouldn't come this time. I couldn't find a comfortable position, and there was a niggling fear at the back of my mind, which as dawn approached, became a stomach-churning worry. What if Martin didn't turn up?

Chapter Sixteen

Thursday, December 21ˢᵗ

The light gradually started filtering through the grey blinds. I couldn't quite make out the clock, so I painfully staggered to my feet to stare at it. A few minutes after six. Where was the through train? What could I do if it didn't come? Then suddenly I heard it. I flew to the door out onto the platform and opened it to a blur of train hurtling past towards Leeds, along with a blast of freezing air. I hurriedly closed the door again and threw the last of the coke into the stove. The trains were running. Two more hours, then I'd be on my way.

I used the ladies again, longing for my toothbrush. Then I stretched out on the narrow bench against the wall, but the floor was more comfortable. Eventually, I heard a car drawing into the car park. I hastily put on my warm dry boots, jumper and jacket, wondering how I was going to explain my presence in the waiting room, behind a locked door. But it wasn't a problem. The station was opened again, but the first thing that happened was that the person in charge went straight into the office behind the ticket booth. I heard a tap running, then the clink of a cup. Priorities.

I waited ten minutes or so, then crept out and opened, then closed, the door to the ticket office. The hatch in the booth was raised, and a woman said. "Morning. Leeds, is it?"

"Please – just a single."

"Four fifty. Thanks. Train's due in about fifteen minutes. Platform One. Through there."

I smiled and went into the Waiting Room.

***

Thirty-five minutes later I was in Leeds Station, jostling my way along the crowded platform, up an escalator, across a bridge, down another escalator, through the barrier and out onto the busy concourse. I should have stopped for a coffee, but by then all I wanted to do was walk across Leeds to get to the Playhouse. I headed off to my left, down the steps and through the covered walkway, past the ticket booths and Starbucks, to emerge onto the street at the side of the station. But as soon as I set foot on the pavement, my feet went from under me and I crashed to the ground onto the sheen of invisible black ice.

I sat for a moment, aware of the cold wet surface seeping through my jeans but too shocked to move. No-one stopped or asked me if I needed help, because people were all struggling to keep their feet. I had fetched up against a railing at the side of the road, so I slowly pulled myself upright, conscious of the return of the sharp pain in my ribs. My jeans had torn at the knee and my hand was bleeding where I'd scraped it along the flagstone trying to break my fall. If I'd had the energy, I'd have howled with despair. But suddenly, into my head came the fleeting vision of that resourceful fox the previous night, out surviving in the bitter cold. I wasn't finished yet.

Leaning against the railing and rummaging in my rucksack, I pulled out a pair of dirty woollen hiking socks and stretched them on over my boots. I put my first foot down tentatively, hanging onto the railing. The difference was amazing – it wasn't perfect, but I had a much better grip. I pulled on the second sock and cautiously tottered on across the road and up towards the Headrow, the broad dual carriage-way that runs through the heart of the city, past the Magistrates' Court, the Town Hall and the Central Library and down towards the Ring Road.

It took me far longer to walk to the Playhouse than I'd anticipated. Going uphill or on the flat wasn't too bad, but the minute the Headrow started to go downhill, the pavement moved from treacherous to lethal. By that point, my socks had great holes in them. I sat on a freezing bench and took them off, turning them round before replacing them so that the holes were now over the laces, but it was obvious that they wouldn't last much longer. But I was so close – I would crawl the last half mile to the damned theatre if I had to.

To make matters worse, a vicious icy wind rattled between the buildings, blowing gritty sleet into my face. As I made my faltering way across the slippery pavements, I noticed large cardboard boxes, piles of old blankets, semi-erected tents in front of many of the disused doorways towards the bottom of the Headrow, where the shops had petered out. I knew that every one of them contained a poor soul trying to survive and keep warm, and I knew that soon there would be deaths, which would probably go unreported. These people had fallen out of the system and ceased to count. But I could do nothing to help, at least not that day. Unless this longed-for rendezvous didn't happen. Then I'd be joining them.

Finally reaching the bottom of the hill, I could see the Playhouse, across a busy roundabout that directed traffic out of Leeds. I couldn't possibly just launch myself into the streams of cars, so I was obliged to detour to my left, crossing several smaller roads that fed into the roundabout until I reached the same side as the theatre. Then I walked slowly up the wide drive that ended at the building, past the rough ground that became a car park at show times, until I arrived at the theatre door.

I pushed it open and went in. There was hardly anyone about, although there were a couple of eager punters queuing for pantomime tickets at the box office counter on the right. I joined the queue.

When my turn came, the woman on the other side barely looked at me.

"Yes, which show would you like?"

"No, I don't actually want to—"

"Sorry? I can't hear you."

I cleared my throat.

"No, I'm looking for someone. Martin Prescott Smith? He's the new Playmaker and due here today for a meeting about his job, which starts after Christmas."

She looked up then, and saw me properly for the first time. A dirty scrap, greasy hair pulled into a straggling ponytail, with a blood smudge on her cheek and a dark purple bruise covering half her face. If she'd looked down, she'd also have taken in the filthy, mud-spattered jeans with the bloody hole in the right knee.

She raised her eyebrows.

"Just a minute."

She disappeared into the room behind the counter and looked at a computer screen. Then she came back.

"I'm sorry, Mr Prescott Smith rang yesterday to say he couldn't make the meeting. He won't be in now until the New Year."

Oh God, no. Please no.

Panic raised my voice and gave it a confidence I certainly didn't feel.

"He told me he'd be here on the 21st – he was coming back from Singapore on the 19th! Are you sure?"

"Of course I am. Actually, he said he couldn't come in because he was trying to find a member of his family who'd gone miss—"

"That's right, that's me! Alison Weston! I'm his partner and I've been homeless for three weeks. Please, *please* could you just ring him and tell him I'm here? Please?"

She looked dubious.

"Do you have any proof of your identity? Why can't you just ring him yourself?"

"Because... because I don't have my phone. It was... it was—"

Thrown under my bed by my rapist, I wanted to say – but of course I didn't.

"—stolen. And I c-can't remember his n-number..."

It sounded pretty lame, even to me.

"Well, I don't know if you are who you say you are – you could be anyone. Our employees are entitled to confidentiality. I can't just be disturbing Mr Prescott Smith for no reason—"

"No, it's really me. I am Alison Weston – look!"

I scrabbled in my rucksack, pulled out my purse and showed her my union card with my name on it.

"How do I know you haven't just stolen this from the real Alison Weston? This isn't proof of your—"

"Oh for God's sake!" came an irritated voice from behind me, "Just phone him or get someone else to do it. What harm can it do? There's a queue here, in case you hadn't noticed."

She looked grim, but disappeared again into the back room. I saw her through the open door, talking to a younger man, who glanced in my direction and nodded. Another woman came out.

"Stand to one side, please," she said to me, rather coolly. "Now, sorry for your wait, madam. Which show would you like?"

The door behind her was closed quietly. I waited and waited, trying not to think, but anxiety was churning my stomach and I felt vaguely sick. Eventually the first woman came back. She looked grim. I thought I'd pass out then, and the world roared in my ears as the foyer went dark.

Dimly, as if from a great distance, I heard her say, "—ten minutes and you're not to leave the theatre."

"He's c-coming?" I managed eventually.

"I've just said so, haven't I? Now move right away from here, so you don't disturb any more of our customers."

I bent over, and the world gradually came back into focus.

There was nowhere to sit, so I hobbled slowly to the stairs going up to the deserted coffee bar and the main auditorium and slumped down, leaning against the bannister. And there I sat as my knee throbbed, my headache returned and a dull familiar ache in the pit of my stomach warned me that I certainly wasn't pregnant. *Perfect timing*, I thought bitterly. How the hell was I supposed to deal with that? I had no more energy left even to watch the door for Martin.

There were a few false alarms when cold draughts of air flooded in as people came and left. *Why was he taking so long? What if he'd had second thoughts? What if he'd had an accident?* As the minutes ticked on, my despair became absolute. He wasn't coming, he'd have arrived by then. I had no plan at all to fall back on, and I'd surely be thrown out of the building before the matinee audiences arrived.

I became aware of someone standing in front of me, and I braced myself to try and argue for a few more minutes.

"Alison?"

Here we go.

I looked up, briefly, and then dropped my head, realising I had no more fight left in me – I doubted I could even walk to the door. With a huge effort I looked up again.

"What the bloody hell are you playing at? I have been half out of my mind since – oh great God in heaven…!"

Martin knelt down and looked at me, then reached out to touch my face. I flinched away.

"What's happened to you? Why didn't you text me? Who the hell did this to you? Oh God… do we need an ambulance?"

"No. I was discharged from hospital last week. I'm ok, just very cold and sore… and tired." I was whispering, but his face was close to mine.

"Really? Christ… Are you *sure* you're ok?"

I nodded.

"Right, well, let's get you up and out of here. Can you stand? That's it, come on, I've got you…"

"B-but… where can we go? Where will we sleep tonight?"

He looked astonished that I'd asked. Then I think some of the implications of where I might have been began to dawn on him.

"No, no, don't worry, don't worry, I've got a room in a hotel near the station. It's really nice – we'll be fine."

I let him hold me then, at last, and I leaned all my weight on him. Even through his thick jacket I could feel the strength of him, and the warmth, and the comfort of another body, and my shivering gradually stopped. Slowly, we walked together towards the door, Martin carrying my precious rucksack. Then we were out again in the bitter air and the grey sky, although the sleet had stopped.

"Look, the car's just there. Not far now, that's it, you can do it. Here we are."

The door clicked open and I was able to get myself in and put on my seat belt. Then I closed my eyes. Martin started the car.

A while later it stopped and I opened them again to find we were in an underground car park.

"Just a ride up in the lift now," Martin said, "then you can relax."

In a couple of minutes we'd reached the top floor of the hotel, and Martin led me to a door he opened with a key card. His room was enormous. It had a huge bed opposite a picture window showing me a panorama of the snowy Leeds rooftops, and the flakes that were once again falling from that grey sky. The bathroom had a walk-in shower and some expensive-looking gels and creams on the shelf by the square wash basin. And it was warm, so warm. I just stood and stared at it, and Martin watched me.

Eventually, I whispered, "Can I please have a shower? I just feel so…"

"Of course you can, you need to get out of those wet things. Look, there's a laundry service, and I've got some washing to do as well, so I suggest we fill the bag in the wardrobe and I'll sort it out. And I'll probably need to nip out and get you some more jeans, won't I? And maybe a jumper. Is there anything else you need?"

"Toothbrush... and tampons," I added bleakly, but he didn't bat an eyelid.

"No problem."

I took off my jacket and he found a large laundry bag and started shovelling in the filthy clothes from my rucksack. Slowly, I peeled off sweatshirt, jeans, socks, tights, thermal tee shirt and then—

"Bloody hell! Look at the state of you! What on earth's happened?"

"I fell. On the way from the station, on the black ice."

"You didn't get those bruises today though, did you? Allie, what on earth? Have you been beaten up? Oh, tell me it wasn't that man from the Blenheim? The one you were worried about? Was it just a beating or did he—"

I held up my hand. "Please, Martin, not now, I can't. I will tell you about it, later, but please can I have some water now? I'm so thirsty... and I could do with something to eat."

He went to the fridge and handed me out a bottle of sparkling water and a packet of peanuts. His face was pale behind his beard.

"Get your shower then, and I'll drop this laundry off as I go out for the stuff you need. And I'll order us some pizza when I get back."

He didn't say anything else, or attempt to touch me again. He just picked up his wallet, threw on his jacket and stalked out, slamming the door behind him.

It was hardly the reaction I'd expected, but I was too tired to be concerned. I went slowly into the bathroom and washed my underwear in the washbasin, using the posh liquid soap, then rinsed it and rubbed it dry on a hand towel and left it draped over the bathroom radiator. Then I had a long, long shower, washing my hair twice and conditioning it. The towels were large and warm. I wrapped one round my hair, a larger one around me, then borrowed Martin's toothbrush to clean my teeth. Finally, I rummaged around in the bottom of my rucksack and found a half-empty, slightly crushed box of tampons, and, right at the bottom, the little picture, still in its bubble wrap, which I'd bought for Martin so long ago. I put that back; now was definitely *not* the time to hand it over.

After going back into the bathroom with the tampons, I found a hair drier in the dressing-table drawer. As I sat blow-drying my hair, I thought, finally, about Martin's reaction to the state of my body. It must have been a shock, I reasoned, but there was nothing I could do to alter that. It certainly didn't excuse his behaviour, running away from unpleasant facts and leaving me like that, alone in a hotel bedroom, when for once I really needed him.

I looked at myself in the mirror properly for the first time in several days. I looked gaunt and haunted, the shadows under my eyes, and the bruise, giving my face an unfamiliar appearance. I certainly didn't look like the woman he'd left four weeks ago, and I didn't feel like her, either. Not anymore.

When my hair was dry, I thought I'd have a rest for a while, just for the sheer luxury of lying flat out with clean sheets and pillows. I dropped the damp towels onto the bathroom floor and put on the white velvet bathrobe that hung on the door. Then I devoured a second packet of peanuts and a bar of chocolate from the fridge and finished off my bottle of water, before getting into the huge bed. It was three forty-five, according to the clock on the table, and the light was almost gone outside.

I lay there, thinking about the last twenty-four hours, and Martin. I had thought of nothing more than getting to the Playhouse and reuniting with him – that hope, and longing, had kept me going through everything. And now I was apparently safe, I felt... nothing. Martin was just a man, after all, who had once loved me and perhaps did so still; but he was far from perfect. He was the sort of man who avoided difficult situations, not facing them head on but walking away instead. Sometimes he came back. Once, long ago, he hadn't. What would he do this time?

I was too exhausted to worry about that. My mind wandered and sleep overtook me.

***

I woke with a start, hearing a rattling at the door. Forgetting the recent past, I thought I was back in Manningham and Hutchinson was trying to get in. Then I remembered where I was, but as I heard the door opening quietly, and someone coming towards me through the dark, I was overwhelmed by complete terror. Pulling the quilt around me, I edged back against the bed head. I could hear a faint whimpering, and realised it was coming from me, but my eyes were screwed tight shut so I didn't have to see what was approaching the bed. Then the bedside lamp went on.

"Allie! Hey, Allie, it's me, it's Martin – you're quite safe. Come on, love, shush. Open your eyes, *please*"

No, no, it was a trick, he was impersonating Martin who was in Singa—

I was suddenly enveloped in a very familiar embrace as Martin sat on the bed and pulled me to him. His hand gently rubbed my back, and he was rocking me as you would a terrified child awakening from a nightmare. And I did wake then, properly, and was instantly mortified.

"Oh God, I'm sorry, I'm so sorry, I thought you were... I thought *he'd* found me..."

"No, you've got nothing to be sorry for. I just didn't want to wake you. I should have said something. Don't worry, don't worry, you're safe now. Just breathe, just breathe... That's better."

He took the crumpled quilt from me and pulled it down and away. Then he took my face lightly in his hands and looked at me intensely.

"I'll never let him hurt you again. I would kill him first. I mean that. Yes?"

It was what I'd needed to hear. I nodded but I couldn't speak.

"Ok then. Now let's stop worrying about that cowardly excuse for a human being and think about shopping and pizza. Right?"

I nodded slowly, and when I looked down, I noticed the large carrier bags he'd dropped near the bed. He'd bought me jeans, a sweater and a red Christmas jumper with a black cat embroidered on the front, sitting next to a green Christmas tree. There was also a pair of black leather ankle boots, some new socks and a smart navy duffle jacket with a hood. In another carrier bag were a toothbrush, a new face flannel, some deodorant and my tampons.

"I'm speechless," I said quietly. "You've even bought my usual size – for everything. Thank you so much."

"Don't mention it," he said. "Not just a pretty face, eh?"

"Not even..." I said – and we laughed, just a little.

Then he said, "Listen, Allie, seriously, I'm sorry for the way I reacted earlier. It was just such a shock, and I was so angry that some slob had hurt you. I just couldn't deal with it. But I tell you this, and I mean every word – *I* will never, ever, ask you to do anything you're not happy with. I'm not an animal and I won't touch you – like that – until you show me you're ready. I promise. And you don't have to tell me anything if you don't want to. Let's just get through this together, ok?"

"Thank you," I whispered. "But there is one thing I have to tell you…"

And I told him about the HIV test I needed in mid-March. He nodded silently and held me again for a long time. Then our food arrived, along with the immaculately clean laundry. They'd even mended the rip in my jeans

Later, after consuming unthinkable amounts and drinking the beer and half a bottle of white wine from the fridge, Martin suddenly said, "God, what a complete klutz I am! Why didn't I think of that before?" and he took out his phone.

"What are you doing?"

"Ringing your number."

"Oh no, don't, please don't. What if he answers? He'll see you come up as Martin on the phone and he'll know!"

"He'll know I'll be sending the police round."

"Oh Martin, *no*…!"

"Sh!"

It was too late. It was ringing, I could hear it. Then it was answered.

"Da?" said a deep Eastern European voice.

"Oh good evening. Am I speaking to Mr Russell Barry Hutchinson?"

Barry?

"Nyet. This man is not… available. Look in papers."

The line went dead.

"What did he mean?" I whispered.

"Let's find out."

Martin had his laptop open and was Googling the name. Instantly several links appeared; at the top of the list was an article from the most recent *Telegraph* and *Argus*, Bradford's local paper. He clicked onto it and I read it over his shoulder.

Canal Corpse Identified

Police today confirmed that the badly-beaten male body pulled from the Leeds-Liverpool canal at Shipley last week was that of Russell Clive Hutchinson, wanted in connection with the death of a man found recently in a Bradford hotel cellar, and also with a serious unrelated sexual assault, which took place at the same location.

An inquest into the cause of death has been adjourned, pending a full post-mortem.

Mr Hutchinson's family has been informed.

"Christ…" Martin said quietly.

Chapter Seventeen
Christmas 2017

On Christmas morning, I woke up in yet another strange bed, listening to the sound of the sea. Martin slept on next to me. We were in a very fine apartment on the top floor of a sea-front former hotel in Filey. Martin had arranged it while he was in Singapore as a surprise, and had fortunately forgotten about cancelling it when he discovered I was missing.

Over the previous days, one issue had been resolved.

It had happened on the 22nd of December. We'd gone into Leeds and found a very expensive chocolate shop. Martin had insisted on buying the biggest box they sold, all wrapped up in glossy Christmas paper, as well as a child's goody bag of Christmas treats, and a chocolate rose for me ("Because it's our anniversary, isn't it? Nineteen years ago today. Remember?"). Then we drove back to Bradford and I left him in the car on Manningham Lane whilst I walked as quickly as I could up the road past the church and round the corner to the women's refuge.

Eunice was quite emotional when she saw me – relieved that I was all right, but also very angry.

"I've something to tell you," she said, "and you won't like it any more than I do."

When she'd come to the refuge the previous Thursday morning, Rosie had quietly told her that, while she'd been in the school toilets the night before, changing out of her Wise Woman costume after the Nativity play, she'd overheard Sharon and Vanessa giggling about a "funny phone call" they'd just made, pretending to be "a nasty woman using a bad word." And they'd found it even more funny, she said, that "the stuck-up cow" wouldn't be able to run away because she didn't have any money or her debit card, and, as Rosie reported, one of them said, "she's given us a brilliant Christmas!".

"When she came home and saw your note, poor Rosie burst into tears. Her mum was upstairs, and Sharon and Vanessa heard her first. They told her if she didn't shut up, or if she told anyone, they'd get rid of her mum as well. She didn't dare ring me up in case they heard, so she'd kept quiet until yesterday morning. Then she waited till they'd gone out.

"I was so angry!" Eunice said. "Especially when I thought about what a vile, cold night we'd just had. I was worried sick about you, but by the time I found out, of course it was too late to do anything to help you. I did ring the theatre, though, and when I explained the situation, they confirmed you had actually met Martin. I was so relieved. But then I got straight on the phone to Social Services and told them I wasn't having either Sharon or Vanessa under this roof a moment longer, that they were dangerous thieves and there was a child living here. Before they knew what had hit them, Pat had come in her taxi to take them to a hostel in Wakefield. Serves them right."

In that moment, I felt a great weight, which I hadn't even realised was there, lift from my shoulders. That terrifying phone call hadn't come from Hutchinson's family, or the gang that had taken him.

I said goodbye to Eunice, promising to keep in touch, and left the chocolates with her – she said she'd put them under the tree before she left on Christmas Eve. "But it'll be my last Christmas here," she said sadly before I left. "The council's closing us down in the New Year. They've no more funding."

I was speechless.

***

Martin then drove me up Marlborough Road, past the still boarded-up Blenheim Hotel and the Marlborough Superstore. I agreed to take him to meet Sabrina and her family when they finally came back from Pakistan.

Next, we drove back to Ilkley and Martin bought a bright bunch of Christmas flowers from a florist's in the town centre. Then we drove on to the supermarket and I left them for Margaret, along with a card. I was disappointed not to see her, but she was due to start work later because the supermarket would be open until nine that night.

Then, because I felt exhausted, we returned to our Leeds hotel.

We talked properly at last, after eating room service burgers and fries. Martin told me about coming back from Singapore earlier than he'd planned, frantic because I wasn't answering his texts. He'd sent the money as he'd promised, but when he'd tried to contact me to check I'd got it, he'd had no reply. The Esplanade management had been very supportive, and agreed to release him a couple of days before the end of his contract. He'd finally reached Bradford on Tuesday and found the Blenheim boarded up as a crime scene, the tape still in place. He'd gone straight to the police, desperate for information.

"I was seriously worried, of course, because it was so unlike you to be out of contact like that. Especially after what you'd told me about the Blenheim."

But all they'd tell him was that I was alive and in a women's refuge somewhere. The next day, "after a sleepless night in a hotel in Shipley", he'd gone back to Bradford and tried the Housing Options office and they did agree to ring the Refuge – but there was no reply. The Duty Officer from Housing Options continued trying to ring into the early evening, but by the time someone did answer the phone, I'd already left. They'd at least passed on my message about going to Leeds to meet him. He'd booked a room in Leeds in despair, because he'd rung the theatre to explain why he couldn't make the meeting, and was distraught when the person on telephone duty that evening had confirmed that I hadn't shown up. She'd promised to let him know immediately if I arrived before the theatre closed.

After another sleepless night ("I was sure they'd be pulling your body out of the river in the centre"), the Box Office had rung. "I ran to the lift, jumped in the car and drove across Leeds like a lunatic. When I saw you sitting on the stairs, I admit I was beside myself – I thought you'd been playing games with me, until you looked up. Then I was so shocked…"

I thought about the state of my face and understood perfectly.

Later, we went to bed. As we rested on our backs side by side, he told me about the Filey trip. Then he turned, took my hand and held it, letting his lips brush my face and linger briefly on my mouth, before turning away and murmuring, "Night night, God bless."

I lay in the dark, grateful that for the second night running it had been so easy. I felt nothing else.

The next day, the 23rd, after checking out, we headed away from Leeds on the A64 and drove past York and on towards the coast. In less than two hours we were on the front in Filey, parking just opposite the white Victorian building that housed our apartment. After picking up our keys on the ground floor, we lugged our bags up two flights of stairs and into our Christmas accommodation. When we got in, we were touched to see that the owners had left a basic box of groceries in the kitchen, a card wishing us a happy Christmas holiday and a real Christmas tree, already trimmed, and complete with a present underneath, in the living room.

We unpacked and then went out into the crisp sea air to walk up the steep hill into the town to find some fish and chips, after we'd stocked up on fruit and fresh vegetables plus a fat free-range chicken and a Christmas pudding. Martin had a miniature bottle of brandy, bought on the plane home from Singapore, with which to flame it on Christmas Day.

All this could have been so romantic. But there was a numbness inside me, an emptiness. I was almost grateful that the HIV test couldn't happen until mid-March. At least I didn't have to explain why the thought of any type of physical contact, beyond hugs and hand-holding, filled me with cold horror. I still loved Martin, and I felt immeasurably grateful for his company, his unquestioning understanding and his unshakeable trust. I just didn't honestly know if I could ever feel anything more again.

So, on Christmas morning, I lay and listened to the rise and fall of the sea, so close beneath our window, and to the calling of the gulls, one of which had cheekily perched on the balcony outside and was eyeing me curiously through the gap in the curtains. Martin slept on beside me.

Quietly, I slipped out of bed and found my rucksack on a chair in the next-door living room. I fumbled about in the bottom of it until my fingers touched the little, bubble-wrapped parcel. I had no fancy paper, but I didn't think Martin would mind. I put it under the tree, noticing that a third parcel seemed to have appeared.

Much later, when we'd showered, dressed and eaten some buttery croissants, we opened the parcels. There was a box of Belgian chocolates from the apartment's owners. Martin had found me a stunning silk kimono in black, with a peacock embroidered on the back in shades of turquoise, jade and vivid blue. And there was something else, something in a little box that he took from the pocket of his jacket.

"I want you to wear it for me," he said. "This isn't a proposal, but I'd like to think of you always with this on your finger. Any finger you like," he added.

It was a silver Celtic ring, an elaborate knotting of strands around a double heart. I looked at him, and I didn't know what to say. Finally, feeling like a complete fraud but unable to do anything else, I held out my left hand, and he slipped the ring onto my third finger. Then he pulled me to him, and hugged me so fiercely I thought my ribs would break again.

"We'll be all right, it'll be good again, I promise. Just take your time."

I couldn't speak.

Eventually, I passed him the final gift from under the tree.

"I saw this in a craft fair in Ilkley," I told him quietly. "The man selling it asked me if it was for someone special, and when I told him it was, but I couldn't afford it, he let me have it for much less than the asking price."

He pulled off the bubble wrap. The sonnet, in a beautifully even, tiny italic hand, began:

Let me not to the marriage of true minds admit impediment.
Love is not love which alters when it alteration finds,
Nor bends with the remover to remove.....

He read it aloud, slowly and with feeling, and closed his eyes. Then he looked at me, and I nodded.

"Yes," I said, "An ever fixed mark, that looks on tempests and is never shaken..."

And I hoped so much that it could be the truth, one day.

On Boxing Day, our last day in Filey, we went for a long, blustery walk along Filey Brig, that spit of land that sticks out at the north end of the bay. It was wild and wet and invigorating; talking was impossible over the roar of the sea, and the blast of the winter gale. At one point the wind was so strong that I clutched Martin for support, and was glad of his instant arm round my waist. We walked all the way back to the car park, welded together at the hip, and when we arrived at the car, finally, he kissed me properly, long and deep and salty, and I didn't pull away. I felt, momentarily, as if the ice was melting.

There was another surprise that evening. We were sitting together comfortably, when something occurred to me. In the emotional upheaval of the last few days, I had totally forgotten that when this break ended, we would be homeless once more.

"What are we going to do?" I asked.

"God, didn't I tell you? I'm so sorry, I'm an idiot yet again. Look at this!"

Opening his lap top, Martin showed me an e-mail dated the middle of December. It was from the estate agents who managed the cottage. They were very sorry, they said, but they'd recently received a message from Mr and Mrs Patel, our tenants. They were both doctors, and both had obtained positions in Manchester hospitals, to start after Christmas. After discussing it, they'd come to the conclusion that they couldn't face the journey across the Pennines, so they'd decided, with regret, to terminate their tenancy and move out at the end of December. They felt it was only fair to pay their rent until the end of March. The estate agents wanted to know whether we wanted them to start the process of re-letting the property, but Martin had replied from Singapore that he needed to discuss it with me.

Now there was nothing to discuss. We were going home.

Chapter Eighteen
January 2018

The cottage was, if anything, cleaner than we'd left it. The coal bunker was full and they'd even filled the scuttle and laid the fire ready to light. It didn't quite smell like home – there was a scented candle in every room including the bathroom – but it was so good to be back, nevertheless.

Pete and Cath were due back from Bali on the 28th, so we couldn't collect our possessions until then. On the afternoon of the 29th (to give them time to recover from jet lag), I sent Cath a text. She immediately invited us round on New Year's Eve, first of all to load Pete's van and deliver our stuff, then to see the New Year in with them, staying the night. So I spent the next day cooking a huge coq au vin and making garlic bread to go with it, as well as a salad. Cath had promised one of her special clementine jellies, and loads of cheese, fruit and red wine. At that point, they had no idea what had happened whilst they'd been away, or why we'd decided to return to our cottage.

Eventually, when we were all sitting together waiting for the casserole and garlic bread to heat through, drinking a mellow Shiraz and nibbling olives and crisps, I told them the whole story. There was complete silence when I'd finished – what could they possibly say? Cath studied her red wine, her face pale, then finally Pete said. "Well, I'm glad that bastard's dead. He had it coming. And if I ever come across those two cows I'm going to—"

"—join the queue." Martin finished. "There won't be much left to do after I've seen them."

That's when I dissolved into tears again. I was home, I was safe, I had my friends around me who were angry on my behalf. So why couldn't I feel good again? Why was I so weepy?

"Oh come on," said Cath, passing me a tissue. "It's over now, you've survived. Think positive – put it behind you."

I knew she meant well – dear Cath, always trying to offer practical help and support – but it wasn't as easy as that. In the quiet moments, it preyed on my mind, and at night I dreamed about the people I'd encountered, and those shapeless forms struggling in Leeds's doorways. There was no-one to rescue them, no-one to surround them in love and warmth – certainly not in a country that had once set such great store by helping the vulnerable. I knew that throughout my life I would always remember a little of how that felt, and I would do whatever I could to explain it to others. But not at that point, not on New Year's Eve.

As we cleared away plates after dinner, Cath noticed the ring I was wearing.

"Does this mean we should open champagne?"

"No," I said, "We're not getting married any time soon. But I suppose it's a sign of commitment."

"Why isn't Martin wearing one?"

"Because I haven't bought him one yet."

She looked at me for a moment, but didn't say anything else. If we'd been alone, I would have confided in her. Perhaps I would, one day. I valued her objectivity and common sense more than I could ever tell her – but I never bought him that ring.

***

At midnight, all of us well-fed and definitely the worse for red wine, we actually joined hands and sang 'Auld Lang Syne' – we didn't usually, but it felt significant to be leaving that old year behind. And I was glad, in years to come, that we'd shared that moment, even if it was drunken and teary. Afterwards, Pete kissed me first and then turned to Cath. Martin backed me away out into the hall, took me in his arms and kissed me with such ferocity that I could hardly breathe. Did I respond? Instinctively I did, and for a split second I thought the night was going to end with a mutual disrobing and a hearty session in the guest bedroom. But we couldn't – of course we couldn't, because apart from anything else, we had my HIV test hanging over us.

"I'm sorry," I gasped, pulling away. "Not yet… But I promise it won't be long now. Just two more months to wait, then… well… I think I will want to, I really do…"

Still holding me, he whispered into my hair, "That feels like a lifetime. I can't begin to tell you how much I miss your body…"

I couldn't in all honesty say the same thing to him. It was a sham, we were a sham, I wasn't being fair to Martin – but I couldn't face losing him – he was my best friend.

The cold January days stretched in front of us.

On the Wednesday after New Year, Martin started his job in Leeds. I wasn't expecting to go anywhere that day, so he left early to drive down and catch the train from Halifax, parking his car at the station. I lay in bed till late, wondering what to do with my time. The Patel's rent, supplemented by some of his Singapore earnings, had given us enough to live on till Martin received his first salary at the end of January. I couldn't face trying to get back into full-time teaching; nothing seemed worth doing.

I embarked, eventually, on a bit of writing – Martin had bought me a new lap top and smart phone, and the *Guardian* offer was still on the table. The problem was that I had to start from scratch with a daily blog, and I just couldn't bring myself to go over it all again. But describing the first few days might not be too difficult, I reasoned, so I made myself sit down and begin. I managed three paragraphs before I found myself staring out of the window at the grey hillside opposite. I gave up and deleted it all, and made a cake instead.

When Martin came back that evening, I was happy to listen to his account of his first day. It hadn't all been plain sailing.

"Christ, I don't know how you did it," he admitted. "Ten hulking great sixth-formers crammed into my airless, sweaty little office and me trying to enthuse them with the finer points of stage management – nightmare!"

"You need to get them out and backstage," I suggested. "Nobody can learn by sitting still and listening for hours on end – get them doing something as fast as possible."

"I will," he said. "Thanks."

He was especially pleased because he'd been asked to help with stage managing, if there was a need, later in the year. They'd pay him extra for that, and it was good to keep his hand in, he said.

"There might be something for you as well, love – they often need people in the Box Office or the coffee bar. It wouldn't be much, but it would give you a bit of money and some company when I was working… if you fancy it…?"

"Thanks for thinking of me," I said. "I might just do that."

But I can't say I much liked the idea of working with the two supercilious women I'd already encountered, on the day I staggered into the foyer to meet Martin. Still, it was kind of him to think of me.

The first weekend after the New Year was crisp and sunny, so we went out for a walk along a road that led to a farm track and petered out on a wild moor. It was easy walking in the good Yorkshire air; the wind had dropped for once, the snow was long gone and our boots carried us safely over the tussocky, springy grass. We reached a high point and stopped briefly to admire the track wending back down the hill, and the grey farm houses and dark green fir trees in the valley below. Martin turned to me, and took my face in his hands. The bruising had disappeared, finally, but my eyes still looked hollow and dark.

"I'm worried about you. You aren't sleeping, and you're not eating much. You're not happy, are you?"

Miserably, I shook my head.

"Is it me? Do you want me to move out?"

That was a shock and I felt cold suddenly. God, I didn't want that. But was I being fair? Was that what he wanted to do? He was looking at me intently. I met his eyes, and again I shook my head.

"I can't think of anything I want less. But I know, I *know* this is hard for you, too, isn't it? I feel as if it's all my stupid fault for being so naive, and for not telling you what was going on. And I know you're suffering too. And I can't… I don't want to… I don't want you to feel that you *have* to stay with me, if you'd rather… if you'd rather… oh God, I'm so sorry Martin…"

"Oh for fuck's sake, love, you don't have to be sorry. I mean, yeah, I admit you were a bit of an idiot – but now you're being a total drama queen. Of *course* I don't *want* to move out – how could you say that? I just want you to talk to me – and I know that's difficult because we just don't, do we? All this psycho-babble that some couples indulge in, we don't do that – but… but I need to know whether you still… you know… fancy me…?"

His voice trailed off. Poor Martin. How could I answer that? I didn't know myself.

But I had to say something.

"Honestly? The truth is I don't fancy anything at the moment. Every time I close my eyes I see something horrible – usually Hutchinson's face – and I still have this crazy fear of going out by myself, even though I know he's dead and his family don't know the first thing about me. But you're the only thing that's keeping me going, and the one thing I do know for certain is that I still love you."

And that, I realised, was the complete truth. Martin looked at me steadily for a minute and nodded.

"Well, that's all right, then." There wasn't a trace of irony in his voice. "My diagnosis, for what it's worth, is that you've got a bit of PTSD – post-traumatic stress whatsit. And frankly I'm not surprised, after what you've been through. But don't worry, you're stuck with me – I'm going nowhere unless you pack my bags and put them in the car for me – although that's not beyond the bounds of possibility if that stunt you pulled last autumn is anything to go by."

I smiled at that, relieved beyond words.

"Right," he said, "that's cleared the air a bit, I think. Let's head for home and put the kettle on. I'm desperate for a brew…"

He turned and headed down the hill, and I followed.

Chapter Nineteen

Spring

And so we carried on, day after day, going through the routines of life together, a little closer than we had been. As spring began and the days grew longer, things didn't seem quite so hopeless. I started taking Martin to the station and using the car to shop; I could cope with a crowded supermarket at last. We shared more laughter, at things we watched on TV, or Martin's stories and wicked impersonations of some of the kids who came for his courses. My appetite was slowly improving, and we went out for the occasional curry with Pete and Cath. And then there was Hartley.

One mild spring day at the beginning of March, I came home with bags of groceries to find a little black and white cat, with striking, black-rimmed golden eyes, sitting on the coal bunker, enjoying the sunshine. When he saw me, he stood up, arched his back in a stretch and purred when I stroked his ears. Then he jumped down and stood by the door, obviously waiting to be let in.

By the time Martin arrived that evening, the cat had polished off two tins of sardines in tomato sauce, been out, come back onto the front windowsill (where he mewed and scratched the glass until I gave in and admitted him) and was now curled up on our sheepskin rug in front of the stove.

"Good grief!" said Martin, bending down to stroke our guest. "Who's this? What are you doing here, eh? This isn't your home, is it?"

I swear that cat looked up at him and winked. But it could have just been a trick of the light.

"We've been adopted," I admitted. "There's no getting rid of him. He isn't wearing a collar and he was very hungry..."

"Hartley. Hartley Coleridge, after the poet's son," he added.

So Hartley moved in. And whenever Martin sat down, the cat jumped up onto his knee, purring and licking his hand or even treading his jeans with sharp little claws before settling down. I was tolerated as the human who fetched the food, but Martin was definitely the favoured one.

After a couple of weeks we bought a luminous collar, had him chipped and Martin fitted a cat flap so he could come and go without disturbing us. He was a clumsy, uncoordinated little wretch who fell over if he tried to jump up after a toy; he had clearly not done much playing, but he used to race around the house like a lunatic and he was terrified by unexpected noises or feet that came too close. He was a delight, really, apart from the time when he brought a live mouse in through the cat flap. We managed to rescue the poor quivering thing, and Hartley got such a rollocking from both of us that he never did it again.

***

In the middle of March, I went for my HIV test at last. Martin took the day off work and came with me; it could be done in Halifax, at a clinic in a new building opposite the bus station. We didn't even need an appointment; we just called in together, waited for about fifteen minutes and then were ushered into a consulting room. The test, administered by a sympathetic but professional nurse, simply consisted of taking a small sample of blood. Martin insisted on having it done as well.

I was expecting a delay of several hours; in fact, it was only twenty minutes later that we were called back for the results. They were both negative.

When we got back to the car, Martin said, "Right, that's that then. So, do I drive you to a deserted bit of moor so we can indulge in wild and uninhibited shagging, like Cathy and Heathcliff, or shall we go for the more sophisticated mutual seduction on the rug in front of the cat? The choice is yours..."

"Hmm. Tough one, that. Maybe... a nice cup of tea and a digestive biscuit instead?" I was only half-joking at first, but then I thought good old cynical Allie was on her way back, and actually it *was* quite funny.

Our laughing eyes met; nothing more was said. But we stopped at Tescos on the way home and stocked up on wine and cheese and crusty bread. I didn't think we'd be doing much cooking that night.

In the end, I had nothing to be nervous about. We didn't head for the hills, or disrobe passionately on the carpet. Martin didn't mention it again, although at eight-thirty he opened the wine, we enjoyed our favourite meal, cleared up, watched the ten o'clock news, had a shower and then went to bed.

But as we lay in the darkness, his hand reached out for mine, and I instantly and willingly moved towards him.

Epilogue
Brief Candle

The trouble with happiness is that it's so hard to pin down. One minute the world is a good place – there is laughter and food and wonderful sex, there is the future stretching away, offering friends and travel and new challenges to meet together. Then, for no apparent reason, the force that runs the universe sweeps a petulant hand over your world and plunges it into darkness.

It was the 28th of May, the Monday of the spring half-term. Martin had no classes to teach that week, but he wanted to discuss a forthcoming show with its director, and do some planning for the new cohort of students who were to start at the beginning of June. I wasn't going out – I would spend the day cleaning the house and catching up on laundry – so Martin took the car to drive down to the station, after carefully checking the times of the Bank Holiday trains. He left at around half-past eight, but I was still asleep; I vaguely remember a kiss on the cheek, and hearing the door close quietly behind him.

It was a glorious day, so I tackled the bed first, hanging out the sheets, pillow cases and quilt cover to dry whilst I whisked round the house hoovering, dusting, washing surfaces. Hartley made himself scarce – he hated the noise of what we called the Hoover monster. By three I'd finished; the bedding was dry, ironed and back on the bed, the house was what passed for spotless in my book, and I'd even washed the lettuce and hard-boiled the eggs for tea. I rewarded myself with a cold drink and took my book, phone, sunglasses and sunscreen outside onto the tiny paved area behind the house. I settled into one of our wooden garden chairs and prepared to enjoy a quiet couple of hours.

After a few minutes, Hartley appeared on the wall bordering the field beyond our little yard. He jumped across onto the fence and from there hurled himself onto the garden table, all but knocking it over. I was apparently preferable to slatted wood, so he picked his way carefully across onto my knee. This was a first. Martin wouldn't believe it – but I could show him. I reached across to the table and picked up my phone, then I photographed the little minx flopped across my legs, and sent it to Martin. Within seconds the reply came back:

- *Ha! Some cats will try anything for a free feed, but thanks for sharing. I'm not insanely jealous or anything. Oh no, not me (grinds teeth in frustration)*
  Seriously though, meeting took a bit longer than anticipated. This director seems a bit of a prat, but I can work with him. Just got planning to do, should be finished about 6. Will text from station so you have time to take off – No! – put the kettle on, I was trying to say. Obviously. xx

I replied:
- *Obviously, but not sure if it would fit... I'll – no – **it'll** be simmering nicely by the time you roll in, never fear. xx*

He replied with a thumbs up.

By six it was turning a little chilly, so I shooed the cat off onto the ground and went inside. I fed him and watched him gobble down his biscuits then shoot back outside, on some vital evening errand. At six-fifteen my phone pinged again.

- *Just getting to the station now. Train in 10. Hope that cat's off your knee because when I get home I'm going to—*

The message stopped abruptly. Idiot! I thought. How many times do I have to remind him to charge that phone? Still, at least I knew I could expect him around seven thirty.

But he didn't arrive. Eight o'clock came and went, and still there was no sign of him. Then it got to nine, by which time I was starting to worry – although of course, I reasoned, if there'd been a delay or a cancellation, he wouldn't have been able to let me know.

Then, at nine-fifteen, there was a quiet knock on the back door. Thank goodness, I thought, but what a bozo for losing his keys – he's probably had to walk from—

But it wasn't Martin. When I opened the door, two uniformed police women were outside.

"Alison Weston?"

"Yes?"

"Did Martin Prescott Smith live here?"

Did?

"Yes," I said, "he's due back at any time, if you need to talk to him—"

"No," said the taller woman. "We need to talk to you, and we need to come in."

Unfamiliar uniforms in our living room. Sympathetic eyes.

"You need to sit down," one of them said. "There's been a tragic accident in Leeds."

It had been absolutely instant, they told me. He'd been standing at the pedestrian crossing in front of the station, waiting for the lights to change. A large van, speeding down the hill on his right, had failed to brake to make its left turn and had ploughed straight into him at about fifty miles per hour. The impact had taken his body under the van, which had come to rest embedded into the building behind. It had taken the fire brigade and ambulance service some time to get to him, but by the time they did, it became clear that they could have done nothing to help. He was already dead. It had happened at six-fifteen, whilst he was texting me.

"But that wouldn't have made any difference," the police woman said, kindly, "He'd have been looking in the opposite direction, down the hill. He wouldn't have expected any traffic from his right; it's a one-way street after the lights."

I sat absolutely still and cold, unable to comprehend what had been said. I can remember little else. I suppose Pete and Cath must have been contacted, because after a while they were there with me. I wanted to go to him, to see him, to say goodbye, but the police officers wouldn't let me.

"Best remember him as he was," one of them said.

That morning, I hadn't even bothered to open my eyes when he crept out.

I can't remember the rest of that night. I can't remember sleeping, or getting up, or showering, or Pete and Cath leaving. I do remember Cath coming back on the Tuesday on her own because Pete was too upset; Martin was his best friend and they went back a long way. A police officer called round to ask about Martin's sister; I told them she was in hospital, about to have a very serious operation for the cancer she was fighting. The officer said he would pass the news on to the Wrexham police, and they would liaise with the hospital. He also said there would have to be an inquest, but it would be a formality and I could start making plans for Martin's funeral whenever I felt up to it.

I had no idea where to start. Cath launched into action and contacted undertakers for quotes, then chose one she thought would do a good job. Flowers and cards started to arrive, until I ran out of vases and the house smelled like a florist's, and was filled with sympathy cards. I even had a letter from Mark, my ex-husband, now divorced again, saying how desperately sorry he'd been to hear the news and offering any help I might need. Eunice came to see me, and has kept in touch ever since – she is a really good person, and I value that friendship very much.

A week later it was all over. The funeral had been brief, although Cath had done her best, with as much advice from me as I could bear to offer. I endured the ceremony surrounded by the friends I needed so much – Pete and Cath, Alec and Sally, Derek – and some of the new people I'd met in Bradford: Eunice and Ian, her husband, and Sabrina and her uncle. Lou couldn't attend as she was still in hospital, too ill to travel, but she sent flowers. Afterwards the body was cremated; I intend, at some point when I can bring myself to do it, to bury Martin's ashes under a sapling, which will grow eventually into his tree.

Then I was alone in an empty house, every room a cruel reminder of our brief time together. The nights were the worst. I would dream he was there beside me, then wake to plunge back into the horror. I sat on our settee on many evenings sobbing, watched by a very bewildered little cat, who seemed to be spending a lot more time at my side or on my knee. One night I went to bed clutching one of

Martin's sweatshirts, because it still smelled of him. When I woke up, it was on the floor by the bed, with Hartley asleep on it.

The summer dragged on, gloriously hot and dry – but that was meaningless to me. I ate very little, spent almost nothing and rarely went out, passing my days trying to sort out the endless paperwork and legal issues surrounding the death of a partner. Cath was tireless in her support, contacting me every day when she couldn't come round, even when they were away on holiday. But if it hadn't been for Hartley's insistence on being fed, and his presence in the house, I think I would have sunk under the blackness. What did I have to live for? Where could I go from here? It all seemed so pointless – and I was a shadow, walking through life towards a dusty death.

Eventually, at the end of July, I felt strong enough to go through Martin's clothes and fill bin liners with stuff suitable for the RSPCA's charity shop. At the back of our wardrobe I came across a plastic box full of the letters he'd written to me after we first met. I took it across to the bed, pulled them out and started reading, crying of course, but inspired by the voice I heard through his writing, his energy and humour, and most of all the love. And I realised that he was still with me, somewhere. I felt his presence so strongly, sensed his laughter at a particularly funny letter and was, for the first time, comforted by the memories. I thought about this clever, funny man I was so proud to have known, of all the things he cared about – his passion for the theatre, poetry and Shakespeare, his love of animals, his concern for our world, his politics – and I thought, *I have to preserve that, somehow. I don't want him to disappear for ever.* Then something extraordinary happened.

I opened one envelope, addressed to me in Manchester and dated the year after we'd met. Folded up inside it was a huge bright blue poster, with an eye and eyebrow staring out; the pupil of the eye was actually a small red approaching aircraft. Under the eye were large white capital letters saying "ALL WAYS ALWAYS!" and it had been issued by the Directorate of Flight Safety (RAF) London. On the back was Martin's letter in his usual, left-handed scrawl. But the thing that really caught my eye was this:

So, you've started your book, eh? Is it permissible for me to see it as far as you've got, or is the whole project to be shrouded in mystery until its completion? I'd like to see it...

I searched my memory, but I had no recollection of telling him I was writing a book, or, indeed, of attempting to do so in the past. But I felt as if he was speaking to me, nudging me to begin, and to get on with it. And at that moment I knew.

I knew I *could* do it – for Martin.

I went straight downstairs, opened my lap top, loaded a fresh page and began:

Death changes everything, and we're all touched by it at some point in our lives – like food and friendship and sex. We all have our worlds altered for ever when someone close to us dies. Death can change the way we feel about other living people, or ourselves, as we realise that we won't walk this earth for ever.

But there is another mysterious force, which also changes everything. I have never, ever believed in love at first sight, and I still don't – it's a myth perpetrated by the purveyors of simplistic romances. For me, it took two weeks. Then I was held in its grip until it was torn from me, leaving me falling into blackness, utterly abandoned, like a shadow walking aimlessly through pointless days. Eventually, losing love taught me something about myself – that I am the type of woman who can function without the support of a partner. I have done so, and will continue to do so, if I have to, for the rest of my life.

The End

Tomorrow and tomorrow and tomorrow
Creeps in this petty pace from day to day,
To the last syllable of recorded time;
And all our yesterdays have lighted fools
The way to dusty death. Out, out, brief candle.
Life's but a walking shadow, a poor player
Who struts and frets his hour upon the stage
And then is heard no more...

William Shakespeare

Acknowledgements

Firstly, thank you to my wonderful publishing team at I Am Books, who have guided me and encouraged me duringto the publication of *A Shadow Walking*. Many thanks are also due to to my long-suffering husband James, my dear friend Abdul Ghafoor and to everyone at the Sowerby Bridge Writers Group, all of whom have provided me with invaluable feedback and boosted my flagging confidence. And I mustn"t forget all the friends, relations, friends, friends of friends and ex-pupils who have read for me and made me believe that I had a story worth telling. You know who you are!

But there is one person I can"t thank, even though he was my inspiration. He shared my past and miraculously reappeared in my life a few years ago, although most of our friendship was conducted by e-mail. I have never deleted his messages –; and they gave Martin his voice in the present.

I was reminded of him in the past by his letters, some of which have found their way into the novel. In the box alongside them I really found the poster that which inspired Alison at the end of the story; it was as if my friend was speaking to me again. I hope I have done him justice.

When the shadows lengthen and we lose those closest to us, what always remains is the love.